YOU BETTER WATCH OUT

SARAH NAUGHTON

■ SCHOLASTIC

Published in the UK by Scholastic, 2023
1 London Bridge, London, SE1 9BG
Scholastic Ireland, 89E Lagan Road, Dublin Industrial Estate,
Glasnevin, Dublin, D11 HP5F

SCHOLASTIC and associated logos are trademarks and/or
registered trademarks of Scholastic Inc.

Text © Sarah Naughton, 2023

The right of Sarah Naughton to be identified
as the author of this work has been asserted by them
under the Copyright, Designs and Patents Act 1988.

ISBN 978 0702 32975 3

A CIP catalogue record for this book
is available from the British Library.

Printed and bound in Great Britain by Clays Ltd, Elcograf S.p.A

Paper made from wood grown in sustainable forests
and other controlled sources.

MIX
Paper | Supporting
responsible forestry
FSC® C018072
FSC
www.fsc.org

1 3 5 7 9 10 8 6 4 2

www.scholastic.co.uk

YOU BETTER NOT DIE

For Bill, who might just read this far.
But probably not.

By the time he is himself again dusk has fallen and it is snowing. The temperature has plummeted and his legs are almost too numb to get up. Reeling about the little clearing, he punches himself in the arms and torso, forcing the blood that has rushed to enfold his shattered heart to flow back into his muscles. He has a job to do.

His nails tear away as he thrusts through the first layers of frost-hardened soil, but the deeper earth yields more easily, retaining even now some of the warmth of autumn. He pauses to stare at the blood welling in the nail beds, like crimson varnish. For a moment he can almost smell it, the intoxicating, secret scent of it. Her fingers draped over his wrist as he strokes the brush along her nails. And then the burning chemical smell of the stripper: the fleeting moment of forbidden glamour over.

In the distance, church bells are calling people for midnight Mass.

This will be his Christmas gift to her.

He glances over to where she lies, unable to extinguish the childish hope that she might yet stir. But the first flakes of snow have settled on a cheek no longer warm enough to melt them, and frost has crept over her amber eyes. Their opaque gaze is focused on something far away, too far for him to reach.

He talks to her as he digs, bestowing upon her the grave goods of their memories. But they run out too soon — there should have been so many more — and then he toils in silence.

Sometime later he climbs out of the sunken bed he has made for her. The full moon has covered it with a silver sheet.

As he lifts her into his arms she seems to sigh into his chest and for a moment he stands there, breathing, as the snow drifts like confetti down through the bare branches of the trees.

On shaking legs he carries her across to the slot in the dark Welsh earth, grunting as he lays her down. She is a weight now. He smiles to think of how he will tease her. Afterwards, when they are together again. When he has done what he needs to do.

It's so cold and she's wearing nothing but a T-shirt and jeans. The T-shirt is baggy, to swamp the body she made for herself: the jeans are tight, leaving cruel marks on her soft flesh. There are other marks too, ugly black stains on the parts of her that lay on the hard ground. The blood is no longer flowing into the atriums of her heart or out of the ventricles. They learned that together, breath mingling, heads touching over the textbook. He smiles at the memory and his frozen skin crackles like wax.

He wants to wrap her up in his jacket, keep her warm in that frigid earth, but then when they find her they will know. And he doesn't want them to know. Not straight away. Because there are things he must do first.

For a long time he sits on the edge of her bed. She is asleep. That's all. A slumbering seed, waiting for spring.

Finally he takes up a fistful of soil. His bloody hand is numb so he doesn't feel the grains slipping between his fingers to dust her cheek. He takes another, and another, watching her features soften and disappear. A handful of earth disturbs the neck of her T-shirt and something catches in the moonlight. Her necklace. He reaches forward. On it is her ring and the key. He unfastens the chain, slips both off into his palm, then refastens it.

When he is done there is a slight rise in the land that might betray her resting place to anyone venturing off the dog walkers' path. He cannot bring himself to stamp it down so he lies on his stomach and lets the earth subside beneath him. With his ear pressed to the soil, he thinks he can hear her whispering. He answers her, making promises.

He's surprised to see the shadow of his profile on the dead leaves. It's morning. Getting to his feet, he vomits until his stomach is empty, even of bile, until he can't breathe, until the blood vessels burst in his eyes and the rising sun becomes a disc of blood, until he thinks, thank you, God, *that he will die too.*

But he doesn't die.

As he staggers back through the woods to where his mother's car is parked, he can hear the church bells ringing out for Christmas Day.

Wednesday December 1

The school lockers are about as far from the 11S form room as it's possible to get, so Eleri only ever goes there first and last thing. Most people do the same, and at 8.25 the corridor is rammed and noisy as hell, but somehow she manages to squeeze her way through and feed the combination into her padlock.

The gaggle of popular girls are squealing as slips of red and white striped paper tumble from their open locker doors. These are the invitations for the upper school Christmas Party, or "dance cards", as the head of year insists on calling them. They read:

Dear…
   Will you be my juggling partner at the Cirque De Elsinore House on December 15?
   From…

Then beneath a dotted line a new section reads:

Dear…
I would love to clown around with you!
Or
It's not trap-easy to say this, but no thanks!
From…

You're supposed to collect one from reception, fill it in and slip it inside the locker of the person you want to invite, then they're supposed to tear off the strip at the bottom, cross out the response that doesn't apply and post it back in your locker. By the look of things the popular girls will be having to send quite a few *trap-easy* replies.

"I'd love to see your big top, Tamara!" guffaws a jock as he tramps past on the way to the hall.

"And I'd love to see your head bitten off by a tiger," the girl retorts and the slim blonde herd sashays off.

Two lockers down, Eleri's best friend is gathering her books.

"Hey, Cal," Eleri calls. "How many invites did you get this year?"

Cal gives a lobotomized grin, "Oh, about a million! How about you, El?"

"Same as last year." She swings the locker open to reveal its cavernous interior, empty but for books and a postcard from her aunt Lynne.

"Don't worry," Cal says with faux brightness. "When

they get their rejections from that lot" – she nods after the popular girls, their long brown legs disappearing through the hall doors – "they'll move to the next level down. And then the next and the next, and the class pets, and then us!"

The crowd is starting to disperse as everyone makes their way to the hall, but Eleri and Calista have promised to wait for Beni, who's always late out of morning drama club, because he has a crush on the teacher. Feeling eyes on her Eleri turns, expecting to see him walking up the corridor. But instead finds herself staring into the glinting blue eyes of Ras Mandip.

She's so amazed that for a moment she just stares back at him.

Though their lockers are only two columns apart, Eleri might have been invisible for all the attention Ras has paid her over the past year. But now he's actually looking at her. And not just looking. The corners of his lips are bent in a faint smile.

Eleri jumps as hands descend on her shoulders. "Ready to pick our Secret Santas then, people? I swear if I don't get someone half decent-looking this year there will be a *rampage*."

The Father Christmas hat balanced on Beni's Afro looks like it came from the pound shop, but he carries it off with his usual panache. "And if I get *anything* pink or sparkly, I'm going straight to pastoral care."

They join the herd moving in the direction of the sports hall.

"It shouldn't be compulsory," Calista grumbles. "I've got way too many things to be worrying about than what crappy gift to buy some total stranger."

"Christmas socks," Beni suggests, linking her arm. "You can't go wrong, especially if they light up and play 'Jingle Bells'."

"Whoever I pick this year, they're getting Quality Street," Eleri says.

They emerge into the chill of the playground and she folds her arms against the cold. Ras is in the queue to get through the doors of the gym, leaning his elbow on the head of his annoying friend Teddy P.

After a whole year of barely speaking to me, why would he suddenly catch my eye? Eleri wonders. It probably wasn't deliberate.

The gym smells of feet and BO and old rubber. The morning sunlight pouring through the high, narrow windows makes the parquet glimmer and throws out long shadows behind the students gathered in their various cabals. The jocks scuff the line marks, chatting in gruff voices and occasionally uttering *her her her* laughs. The bad kids (Ras Mandip front and centre) lean against the crash mats looking bored. The popular girls sit on the floor with their knees pulled up, playing with their hair. The hockey team is gathered on the other side of the room and Eleri smiles as the centre back glances in her direction, but her team member's eyes just skim over her.

You would never know someone was missing. There

isn't even a gap where she should have been because the school has filled her space with a new kid.

"It's freezing in here," Calista complains. "I hope this doesn't take too long."

"Who do you want, then?" Beni raises an eyebrow.

"I couldn't care less," Cal grumbles.

"I want Daniel or James C, or that new boy. If I get Daniel I'll get him a new cricket box."

Calista wrinkles her nose. "Yuck."

"Not at all. I care about the integrity of his testicles." Beni sticks out his lower lip and blows the Santa hat pom-pom away from his forehead. It gives an elven tinkle. "What about you, El? Who do you want?" He winks at her over Calista's head.

Eleri shrugs, but her eyes automatically flit to the crash mats.

"Right!" Miss Merrion yells over the hubbub. "Are we all ready for some festive fun?"

There are equal numbers of groans and cheers.

"Who wants to go first?" Miss Merrion gives a wry smile as she shakes the plastic bin on the trestle table in front of her, knowing she will have to start summoning people by name.

But then a hand shoots up from the kids lolling against the crash mats: "Me, miss!" Those around him laugh, but now the gangly frame straightens and Ras Mandip lopes towards the table. His trousers are too short and his shirt is flapping and the skin fade he got on one side of his head, the one he was suspended for, is just starting to grow out. You can see his ridiculously gorgeous eyelashes from the back of the room.

On the way past the gaggle of nerds he snatches a pair of glasses from one of the girls and puts them on top of his head.

"He is such a dick," Calista mutters.

As he nears the trestle table, Miss Merrion's frown melts: Eleri guesses it's because he is treating her to one of his beaming smiles. None of the teachers can stay angry at Ras for long, which is a source of constant irritation to the more strident parents who are always marching in to complain about him disrupting classes.

"Be sensible, please, Ras," Miss Merrion murmurs.

Eleri holds her breath, waiting for him to do something, but instead he just leans over the wrapping-paper-covered bin, biting his lip in exaggerated concentration as he rifles through the slivers of paper inside. Then he gives a subtle flick of his head and the glasses slide off and fall in.

"Oh bother!" he cries, and before Miss Merrion can stop him he has taken the bin from her hands and is delving inside.

"Ras…" the teacher warns, at the clear attempt to sabotage proceedings.

"I have to find them, miss. They're Jeany's. Aha!"

He extracts the glasses with a flourish, and with them a slip of paper.

On the way back to the crash mats, the paper hidden

in his closed fist, Ras tucks the glasses gently over Jeany's coarse red curls, and her cheeks turn the same colour as her hair. As he rejoins his friends, Teddy P joshes him, trying to snatch the strip of paper from his hand, but Ras screws it into a ball with his long fingers, then puts it into his mouth, grimaces, and swallows it down.

"Not fair!" one of the rugby boys shouts. "He was looking at the names!"

But Miss Merrion shouts over him, "Next!"

Other students trickle up to the table. Some respond to their chosen name with poker faces, others are obviously pleased or horrified. The nerds slink up and scurry away, then the jocks approach en masse.

"*Oh man*," sings a voice from the crash mats. "*Look at those cavemen go…*"

Eleri's mouth twitches.

The rest of the crash-mat kids go up then amble out of the hall, laughing and grimacing over their slips of paper. Ras doesn't look at her as he passes.

"Come on," Calista says. "Let's get this over with."

They join the queue, shuffling through the shafts of dusty sunlight. Calista picks. Then Beni. And then it's Eleri's turn.

She walks forward, towards the gaping mouth of the bin.

"Go on, Eleri," Miss Merrion says, and suddenly Eleri is back there, last year, standing at the same table in front of the same plastic bin, picking out a slip of paper inscribed with the name *Nina M*.

"I don't know who this is," she had whispered, frowning down at the tiny, neat hand.

"The new girl," Miss Merrion murmured. "Over by the monkey bars. Black hair, glasses."

Walking back to her friends, Eleri glanced over. Nina M stood alone, shoulders hunched, head bent as if desperately trying to shrink her oversized frame, to make herself invisible to the sharp eyes of the popular girls and hot boys. Eleri felt an immediate rush of pity. She wouldn't have it easy here, looking like that. They'd make up names for her: *the Hulk* or *the Blob*, or something similarly cruel and unimaginative.

She resolved then to get Nina M something really nice for her Secret Santa present. Perhaps the new girl was into something, like art or books. Eleri would give it some proper thought, she decided, get to know Nina a little better, and do everything she could to make her first Christmas at Elsinore House a happy one.

But Nina never made it to Christmas. On December 15th of last year the new girl went missing, and despite the coverage on the local news, the posters slapped on every bus stop and lamp post, the flyers handed out by an army of volunteers, she might as well have vanished off the face of the earth.

"Eleri?"

"Sorry. I was miles away."

Miss Merrion shakes the bin. The slips of paper whisper against her fingertips: *pick me, pick me*. Eleri grasps one and snatches her hand out.

As she walks quickly away to join her friends, she glances at the note and feels a rush of relief. It's Beni.

Wednesday is pasta day and Eleri gets a ladleful of flabby spaghetti in a glutinous brown sauce that smells like a laundry basket full of socks. She, Cal and Beni head for their usual spot, a small round table in the far corner of the room, away from the hustle and noise of the long tables. They've been sitting here since the three of them joined the school from the same primary five years ago.

As they pass she doesn't glance at Ras's table, but she can hear his friend Kika nagging him to tell her who he picked.

Beni falls into step beside her. "I reckon he deliberately dropped the glasses so he could choose. Perhaps it was you, El." He waggles his eyebrows.

"Yeah, right. He hasn't spoken to me in a year."

"Maybe he realized the error of his ways."

"He was probably going for Tamara George."

"You're probably right." Beni sighs. "I would totally kill for her lips. And eyes. And hair."

"And money."

They've reached the table. It would seat four but Calista always moves the fourth chair away to give them more room.

"So-o-o…" Beni drawls as they sit down. "Who did we all get?"

"Can't say," Eleri says, poking the greasy tentacles of her meal.

"Er, why?" Calista looks at her suspiciously.

"It's in the name! *Secret* Santa."

Cal rolls her eyes.

"So who did *you* get?" Beni says.

Calista's lip curls. "Matthew H."

"Ooh, he's hot!"

"If you like dumb jocks."

"We *all* like dumb jocks! I got that girl with the eyebrows that join up."

"Who cares? It's all cringe," Cal says, forking up a tangle of spaghetti.

Beni starts talking about football. About how the new boy has signed up for the team and he hopes he's better than their current striker who couldn't hit a barn door at five paces. Beni can talk for England and doesn't require much in the way of a response. Soon his voice merges into the general hubbub around them.

"… and supposedly he's a Millwall fan. What kind of normal human being supports *Millwall*? I mean, you'd have to be…"

Something makes Eleri look up.

Ras's eyes are all wrong. How many other Indian boys with jet-black hair and dark skin have aquamarine eyes? They're so clear as well, like the irises are tinted glass or seawater, and you might see silver fish swimming behind them. She knows all this because, for the few seconds it takes for the thoughts to pop into her mind, those improbable eyes are looking right into hers.

*

14

The afternoon drags. History is as dull as usual and Eleri spends most of the lesson gazing out of the window. When the bell goes she gathers her books, then waits while Cal explains to Mr Scarf why her homework was late again.

Beni is waiting for them outside.

"We're going for a milkshake in Maccy Ds. Wanna come?" By *we* he means his new drama friends. Last term he finally plucked up the courage to audition for the school play. "Come on, it'll be fun!" He waggles his head in exaggerated encouragement, knowing full well what the answer will be.

"I need to check on my dad," Calista says, then turns to Eleri. "Come on, let's get our bags."

"*You* could come," Beni says casually to Eleri.

Calista clutches her hands together. "Oh my *god*, Eleri, you are *so super blessed* to be asked to join the tits and teeth, jazz hands gang…"

Eleri can't help laughing. Cal's right, some of the drama girls are super annoying. Besides, the two of them always take the bus home together, and even on the days Eleri has hockey practice Cal waits for her, so it's not fair to abandon her when she needs to get back.

"Have fun, Ben. See you later." She smiles.

They set off for the lockers, passing the evidence of various EHS student endeavours: 3D collages made up of plastic bottles the Year 7s collected, display boards and framed artworks from the kids studying art GCSE. There's a pastel picture of a forest, the sun breaking through the trees dissolving into flares like an overexposed photograph. It's so well done that you almost want to squint when you look at it. Half visible behind the floating discs of light is the figure of a girl with her head bent. Something in the line of the shoulders communicates perfectly the girl's solitariness and sadness. The initials underneath are NM. Eleri sometimes wonders whether she should ask the school if she can give the picture to Nina's mum, but she can't quite bring herself to. It would be a kind of acceptance that Nina isn't coming back. Plus it might make Nina's mum sad that her daughter was lonely. *Was that the reason?* Eleri wonders for the millionth time. Was Nina depressed about not having a boyfriend?

The lockers are crowded with kids collecting their stuff and, as usual, Eleri hangs back waiting for a space while Calista dives straight in. She and Cal have been at school together since they were four years old, and she can't imagine what it will be like when they're not with each other every day. Calista clearly can't either, because she's already planning what unis they'll apply to. They both want to do English. Or at least, they did. Eleri's been thinking she might choose biology and phys ed for A level, so she can do a degree in physiotherapy. Her mum always feels so good when she comes home from her physio sessions: she can move more freely and comfortably, and even sleeps better. To be able to help people like that would be really rewarding. Cal won't be happy about it, but Eleri will have to tell her soon because they have to make their A level choices at the beginning of next term.

Finally there's a gap. Eleri squeezes into it and opens her locker.

She frowns.

Her jacket is hanging on the hook but her backpack isn't there. Pointlessly she moves the jacket aside, as if the bag could have somehow shrunk down enough to be hidden by it. Nothing but paper clips and dust bunnies. She turns round. Calista is leaning against the wall, on her phone, her own bag slung over her shoulder.

"My bag's gone."

Cal helps her look on top of the lockers, in the empty ones and around the floor, but there's no sign of the bag. Finally, at a loss what else to do, they head to reception to tell the secretary.

"What was inside it?" Mrs Banwa asks.

"Books. My laptop and my phone."

"Your laptop? Oh dear."

"It's OK." Eleri shrugs. "It's a piece of crap anyway."

"Do *find my iphone*," Mrs Banwa suggests.

They do this, heads bent over Calista's screen, her straight blonde hair mingling with Eleri's black corkscrews.

"That's weird," Eleri murmurs.

"Got it?" Mrs Banwa says, leaning over the desk, her huge bosom almost knocking off the sign-in book.

"It looks like it's on my bus route home."

"Yeah, look," Calista exclaims. "It's just turned off on to the high street."

They follow the bag's progress all the way back to the Benjamin Estate, where it stops moving.

"That's where I live," Eleri says, frowning.

"Well, perhaps whoever took it had second thoughts and decided to return it. The number of times I've spoken to Mr Roberts about the security of those lockers." Mrs Banwa shakes her head.

"But who actually knows where you live?" Cal says. "Apart from me and Beni?"

The answer is no one. Since joining EHS Eleri has kept as low a profile as possible, sticking with Calista and Beni and avoiding any clubs or performances that might tempt her mum to visit school. Cal has done exactly the same: it's only Beni who has managed to branch out and make new social connections.

They call him, but he's already in McDonald's and doesn't know anything about the bag.

"I'd better get back," Eleri says. "Before someone takes it."

Thanking Mrs Banwa, they set off for the bus stop.

Cal's always quiet on the journey back. It's different in the mornings when they chat and laugh over TikToks, but having to go back home always seems to diminish her friend, shrinking her, draining her of colour. Normally Eleri would attempt to cheer her up, but she can't relax until she's got her bag back. Losing her books and laptop are bad enough, but the feeling of not having her phone is worse. Like she's lost a limb.

Cal's stop comes up first.

"Call me when you get in, OK? Let me know if you find it."

Eleri nods, watching her friend step down on to the pavement and set off in the direction of her street. Eleri used to be envious of the Szajna house: two floors, a back garden, a bathroom with an actual bath, a massive TV and a PlayStation where Cal and her dad Paul had FIFA battles. But not any more. And if Paul doesn't go back to work soon his company will fire him and they'll lose the house.

Ten minutes later the two towers of the Benjamin Estate come into view. One lit up cheerfully, the other a bony finger of darkness pointing up at the sky.

They were only finished five years ago – Shiloh first – and Eleri can remember being so happy when they moved in. Covered in attractive cladding that looks like limestone until you get close, they were really popular. Families like theirs couldn't wait to get out of the cramped Peabody Trust buildings that were in the process of being demolished. Their middle-class neighbours were always protesting that the "classic Victorian architecture" must be preserved, but they should try living in one, with its two-hundred-year-old plumbing, sagging ceilings and rising damp.

She and her mum had been on the waiting list for years, and when a flat in Shiloh came up it was a dream come true. When they finally moved in, Eleri would sit by her window watching them finish work on the tower next door, wondering who would have the window opposite hers. She hoped it would be a kid so they could flash messages to one another, like they were in a fairy tale or a spy film. But then the Grenfell fire happened and no one ever moved into Gibea.

The construction company went bust shortly afterwards, presumably to avoid having to pay to get the flammable cladding removed, but it was too late for the residents of Shiloh. There was nowhere for them to move back to. Ever since, there have been endless arguments between the council, the government and the residents' association about who's responsible for removing it, but Eleri's mum says it'll never get sorted: they just need to make their fortune and move out. Which isn't likely now.

The bus pulls in and Eleri disembarks, stepping off the pavement on to the broad expanse of scrubby grass. The plan was to build more blocks here, but now everything's on hold, they haven't even put street lights in. There are just a few lamps along the gravel path that leads to the towers, and they flicker and buzz as if there's something wrong with the electricity supply. As she moves further away from the high road, the only sound is the wind racing around the base of the towers.

And something else.

Eleri stops dead, fingers of wind lifting the ends of her hair.

Her phone is ringing.

Someone really did bring the bag home for her. But hurrying towards the door of her block, her steps falter. The ringtone is getting quieter, not louder.

She stops and slowly turns around. The black windows of Gibea Tower stare back at her.

But the tower is not entirely dark. A thin yellow

rectangle falls on the grass on the far side of the building. It is coming from one of the empty flats on the first floor. But how could that be? The double doors of the main entrance are chained and padlocked and the electricity was never turned on.

The ringing stops. Was she imagining it? She stands in the semi darkness breathing heavily, then jumps as it begins again, shrill and insistent. She takes a few tentative steps towards Gibea. The ringtone gets louder. Swallowing hard, Eleri sets off towards the building. Out of the shelter of Shiloh the wind picks up, snatching at her jacket. On this side of the estate there is nothing but darkness, stretching all the way to the railway embankment – and that one sliver of light trickling down from the first floor window. She walks up to the building, feeling the hugeness of Gibea leaning in on her, and looks up. Her heart is in her mouth as she waits for the jump-scare of a leering face: someone setting her up for a laugh.

The phone stops ringing. Eleri listens for muffled giggles, but all is silent. *In and out*, she thinks. Get the phone and go. But how will she even get in? Taking a step back, she looks left and right. Then she sees the fire exit. The door is ajar.

She crosses the dark grass. *Deep breaths. Get this over with. You'll be home soon.*

The exit has been levered open, leaving a splintered gash in the frame. The door is several centimetres thick, so whoever did it must have used a crowbar or other tool. It's this more than anything that makes her properly uneasy.

The thought and planning and purpose required to hide her bag in this abandoned building. The door swings open and shut again in the wind, as if the tower they all thought was dead is still breathing. Far away, across the ocean of grass, the high road is strung with the red and white fairy lights of the traffic, the phone shops and takeaways blaring their neon welcomes. Eleri can hear music, the low rumble that is the beating heart of the city. But she is alone here in the hushed dark. The door swings open again and she grasps it and steps inside.

It takes a moment for her eyes to adjust to this deeper level of darkness, but there's still enough ambient light to enable her to see where she's going as she walks down the corridor that leads away from the door. If Gibea is modelled on Shiloh there is nothing on this ground floor but the entrance hall and utility rooms accessed by the maintenance teams, but if she turns left at the end of this corridor she should reach the entrance hall that leads through to the stairwell.

There's a chance that the lift still works, but she doesn't fancy getting trapped in it. Besides, it's only a couple of flights.

The corridor can only be twenty metres long but it seems to take an eternity to reach the end of it and step out into the entrance hall.

It's eerie, she might be in Shiloh – but a post-apocalyptic Shiloh: like the pictures she's seen of the Chernobyl apartment buildings. The floor is littered with rodent droppings, and drifts of dust and detritus have collected in the corners. There's a smell, astringent and metallic. Against the far wall, the mailboxes glimmer, their number stickers still pristine white, but other than that the darkness is total, thanks to the metal grilles across the entrance. A sudden claustrophobia accelerates her heart and makes her muscles twitch.

In and out.

Crossing the atrium, Eleri pushes the swing door. Sure enough it leads to the stairwell, flooded with moonlight from the tall windows running up the side of the building. With its grey lino floor and white metal railings, it's just like Shiloh, except there are no scorch marks from cigarettes, no names carved into the paintwork, no crayon scribbles up the walls. Her mum complains about the casual vandalism by the younger residents of their block, but there's something comforting about the signs of humanity. This place is lifeless.

Setting her foot on the first step, she takes a deep breath and begins to climb.

The first flight rises towards the window and the moon's round face gazing down on her, but then it turns back on itself and she is climbing into the dark. At the top is a door. As she reaches for the handle, she notices how the moonlight has leached all the colour from her hand, turning it corpse-white.

The hallway beyond is much darker. Closed doors stretch away to a tiny window at the end, through which she can make out a slot of night sky, clouds scudding against the moon. Yellow light spills from beneath the door beside it. Her heart sets up a painful banging. Is someone going to leap out at her?

The image of laughing idiots filming her with their phones has gone: they used a crowbar to get in here. To lure her in here. Mum is always telling her not to go anywhere alone after dark. To keep her phone with her, the location on, not to make any bad decisions. Well, isn't this the worst decision she's made in a long time? Why didn't she wait for Mum to get back? Or even call the police? They could have escorted her to retrieve the bag. But to have taken it in the first place, it has to be someone from school. And while there are certainly some weird kids at EHS, there's no one particularly creepy, apart from maybe Ray the groundskeeper, and he doesn't venture much inside the school building. Still, Eleri wishes she had her hockey stick.

She sets off towards the illuminated door, her steps unfaltering, despite the pounding of her heart. She learned this from her mother: it doesn't matter how much it hurts, you keep going.

She passes silent door after silent door, until she reaches the end. The brass number on the door gleams. *One.* She pushes it open.

The room is empty: no furniture, no carpet, just bare plastered walls and a concrete floor, and a single item lying on the floor, starkly outlined by a light on a tripod in the corner of the room. Her backpack is bathed in the harsh glare from the bare bulb. The sort of light you have in building sites where there's no power. That sense of unease again: this whole endeavour took thought and planning. Crossing the room, Eleri snatches it up, then runs back the way she came – down the stairs, through the entrance hall, out of the splintered door – and doesn't stop until the lift doors of Shiloh Tower close behind her.

The text message comes through as she's chopping bacon for the carbonara sauce.

It's her night to cook again. Usually they take it in turns, but Mum's taking extra shifts at Sainsbury's to try and make more money for Christmas and she's working late tonight.

Eleri's already texted Calista and Beni to tell them what happened, so she's expecting the message to be from them.

But it's not. It's from the unknown number that guided her to her bag through that insistent phone call.

She opens it, leaning on the counter with the sauce bubbling behind her. It's brief, just two emojis: the shush face and the Father Christmas.

Who is this? she types, but when she tries to send the message it bounces straight back.

Her mum gets home at just gone nine. She takes a long time opening the door and Eleri's heart sinks. This means her muscles have stiffened up again and she'll need to do her stretching exercises later, which take ages to do properly, especially when she's already exhausted.

Though the supermarket has done everything they can to accommodate Mum's cerebral palsy, some strenuous tasks are unavoidable. There's no getting away from the fact that she would be better off in an office, but the whole experience with AWP, where she used to work, has knocked her confidence.

A year ago Mum's nice old boss retired and was replaced with a new guy who had pledged to "trim the fat" from the company. Within a few weeks Mum had been relocated to an office at the top of the building, only accessible by stairs. Because it took her so long to get down to the sales team and back up again her work rate decreased. She started getting verbal and then written warnings. In the end she resigned before she was fired.

Her mum looks so tired when she comes into the kitchen that Eleri decides not to mention what happened with the bag.

They eat in front of the TV, but she can't focus on the drama playing out on-screen. Her backpack is hanging on a peg by the front door and her eyes keep flicking to it. It feels strange that someone else has been handling it, looking inside, touching her stuff. As intimate as eyes moving across her body.

That night it takes her a long time to fall asleep.

Thursday December 2

The alarm wrenches Eleri awake and she lies there for a few moments, steeling herself for the shock of the cold when she pulls back the duvet. When she does get up she goes straight to the window and opens the curtains, wiping condensation from the glass. The morning is overcast and Gibea Tower is a black spear against the lowering sky. The day is so gloomy that you'd be able to see light from one of the flats falling on the grass, but the tower is in darkness, so whoever left the bag must have switched it off. In which case they must have been watching her. Perhaps they were inside the tower with her all along.

Eleri shivers in the chill seeping around the windowpane.

Above her head the little kids on the fourteenth floor are running up and down, probably trying to put off the moment they have to go to school, and Mr Vaseli next door is listening to talkSPORT, the burble of conversation

27

occasionally interrupted by the burst of a jingle or an advert, but Eleri exists in a little box of silence. A silence she shares with the abandoned tower. For a moment it feels as if they are somehow connected. Shaking off the unpleasant notion, she heads to the kitchen for breakfast.

She's halfway through her cereal when Mum comes in, ready for work. At her expression Eleri lays her spoon down, instantly on edge. There have been times in the past year, since Gran died and Mum lost her job, that she has been so low Eleri's been seriously worried about her.

"Everything OK?"

Her mum bites her lip. "Erm, when we go shopping on Saturday, you were probably hoping we'd look for a dress for you, for the school Christmas party."

Eleri wasn't hoping this at all. Even the Primark ones cost forty quid or more. She was actually hoping the one she wore last year might still fit.

"Well..." Mum's smile is rather forced. "I spoke to Aunty Lynne and she's going to send you Isla's prom dresses. She's got two, apparently." Mum rolls her eyes. "And she doesn't need them any more, so Isla said you could keep them. One's Next and the other's Zara. What do you think?"

Eleri nods and forces a smile. Isla is half a foot taller than her and reed-slim. If a dress looks good on her cousin it will look bloody awful on her.

"You're OK about that, yeah? Otherwise we could try and sell them on Gumtree and get a new one."

"It's fine. I'll wear Isla's."

"Great." Her mum looks relieved. "Well, I'm off, so have a lovely day." She comes over and kisses Eleri's forehead then limps out with her usual lopsided gait, left leg twisted in at the knee, left arm curled into her body. Her hair looks lovely today, all piled up on the top of her head in loose curls (she's past forty but still hasn't got a single grey), and her burgundy wool dress hugs her slim figure, but all people ever seem to see is her disability.

Dumping the rest of the cereal down the sink, Eleri goes to get showered.

When she steps outside half an hour later she is buffeted by a stiff wind. Sometimes on days like this the two towers act like a tuning fork, making the air hum with a deep low tone that sets your teeth on edge, and she's glad when the dark tower is behind her.

The bus stop is in front of the community centre and a single poster is still pinned to the noticeboard, yellowed and half covered by adverts for jumble sales and yoga classes. Nina's liquid eyes gaze at her through the pitted glass of the bus shelter.

Have you seen this girl? Call 116 000. All calls confidential.

But there were no calls, no sightings, and now, a year on, no one except Eleri even seems to remember she existed.

"I know what it means!" Beni looks up from the phone, grinning.

Huddled around her desk before morning registration, Eleri showed her friends the messages from the unknown number.

"What?"

He points at the shh emoji: "That means *Secret*." And then at the Father Christmas: "And *that's* Santa, so...." He widens his eyes, nodding at them enthusiastically, encouraging them to make the leap of logic.

"Secret Santa?" Eleri ventures.

"Yes! It was your Secret Santa! Oh my god, that is so cute."

Eleri isn't convinced. "What, so my gift is stealing my bag and then giving it back again?"

"You should go to Mr Roberts," Calista grumbles. "They were putting you in danger making you go inside that building."

Beni rolls his eyes. "It was just a bit of fun."

"Why go to all that trouble for a bit of fun?" Eleri asks.

"They obviously wanted to freak you out," Cal says. "Go to Mr Roberts."

Fortunately Mr Ekudo comes in then and they have to go back to their seats. The absolute last thing Eleri wants, if this *is* something to do with the Secret Santa draw, is to attract attention to herself by making a fuss and getting someone into trouble. The safest way to be, she has learned from bitter experience of her mum being heckled by idiots on the street, is for no one to notice you.

"So how was your dad when you got home?" Eleri asks when Mr Ekudo dismisses them for their lessons.

After gathering her books, Calista stows her bag in her locker but Eleri has decided to keep hers with her all day.

"Asleep on the sofa," Calista says quietly. "There were two empty bottles of wine on the floor. He's been told he shouldn't mix alcohol with his medication but he doesn't listen. I got up every hour to check he was still breathing."

It's been almost two years since Calista's mum Sally left, and Eleri can count on one hand the number of times her best friend has smiled since then. Now Sally lives with her boyfriend and his seventeen-year-old daughter Freya. It's Freya who gets to eat Sally's blueberry pancakes, borrow Sally's shoes, laugh at Sally when she's drunk, kiss her goodnight, while Cal lives with her father. Paul is on sick leave from his job due to depression: he drinks too much and takes antidepressants and sleeping pills and sometimes Cal has to stay home from school to make sure he actually wakes up.

"Can you talk to him about it?" Eleri says gently as they set off down the corridor. "Tell him how it's affecting you?"

"It'll just make him feel worse, that he's screwing up my life too."

They pass the art display and Eleri glances automatically at Nina's picture, then double takes. It looks different somehow. She's passed by when she realizes what the change was — there are two figures standing in the wood. She wants to go back and check she wasn't imagining it, but Calista is obviously upset.

"If he thought he was doing that he really would kill himself."

"He'd never do that to you. He loves you."

"I thought my mum loved me." Her voice cracks.

Putting her arm around Cal's shoulders, Eleri pulls her towards the door of the girls' toilets. When they get inside, a couple of Year 7s are in there looking at something on a phone. They glance at Calista, who has turned to the wall, then slope off, trying to look like they were going anyway.

Eleri turns Cal around, and lifts her face to look at her. "He's not going to kill himself, OK?"

"If he does, I'll have no one," Cal whispers. "I'll have to go to a children's home."

"No you won't. Firstly, it's not going to happen. And even if your dad did die, not because of this, cos it's not going to happen, but like an accident or something, you'd go and live with your mum."

Cal shakes her head, stirring the lank strands of hair that looks like it hasn't been washed in a week. "She wouldn't want me."

"Of course she would. You're her daughter. She loves you!"

"If she loved me she wouldn't have left."

"She thought it was better for you to stay with your dad, so you didn't have to change schools and everything."

"Know how many times a week she actually bothers to call me? Once. On a Sunday evening because that's Steve's pub quiz night with his mates."

Eleri sighs. Sometimes she wants to go round there and shake Sally, tell her exactly what she's putting her daughter through.

"What's wrong with me?" Calista is picking at the cuticle

32

of her little fingernail again, drawing beads of blood from the ragged skin. "Why doesn't she love me?"

"Nothing's wrong with you! You're lovely. Your mum ... well, she's just distracted at the moment. You know what it's like when you fall for someone, how they're all you can think about, how everything else seems totally unimportant. We all think that by the time you're their age it doesn't happen like that any more, but maybe it does. She fell in love and it sent her off her head. She'll come back. She'll come back to you, Cal, I promise. And your dad ... well, he'll get better."

It's a weak argument and Eleri knows it. How can she promise Cal anything? And the truth is, Calista isn't so lovely any more. She never has a good word to say about anyone, she pours cold water on every plan, and sometimes Eleri is so exasperated with her friend she wishes she could just move on. It was nice, last year, to have Nina to talk to.

But Cal is looking up at her gratefully now, snatching at any fleeting hope.

It's to avoid her gaze as much as anything else that Eleri pulls her into her arms, stroking her damp cheek, rubbing her back until the fluttering bird in Calista's thin chest settles its wings.

On the bus home, Eleri keeps up a steady stream of conversation to try and distract Cal, so it's a relief when her friend finally gets off and she can relax for the rest of the journey home. Yawning, Eleri scrolls idly through her phone. Then an uneasy thought occurs to her. Whoever took her stuff yesterday might have installed some kind of malware to track her or steal her personal information. She looks through her phone and laptop, checking all the apps and recent installations: there is nothing. Perhaps Beni is right: perhaps the whole thing was just a bit of fun arranged by her Secret Santa.

Eleri looks up just in time to see they have arrived at the estate. Scrambling off the bus moments before the doors close, she sets off down the flickering path, the two towers rising up ahead of her, one speckled with brightly lit windows, the other in complete darkness.

Or not complete darkness.

On the second floor of Gibea Tower a light is on.

Eleri stops. The wind stirs the zip of her backpack, making it clink softly against her metal water bottle. Shreds of cloud scud across the sky, concealing and then revealing the white face of the moon.

She had almost forgotten the phone was still in her hand and when it trills she jumps and drops it on to the grass. The screen lights up with another message from the anonymous number.

Door 2

After a few rings the video call connects and Cal's face fills the screen. For once there's some colour in her cheeks. She's eating what looks like half a poppadum.

"Cal?"

"Hey." Cal is in the kitchen and in the background her dad is chopping something, humming along to a radio playing nineties pop.

"You OK?"

"Yeah. Dad's cooking us a curry." Her tone is bright.

"That's nice. Listen, I, um… I had another message."

"Shit. Hold on… Dad, I'm just going to speak to El."

The screen blurs as Cal carries the phone out of the kitchen, and then she's back, her face close to the camera.

"What did it say?"

Eleri tells her.

"*Door Two*? What, so yesterday was *Door One*?"

"I guess. I'm going over there now."

"El, no! Are you off your head?"

Eleri pauses, gazing at the little golden light. Maybe it *is* a bad idea to go. Maybe this whole thing is super creepy, like Calista thinks. Or maybe it's cute and fun, as Beni sees it. She just doesn't know. But what she does know is that in her dull routine of school, cooking dinner, watching TV with Mum and going to bed, this is about the most exciting thing that's happened to her in years.

"I just want to see," she says. "Will you stay on the line with me?"

"It could be anyone! Some paedo who got your number from somewhere. They could murder you!"

"It has to be someone from school though, right? And I'll have you with me all the way."

35

"Like that's gonna make any difference when they drag you off and rape you!"

"I'll be super quick, in and out. I just want to see."

"No way. I'm hanging up now. You are not going over there."

"In that case I'll have to do it without you."

Cal growls with frustration. "For god's sake, El, why?"

"I'm just curious. Right, here goes. Now be quiet and just watch my back." Eleri sets off across the grass holding the phone up to her shoulder so that Cal's seeing what she is.

The phone torch dances on the grass, leading her on like a marsh light or a will-o'-the-wisp towards the dark tower.

"Is that it?" Cal's voice is tinnily distant. "Shit, that is so creepy."

Eleri says nothing. Her breath is coming too fast. Circling the building, she comes to the splintered fire exit. "See? Someone broke it open."

"Don't go in!"

Eleri grasps the edge of the door and the chill darkness on the other side closes its hand over hers. Her skin prickles. The lights of Shiloh Tower wink at her. *So long. It was nice knowing you.*

"Eleri, please."

She slips inside. This time the illumination from the phone means she doesn't have to wait for her eyes to adjust and she sets off straight away, down the corridor to the stairs.

She passes through a door that leads to the entrance hall and then through to the moon-washed stairwell.

"Oh my god…" Cal murmurs.

"Shh!" Eleri hisses, partly because if the messager is here, she doesn't want to announce her presence, but mainly because the echo of Calista's small voice, swallowed by the soaring darkness, makes goosebumps ripple across her skin.

Setting her foot on the first step, she takes a deep breath and begins to climb.

Calista gives a high-pitched moan as Eleri reaches the second floor and passes through the door that leads to the flats beyond. Doors march away to the left and right. From one on the left, near the end of the row, yellow light bleeds on to the grey lino.

She sets off towards it, her steps unfaltering, despite the pounding of her heart.

"Talk to me," she murmurs.

"What do you want me to say?" Cal squeaks. "*Lovely evening, isn't it? I can't think of anywhere I'd rather be?*"

"How's your dad?"

"He only drank three beers today. He says he's going to stop the wine."

"Excellent," Eleri breathes.

As she approaches the illuminated flat, she wishes she hadn't asked Calista to talk because she can't listen for any sounds coming from it, but Cal's voice falters and dies. All she can hear now is the wind moaning around the tower, high and keening, the wail of a distant police siren and her own blood pulsing in her ears.

Eleri takes a deep breath, and steps into the pool of light spilling from flat 23.

The bare concrete room is identical to the one she collected her bag from. Wires and pipes protrude from holes in the walls like severed arteries and veins, and the tripod lamp shines down on a figure sitting in the middle of the floor. She gasps.

"What?" Cal yelps. "El? Are you OK?"

Eleri holds the phone up for Cal to see.

It's a doll. Head drooping, long arms dangling, striped legs splayed out, a gold bell glinting on its pointy hat.

"It's an Elf on the Shelf." The head lolls back as she picks it up and a rosy-cheeked face beams up at her.

Tucking the elf under her arm and holding the phone out like a shield, Eleri turns in a slow circle. Apart from a scatter of dead flies on the window sill and some white plastic clips littering the floor, the room is entirely empty. There isn't even a footprint in the grit and dust.

"Come on, let's go!" Cal whimpers.

The elf's boots jiggle against Eleri's hip as she runs back down the darkened hallway and down the moonlit stairs. She bursts out into the night, gasping in the clean night air, her heart pounding so hard the face of the moon jumps in her vision.

Calista's face is pressed close to the screen, round-eyed and blinking. "Oh my days! That was messed-up!"

For a while they just pant and swear, and then Calista

says, "Oh wait, my dad's calling me for dinner. Will you be OK to get home on your own?"

"Sure, yeah. Go."

"OK, well, text me when you get in to let me know you got there safely."

"I will."

Calista hangs up and Eleri is alone under the shadow of the tower. A cold breeze racing across the flat expanse of grass makes the elf's little bell ring softly. She needs to get home before she catches a chill (as her gran would say).

When she gets to Shiloh a woman is just getting into the lift and Eleri calls for her to wait. The woman smiles when she steps into the little box carrying the elf, and says she must get one for her own kids.

Eleri turns round to press the number of their floor and the lift doors rumble closed, shutting out the sight of the black spike of Gibea Tower. And now her heart starts banging again because the light in the second floor window has gone out. The messager must have been there the whole time.

Friday December 3

On the bus next morning, Calista is bright-eyed and cheerful. Eleri would really like to talk about last night – she barely slept for turning the whole thing over in her mind as the elf gazed benevolently down from her bookshelf – but Cal is too excited about the weekend ahead. She and her mum will be going Christmas shopping, alone (i.e. without Sally's soon-to-be husband and stepdaughter).

"I feel kind of sorry for Freya really," Cal says with uncharacteristic magnanimity. "Her mum is really tight and gets all the Christmas shopping done in the summer sales, so she misses out on all the atmosphere – the lights and music and decorations and everything. Plus everyone gets things that are six months out of date. Do you think I should get her something?"

"Freya?"

"She has this gorgeous waist-length blonde hair, totally straight, like it's ironed."

Eleri raises her eyebrows. The shopping trip must have put Cal in a really good mood to be describing any attribute of Freya as "gorgeous".

"Maybe an Alice band. One of those fabric ones with a knot in the middle."

"Yeah…" Eleri gazes out of the window as the bus turns on to the main drag to school and slows down in the rush-hour traffic. A helmetless cyclist pulls up to the side of the bus, his tangled black curls bouncing as he bumps over a drain.

Her heart slams against her ribcage.

A logjam up ahead means that neither the bus nor the bike can move, and for a moment she's within touching distance of him, separated only by glass. She can see the little hole in his pierced right earlobe and the sweep of his unfairly long eyelashes, the muscles of his arms outlined by the clingy sleeves of his jacket.

Then, as if he has felt the weight of her gaze, he turns his head and their eyes meet. His irises reflect the interior lights of the bus.

He raises his eyebrows at her, in a way that could mean anything – *Hi/What are you staring at?* – and then the logjam eases and both vehicles can move again. Ras pushes off, then immediately sits back in the saddle, folding his arms, nodding his head in an exaggeratedly chilled way as he rides hands-free. This is somewhat undermined by the fact that

41

he has filled his wheel spokes with coloured plastic beads, like an eight-year-old. Eleri can't help smiling, especially as the bike begins to weave precariously from side to side and he's forced to grab hold of the handlebars.

When he looks up at her again she shakes her head.

What? he mouths back, opening his arms. The gesture unbalances the bike and the front wheel gives a sudden twist. Eleri's breath catches in alarm as it looks like the bike is about to swerve under the wheels of the bus – but just in time Ras grabs the handlebars and jerks them to the left. The bike comes up sharply against the kerb and he is thrown on to the pavement, landing heavily on his backside in front of a group of highly amused primary school children.

The bus pulls away and he is lost to sight.

"How about this one?" Cal says, holding out her phone displaying an image of a turquoise hairband.

Eleri suppresses her smile. "Yeah, nice. She'll like it."

Friday is fish day. As Eleri emerges from the maths room she can smell it, like sweaty socks, and it does nothing for her appetite. She couldn't concentrate on her chemistry homework last night so she could use the lunch hour to get it done, but then Calista texts to say she needs to call her mum and will meet Eleri and Beni in the canteen.

It's quieter than usual because the kids studying catering are on a trip. Eleri joins the back of the short queue and eyes the silver trays glinting under the warming lights. Greying slabs of cod float in a scum of watery white sauce flecked with what is supposed to be parsley. The accompaniment of sloppy mash and wrinkled peas make her hanker for the old days, before the formation of the School Nutrition Team, when they used to get chicken nuggets and hotdogs and actual pudding.

Beni pushes in beside her. He's panting and his brown cheeks are red with extertion. "I know something you don't know!" he sing-songs.

"What?"

He lowers his voice, glancing around theatrically. "I was in the toilet, right, in a cubicle because I don't like anyone looking at my winkie, when Teddy P and Pasha come in. They're talking about who they got for Secret Santa and one of them says it's not fair he has an ugly girl when Ras got to choose his. The other one asks who it is and he says…" He gives an agonizing pause, like he's on *X Factor*, one eyebrow arched. "Eleri Kirdar."

She concentrates on keeping her breathing steady. She can see Ras's table out of the corner of her eye.

"Hey, bitches." Calista pushes in behind them, to the irritation of the girl next in line.

"Guess what," Beni says. "Ras deliberately picked Eleri for Secret Santa. I heard his friends talking."

"So that was him with the bag?" Calista says, grimacing. "What a freak."

The disappointment is sharp and Eleri struggles to swallow her irritation as they shuffle up the queue. Why did Cal have to ruin it? Whatever she thinks of Ras, it's nice to have been deliberately picked by anyone.

"I couldn't get through to Mum," Calista goes on, as if the news wasn't even worth discussing. "It was probably to let me know what time she's coming to get me tomorrow. Oh my days, I swear something just moved under there." She grimaces at the tray of cod and sauce.

When it's her turn, Eleri slides her tray along to the end and helps herself to salad and grated cheese. As she's waiting for Beni and Calista, there's a sharp whistle behind her. Quite a lot of the catering students are Ras's friends – it's an easy choice for the less academic kids – and there are now several free spaces on his table. He nods at the free chairs and then back up at Eleri.

The blood rushes straight to her face and she turns to Beni, who's just collected his own meal.

"Shall we sit with Ras?" she says, her voice several tones higher than normal.

"Yeah," he says, surprised. "Sure."

"Cal?" Eleri says, as Calista gathers her cutlery. "Ras is asking us to sit with him…"

She tails off at Cal's expression.

"Only for today," Beni says. "Look, he's all lonely, poor lamb, with his little pals gone."

"If you two want to, be my guest."

Eleri experiences a stab of irritation. She would do it for Cal, if there was a boy Cal liked, but now Calista walks purposely away from the serving station in the direction of their table.

"You know what," Eleri mutters as she catches up with

her. "We *can* actually sit with other people sometimes. We're not going to catch anything."

Cal stops and turns to face her. "Look, he's only going to drop you again like he did last year. I just don't want you to get hurt."

"I can look after myself, thank you. I don't need your protection."

"You did last night."

Eleri is tempted to dump her tray and walk out of the room, but Calista immediately apologizes. "I didn't mean that, really. Let's go and sit with him, then. I don't mind."

"It doesn't matter."

Beni has already reached their little table and to turn back now would look like a big deal. They sit down and when she glances back at Ras's table, Tamara George and her friends have filled the places. The gorgeous blonde girl is laughing at something Ras is saying, and the way she's looking at him it's pretty obvious she likes him. Eleri's heart sinks.

"Soooooo," Beni drawls, shovelling a forkful of sloppy fish into his mouth (he will literally eat anything). "Last night...?"

Eleri had messaged them both when she got back home, and Beni replied with his usual splurge of emojis, but now he's leaning over the table, eyes bright with curiosity.

She gives him the blow-by-blow account she knows he wants. Her pounding heart, the echoing stairwell, the creepy doll, the dead flies, and finally the darkness of Gibea Tower as she hurried home.

"OK, I get it." A smile creeps across Beni's face.

"What?" Eleri says.

"That is cool. Oh my, I think I fancy him myself."

"What?"

"He made sure he picked you for Secret Santa, and now he's going to make it really special. A different gift for every day in December, all the way to Christmas! Just think about it. The day before yesterday was the first of December and the message said *Door One* – it was your bag, on the first floor of that tower block. Yesterday was *Door Two*, he leaves the elf on the second floor. Today is *Door Three*. There'll be a gift waiting for you on the third floor, like a real-life advent calendar!"

Eleri smiles and shakes her head, but a warmth is spreading up from her stomach. If he's right, then this has taken a level of thought and planning you'd only bother with if you really cared about someone.

"I wonder what it'll be!"

"A rope and some cable ties," Calista mutters.

"Honestly, if some handsome boy was doing that for *me*, I'd be totally gassed."

Dipping her head, Eleri glances over at Ras's table through her hair. He's scrolling on his phone, apparently oblivious to her presence, and she experiences a pang of doubt. "What if it's not him?"

"Then who? You literally don't talk to anyone else."

"A stalker," Calista retorts. "He's got a dungeon waiting for you with a stained mattress and a bucket to pee in. You'll have nineteen of his babies before they rescue you."

"Wouldn't I know?" Eleri says. "If I had a stalker? Wouldn't he have got in touch before?"

"Exactly," Beni says, picking strands of fish from his expertly whitened teeth with a pointed fingernail. Then he frowns. "I wonder what his beef was last year, then. I did ask around but he obviously didn't tell anyone."

Eleri winces. "You *asked around*? Beni!"

"Of course! He goes from puppy-dog eyes to blanking you overnight. Didn't *you* want to know why?"

Eleri pokes her salad. This question has been revolving in her mind for exactly a year. Ras only joined EHS in Year 9 and they didn't have much to do with one another. Eleri was mostly in higher sets than him, but that was because he was dyslexic – you only had to hear him arguing with one of the dick jocks to know he was intelligent. But they were right, the jocks, when they finally gave up arguing a point (that Ras was winning) and resorted to insults – he *did* seem to have some kind of screw loose. That was the only way she could think of to describe it. He just wasn't as tight and controlled as other people. He didn't seem to have any inhibitions or fears and he wasn't the least bit deferential to authority. Some of the teachers liked it and found him hilarious, but others detested him. And that was how it was for her and Calista – she'd liked him immediately, and Cal had hated him.

They met properly at an art club session, with Nina, and after that they just hit it off, until after the party, when he just stopped speaking to her. Wouldn't even look at her.

47

She's tried to figure out what she did wrong ever since. Was he the type that would go off you if you flirted with other boys? If so, good riddance – but she hadn't been flirting. She'd danced with Beni and that was it. And now, out of the blue, he's speaking to her again, just as these messages start coming through.

"He's a dick," Calista says. "Come on, let's go."

"So will you go," Beni says, getting up from the table, "when the next message comes through?"

"*If.*"

"If, then. Will you?"

She glances automatically at Calista. Cal shakes her head. At that moment a burst of noise announces the approach of Ras and his friends. He passes their table without a glance, too busy roaring with laughter at something on a phone screen. Eleri watches his retreating back. After the knockback he probably won't ask her to sit with him again. Sudden irritation at her friend makes her snap. "Yes, I'm going."

Cal stares. "Are you off your head?"

Eleri shrugs, getting up and walking away towards the tray drop.

Calista catches her up. "In that case, I'm coming with you. I'll tell Dad I'm going to be late home. Beni, you should come too. Safety in numbers."

Guilt washes over Eleri. Cal is her best friend. She's only trying to protect her.

"I've got art club," Beni says, stashing his tray on the

trolley. "We're making party decorations. Come. We could use more people, and then afterwards we can all go and see what your next present is..." He links arms with them and skips them out of the canteen.

Taking up an entire quarter of the second floor, the art department is the pride of the school. There's a darkroom, a kiln, a 3D printer, laser cutter, sewing machines and an etching press. Huge papier mâché sea creatures drift beneath the ceiling and the walls are covered with the sort of paintings and sketches you might see in a gallery. Head of art, Mr Hake, is young and handsome and at break and lunchtimes the room is usually filled with girls, but art club is run by one of the other teachers, Miss Hanson.

Peering through the porthole windows, Eleri glimpses the teacher's dumpy frame bent over a table, gathering up cuttings from magazines. The fluorescent lights spark off the rings clustered on every plump finger and make her frizzy magenta hair glow. Rather than make awkward conversation with a teacher she barely knows, Eleri decides to wait outside for the others.

As on the floor below, the girls' toilet is this end of the corridor, and glancing over at it she can't help smiling. Art club is always on a Friday, so it must have been the exact same day the previous year that she was last here, the day she first got to know Nina and Ras.

*

49

"Just get her chocolate," Calista had said when she'd announced she wanted to get a nice Secret Santa for the new girl. "She looks like she likes sweets."

"Me-ow!" drawled Beni. "She's totally nice actually."

"How do you know?"

"She goes to art club."

"What's she like, then? Does she have hobbies and stuff?"

"We haven't talked much. Oh wait, hang on, why don't you come tonight and I'll introduce you? We're making decorations for the Christmas dance. Everyone's welcome. Apart from Ras Mandip."

"How come?"

"Didn't I tell you? *Well...*" Beni leaned over the table delightedly.

It had happened at art club a few weeks previously. It was a busy afternoon so Miss Hanson had divided the class into three and set them all doing different tasks in each of the three rooms. One group would be life-drawing in pairs, while a second group was in the sewing room embroidering an eye, and a third attempting to throw beakers on the pottery wheels. It was this last class that needed the most attention so she didn't get a chance to check on the life drawers until the club was almost over. When she walked back into the main room she stopped dead. Ras Mandip was posing patiently for his partner; lying on a table, head propped on his hand, one knee bent, completely naked. The drawing was excellent, apparently, but Ras was suspended for a week.

"Gross," Calista said and flatly refused to waste her evening making paper chains, so they'd gone alone, Eleri and Beni, and he had introduced her to the new girl, who was sitting on her own at a table by the door.

Beni was right. From a distance Nina just looked hunched and bulky, her frumpy bob falling over her face, but up close, when she lifted her head to greet Eleri, she was really pretty. Her hair was glossy black and the kink by her ears suggested that it would tumble in luxuriant waves if she allowed it to grow. Behind the heavy-rimmed glasses, her eyes were such a light brown they were almost gold, her lips were perfectly bowed, and if she lost a little weight her cheekbones would be to die for.

Nina had shifted up immediately to let Eleri sit down, then handed her the best scissors (the others were blunt, apparently) and showed her patiently how to fold strips of paper into origami stars. They were so engrossed in this, laughing at Eleri's attempts that looked as if she had simply screwed the paper into a ball, that Eleri didn't remember she was supposed to be finding out about Nina until Miss Hanson announced that there would be a special treat for them tonight, as it was Christmas. Asking one of the younger girls to help her, the teacher left the room.

"So," Eleri said, trying yet again to slide the end of the paper strip through the right loop. "What are you into? Hobbies and stuff? I guess you like art?"

Oil pastels? she mused. *A sketchbook? A set of watercolours?*

"Kind of. I just wanted to help with the decorations really."

Eleri was about to ask if she liked any sport but stopped herself. You didn't have to be slim to be fit, but Nina's breathing had a heavy, nasal quality to it, as if she wasn't very fit at all.

"How about at your last school? Were you in any clubs there?"

Nina shook her head and the dark curtains fell across her face.

Miss Hanson returned then, holding the doors open for her helper who entered pushing a trolley. On it was a silver tray of mince pies and some of the large jugs from the canteen. But instead of tap water these now contained a dark red, steaming liquid, with pieces of apple and orange bobbing on the surface. The room was filled with the pungent aroma of spices.

"Help yourselves to Christmas punch, everyone!" She beamed.

The trolley was immediately surrounded and by the time Beni, Nina and Eleri got there only crumbs and dregs were left.

Back at the table, with Nina concentrating silently on her stars, Eleri glanced helplessly at Beni. Had she made a mistake bringing up Nina's last school?

He saved the day by telling Nina all about the art trip they had gone on last year to the National Gallery, where one poor child had tripped over the wire that was supposed to keep you at a distance from the paintings. Throwing his hand out to steady himself he had planted a greasy palm right in the middle of a Tintoretto. An alarm had gone off and the security team immediately surrounded him and Mr Hake had to stay with him until a review of the CCTV footage proved that it had been an accident.

That made Nina laugh and soon the conversation was flowing again.

Miss Hanson had come over to their table with reels of cotton to thread their stars on to when one of the younger children crept up to the teacher's side, her face a delicate shade of pastel green. "Miss, I don't feel well."

Before Miss Hanson could react the child vomited on the floor. If they hadn't known about the punch, the colour would have been seriously alarming.

"Girls, go and get some paper towels," Miss Hanson sighed to Eleri and Nina. "Klara, sit down and I'll get you some water."

"It was the drink, miss. It tasted funny."

As Eleri and Nina got up, Miss Hanson went to the trolley and sniffed one of the jugs. Frowning, she poured the dregs into a cup and sipped.

"Oh shit," she muttered. All the attention in the room was on her, and in the sudden silence Eleri heard a scuffle in the corridor outside. Miss Hanson must have heard it too, because her gaze snapped in the direction of the door, but then another child whimpered that he too felt sick.

Eleri and Nina made for the door.

"Food poisoning from the mince pies?" Eleri said, as they walked up the corridor to the toilet.

"Nah, I reckon the punch had alcohol in it," Nina said.

"Oh my god. She'll totally get fired."

"I don't think she knew."

They went into the toilets. One of the doors was engaged and it sounded as if someone was crying on the other side.

"Hey," Eleri said, tapping on the door. "Are you OK?"

"Fine," squeaked a high-pitched voice.

Eleri frowned. "Open the door."

The door opened a crack and Ras Mandip peered out. "Sup."

She folded her arms. "What did you do?"

It didn't take much for Ras to spill. He'd heard the dinner ladies talking about Miss Hanson. That she'd put some grape juice in the kitchen for art club, so he brought in some wine, then refilled the bottles. At the end of the explanation he opened his arms as if it had all been an innocent mistake.

"Why would you even do that?" Nina asked, shaking her head and smiling.

"I figured you'd all have more fun with real wine! And also because she chucked me out. What can I say? Don't cross me." He grins.

"The Year Sevens are all puking in there," Eleri said sternly. "You are in deep shit."

Then all three pairs of eyes darted to the door. Miss Hanson was approaching, telling a child to *try and hold it in until she got to the toilet*.

"Hide me!" Ras hissed.

"Get into a cubicle!" Nina whispered.

Ras jumped into the nearest one. "You have to come in too!" He beckoned frantically. "Or she'll know!"

Eleri was closest so she joined him, closing the door just at the moment the outer door opened and Miss Hanson came in, her arm around the shoulders of another green-tinged Year 7.

She must have slammed the door too hard, or shot the bolt too fast because Miss Hanson said. "Eleri? Is that you? Are you OK?"

"Yes, fine!" Eleri said, somewhat shrilly.

It was a small space and her and Ras's bodies were almost touching. His warm breath pulsated against her ear as he tried to stifle his laughter.

"I think she's feeling a bit queasy too," Nina said heroically, but there was an ominous silence and a moment later, under the door, a bejewelled hand came into view, followed by burgundy frizz, and Miss Hanson's glasses were peering at them.

"Out. Both of you. Now."

The following morning the three of them were marched straight to the head, but as there was no real evidence, and since Eleri and Nina didn't mention Ras's admission, he was let off with a detention for going into the girls' toilets. Miss Hanson shouldn't have looked under the door, so she couldn't really protest, but she knew full well that Eleri and Nina were lying for him, so she also concocted a detention for them – not alerting a staff member that there was a boy in the girls' toilets. It was that detention, three days later, when Eleri decided that she liked Ras. A lot.

"Hey, sorry I'm late." Beni runs up the corridor, panting. "The new boy was in the playground so I had a kickabout with him.

"No worries."

"Where's Cal?"

"Dunno. I'll text her."

But when she takes out her phone there's a message from Cal. She didn't feel well and has gone straight home. Clearly she had entirely forgotten her promise to go with Eleri to the tower if a message came through. But that was typical Calista these days, only ever thinking about herself.

And right then, as Eleri's holding the phone, thinking mean thoughts about her best friend, it trills.

Door 3.

As they tramp across the grass towards Gibea Tower an hour later, Beni keeps up a steady stream of excited chatter. He is the polar opposite of Calista, seeing fun and excitement in everything, and Eleri often wonders why he bothers to hang out with them, when the drama or art crowd is far more his style. They were all together at primary school, which bonded them, and they were the first people he told he was gay, in Year 5, so maybe it's that, but whatever it is, she's glad of his friendship. It had been fun making decorations with him, chatting to the other students there without Cal scowling and muttering.

He gasps and squeezes her arm. "Look, look! A light on the third floor!"

He's right. It glimmers in the mist creeping across the expanse of grass.

She leads him around to the splintered door and they creep through into the darkness.

He sniggers as they set off down the corridor towards the stairwell. "This is the moment in a film where you're shouting at the TV, *Don't go in there!*"

"Yeah, well, if it was a film then you're dead cos I'm the final girl."

"Oh my days, you are!" he exclaims. "So how do I die? Oh wait, I know, there's gonna be a tripwire that sets off a crossbow. Or … the walls start closing in and my head explodes like a watermelon…"

"Seriously. Stop."

He jerks and chokes in melodramatic death throes and Eleri can't help laughing. She's actually glad Calista's not here: she'd only be jangling all their nerves with her stress.

The stairwell is dark this evening, the moon lost behind thick cloud, and the tall windows reflect their wide eyes in the glow of Beni's torch app. He shines it straight upwards and Eleri's heartbeat quickens as she follows the beam, half expecting to see a face peering down at them from one of the upper floors. But there's nothing, only smoky blackness swallowing up the frail light.

As they set off up the stairs, Beni starts whistling and Eleri recognizes the horror film favourite, "Tiptoe Through the Tulips".

"Shh!" she hisses, only half amused.

"Why?"

She opens her mouth and closes it again. Why *does* she feel the need to creep around when it's clear whoever is doing this is tracking their every step?

"Hello-oh!" Beni sings loudly. "It's only us, come to get our prezzie! It better be a good one!" The echoes of his voice bounce around the stairwell.

"Shut up!"

"I'll have some Jordans, and El wants diamond earrings!"

"Beni, stop!"

"Race you up there!" he cries and then scampers on ahead, the torch jumping in the darkness. Unwilling to be left behind, she races after him and a moment later they emerge, panting, through the door to the third floor.

The corridor is completely black and her heart leaps – the light has gone out: the game is over. But then she remembers. The light they saw was on the other side of the building. They will have to walk deeper in.

"This way," she says.

They walk in silence, past the ghostly glow of the white painted doors. Then suddenly Beni grabs hold of her arm and gasps. Her heart slams against her ribcage as she follows his wild stare: one door is open! Then she realizes: it's the lift shaft, gaping like a black throat. A cold draught seeps through the open door.

"Jesus. Anyone could fall down that!"

"Yeah, well, they don't expect anyone to be stupid enough to wander about here at night," Eleri mutters. "Come on, I think it's just up here."

Sure enough, as they approach the corner, a yellow glow spreads across the floor.

"Once more unto the breach, dear friends," Beni murmurs, taking her hand.

From the middle of the floor of flat 35 a pink cuddly octopus smiles up at them. Beni squeals, rushes over and scoops it up in his arms. "Hello, little fella. You're a cutie, aren't you?" He turns and holds it out to her, making its ribbed tentacles jiggle. "It's Jellycat. They cost a bloody fortune!"

Eleri takes it from him. The fur is soft as velvet and has a slight scent of dried flowers.

"No label, though. He totally regifted it."

"You think?" She feels a pang of disappointment.

"Or maybe it was his when he was little? That's cute."

The corner of her mouth lifts as she looks into the octopus's glossy eyes. Has Ras given her this because it was special to him?

As they pass back through the darkened building she feels weary and relieved, as if she's just run a particularly arduous cross-country race. She wants to get home, slump on the sofa and eat toast.

"Are you going to thank him?" Beni says when they get outside. There's no wind tonight but the cold is heavy and oppressive.

She shrugs. "No one replies when I message back."

Beni pouts. "That's no fun." Because he can't resist any opportunity for a kickabout and doesn't want a big coat cramping his movements, Beni never wears enough layers and in the lights from Shiloh, Eleri can see that he's shivering.

"Go home before you freeze."

"OK." As he leans forward to kiss her on the forehead, she pulls him into a hug.

"Thanks for coming. I'm really glad you were here."

"No problem. That's what friends are for."

They pull apart. "Wish Calista felt the same."

"Hey." Beni's smile softens and his slim dark fingers rest on her arm. "Don't be too hard on her. It's tough, your mum leaving. Dads are different. They're ten a penny, but your mum, she's supposed to stay, to love you whatever. Can you imagine how you'd feel if your mum left you because she'd got the hots for some guy? How hurt you'd be?"

Eleri drops her gaze, ashamed. "Yeah, I know."

"Remember what Cal was like at primary school? She was wicked, right? Funny as hell and up for anything. That girl is still in there somewhere, and we just have to hang in there and support her until she's ready to come out again."

"Yeah." Eleri lifts her gaze to Beni's face. "You're a better person than me."

"Damn right. Now go and press that octopus to your heaving bosom and dream of Ras Mandip."

"Beni!"

He skips away, laughing. Feeling suddenly protective, Eleri watches until he's safely back at the road. Once he's crossed to the other side and disappeared behind the stream of traffic, she heads into Shiloh.

Her mum's home, but she's cooking onions with the radio on, so the noise masks the front door closing, and Eleri only shouts hello when she's past the kitchen. If Mum sees the octopus, she will have to lie to her face, because if she admitted the truth, that she has been creeping around an abandoned building after receiving messages from a stranger, she will get a massive lecture. Rightly so. Haven't they had enough visiting speakers at school, recounting horror stories of how their kids died after meeting up with strangers they met online? Only this morning, in assembly, Mr Roberts warned them about a rough sleeper who's been hanging about the area and had approached some Year 8 girls asking for money.

But even if the messager isn't Ras, it's someone from school, so that doesn't strictly count as a stranger. She hates lying to her mum though, so she just won't mention it.

Taking the octopus into her room, she throws herself down on the bed and checks her messages. There are a few on the hockey group chat talking about a bunch of private schoolboys they met in the cafe after last week's practice: meaningless to Eleri as she didn't go. There's also one from

Calista, asking how it went. Remembering Beni's words, Eleri decides she ought to check up on her, even if Calista can't be bothered to call her.

"Cute?" Calista snaps when she hears about the octopus. "How is that cute? That is totally inappropriate. He probably had that in his bed!"

Eleri's heart starts to beat faster because now she's picturing Ras's smooth brown limbs stretched out on a white sheet, his dark hair tousled on the pillow, the octopus pressed to his chest. When she thinks about Ras she often pictures him naked, but probably only because of the art club story.

"Eleri? You still there?"

"Yeah."

"I said, what are you going to do with it?"

"Keep it, I guess."

"Bin it! It's probably crawling with germs."

"So," she decides to change the subject. "Are you feeling better?"

There's a pause, then when Calista replies her voice sounds different. "Not really."

"What's up?"

"Chest infection."

"Ew. How are you feeling?"

"Not me. Frigging Freya. Mum doesn't want to leave her alone in the house, so she's cancelled our shopping trip. We had a massive row."

Eleri sighs. "Oh no…"

"She said I was being selfish, but it's only a bloody bug. She doesn't seem to mind *me* being alone in the house." Calista's voice cracks.

Eleri listens patiently and tries to comfort Calista as best she can. Midway through the call her mum comes in with her dinner, but Eleri shakes her head and jabs a finger at the phone, mouthing *Calista*. Mum nods wearily, points at the food and mouths *oven*.

By the time Calista's sobs subside it's gone seven. Her dinner is probably dried out by now, her and Mum's plan to rewatch the whole of *Stranger Things* Season Three in tatters, and the warm feeling she had about the octopus has been well and truly extinguished. Her tone is curt as she tells Calista to sleep well and that she'll see her on the bus tomorrow, but before she hangs up Cal thanks her for always being there for her.

"Don't be silly," Eleri says, smitten with guilt yet again. "That's what friends do."

Saturday December 4

Eleri wakes to find fingers twined in her hair. Crying out, she tears at them, and the pink octopus sails across the room, striking the wall and sliding down into a quivering heap on the carpet.

She dreamed about Nina again. They were making paper stars for the Christmas dance and this time Eleri had mastered them. In fact she was working so fast the pile of white stars soon became a drift. It got higher and higher until eventually she had to climb on the table to be able to lay the last one on the pinnacle. But this fragile knot of paper was enough to unbalance the whole pile and it slipped down, burying Nina in a drift of white. Eleri was scrabbling at the pile, trying to find her, when a clawlike hand burst out to pull her under.

She lies there, gazing up at the ceiling, as her heart rate returns to normal.

Sometimes she has to remind herself that Nina was her friend. That whatever the reason for her vanishing, it was nothing to do with Eleri. At the beginning there were salacious rumours that she had been abducted and murdered, but there was never any reason to think that Nina had been killed. She went of her own free will, according to police, taking her card and phone, and the last supposed sight of her was on CCTV at Paddington station, where she vanished into the crowd, never to be seen again. Just another troubled teenage runaway, living on the streets somewhere.

But however much Eleri tries to reassure herself of this, the creeping dread that something far worse has happened to Nina comes out in her dreams. The Nina of her dreams is a darker, more ambiguous presence than the kind, quiet, funny girl she knew. Eleri thinks she knows why her brain has done this but it's just paranoia. Whatever the reason for Nina's disappearance, it could never be something so trivial. She puts it out of her mind and gets up.

Today she and Mum are going Christmas shopping. They don't have that many people to buy for this year: only Aunty Lynne, Uncle David, cousin Isla, her godmother Lauren, and each other. Last year there was Gran too, but she only ever wanted a nightie or pairs of knickers so massive you could use them as tents. This time last year Gran had just gone into the home. She'd complained that the other residents were simple, but she seemed to like the nurses who would make time to chat with her, even though they were rushed off their feet. Covid got her the following Easter and for a while Eleri thought her mum would never stop crying.

It's Gran's birthday tomorrow. She would have been seventy-eight. Mum says that's "no age" these days, but it seems impossibly remote to Eleri. She's not sure she would even want to get to that age if she had a choice. Apart from her and Mum, Gran had no one. All her friends had died or fallen away, losing their minds or their health, marooned in other pastel-coloured rooms, surrounded by photos of people who had either died or never bothered to visit. Eleri and Mum visited Gran every single Sunday, and even though Eleri complained about it, she knew it was the right thing to do. You don't just forget someone when they get old. Not even when they die. They will be making the pilgrimage to Gran's grave tomorrow, even though the weather is due to be awful and the grave is miles away from the bus stop so it's a real pain for Mum.

They take the tube to the big shopping centre at White City. It's always fun going round these places, but realistically the only shops they can buy anything from are Primark, Claire's and Tiger. Emerging from the tube station Eleri is briefly overwhelmed by the crowds and the noise and the riot of colour and sparkle. Every shop has been decorated to bewitch and bedazzle, to draw you in like a gingerbread house. They join the shuffling throng of shoppers, passing windows full of perfume bottles and iPhones and party dresses. Everything is the Perfect Gift: *for a football mad teen, for a baker, for his man cave.* There are drinking games and cake-pop makers and chocolate "reindeer poop". But as much as she knows it is all junk and by Boxing Day it will be piled up ready to be chucked out for half the price, she's not immune to the tug of longing. Maybe she *would* like a glass jar of rainbow cookie mix or a head massager. They pass a toy shop and she spots her octopus's enigmatic smile on the shell of a cuddly lobster. The fabric label says *Jellycat* and the tag reads £45. She smiles: who needs cookie pops anyway?

While Mum goes into M&S to get a tin of biscuits for Mr Vaseli who often brings up their post for them, Eleri waits outside the clothes shop next door.

A huge window poster shows a beautiful mixed race girl and boy, with amber freckles and caramel curls. Their slim arms are entwined and they gaze at one another with matching turquoise eyes. Eleri has boring brown eyes, boring brown hair and her granddad's Turkish nose that dips down at the end when she smiles. Beni says it's cute, but the cuteness seems to elude most of the boys at EHS.

People do grow into their features, though. Her mum was a weird-looking kid, but by the time she turned eighteen she was beautiful. And whatever Mum says, it matters. It takes a brave person to reject the tyranny of it all – the dieting and make-up and clothes posts on social media – and not care about your looks at all. Like Nina. So much easier to be Tamara George, adored by all.

Mum comes out, tucking a tin in the shape of a fairground

carousel into her Bag for Life. Eleri catches a glimpse of the price label. £9.99, which seems steep considering they never have much post. She has also bought a box of mini baubles. Seeing as they have loads of Eleri's tatty handmade decorations in a box and Mum's always saying how much more *special* they are than bought ones, this seems like an unnecessary extravagance.

"OK, Primark is on the second floor, so let's get the escalator."

Piped music from overhead speakers is playing "Stop the Cavalry". Eleri has always considered this song way too sad for Christmas. It's about a man who is fighting a war and just wants to be home with his family. The song ends and "Fairytale of New York" begins, and people immediately start singing along. She waits for the line with the F-slur: sure enough, no one has thought to censor it, and the singing continues unabated. Beni would be scandalized.

Realizing her mum is no longer at her side, she cranes her neck to peer over the heads. Mum has paused outside a jewellery store lit so that it looks like a window full of stars. When Gran died they inherited her gold jewellery, but almost straight away Mum sold it all to catch up with the mortgage arrears that had built up since she resigned. For a couple of months she wore Gran's engagement ring on her right hand, a twenty-four carat gold band with a huge square emerald surrounded by diamonds, but eventually that had to go too. The thousand pounds they got for it was gone in a month.

Eleri goes over to where she stands, slightly lopsided, with one shoulder higher than the other.

Close up the jewellery store is just tat. Cheap plated metal with stones of glass or plastic. You'd wear something a week and the gold would rub off to dull grey.

"What do you think of those?" Mum points at a tiny pair of faux-diamond studs. "For Isla."

"They're thirty quid. You said twenty pounds was the budget for everyone."

Her mum doesn't reply to this, only lowers her head and limps away. Eleri experiences a lurch of guilt. She's hurt her feelings, made her feel like she can't provide for her family.

It's boring shopping with no money, so while her mum browses the Primark onesies and pyjamas for Aunty Lynne, Eleri sits on a faux-leather cube nearby and scrolls through her Insta feed.

Her finger pauses at a post from Ras. His chin is resting on the head of a black pug, and he's doing a very accurate impression of its lolling tongue and slightly crossed eyes. Sunlight pouring through the window behind him has given his hair a kind of halo.

The comment reads: Gotta love pugs.

Kika has commented: Seriously pugly.

Beni always says she doesn't flirt enough, that no one would ever know if she liked them, and she has wondered if that was the reason Ras gave up on her last year.

Maybe she should try. Because she doesn't want this

to stop, whatever it is. The unnerving part of what's been happening at Gibea Tower is what makes it so exhilarating. The sense of unpredictability, of wildness that perfectly encapsulates Ras himself. And if he gets no response at all, maybe he'll lose interest.

She types a comment beneath Ras's post then, before she can change her mind, sends it.

```
I prefer octopuses.
```

Almost immediately a red heart pops up in the corner. He has liked the comment.

Predictably enough this is followed by a comment about pussies from Teddy P, and then the feed refreshes and his post disappears.

Mum is still rummaging around in the nightwear section, so she messages Calista.

```
How r u?
```

Calista must be on her phone because the reply is immediate.

```
Ok. Thnx 4 last nite. Sorry 2 b a
pain.

U werent. Its fine.

Wot u doing?
```

At Westfield with mum.

She kicks herself straight away when the message is marked as read, but Calista makes no response. *Don't mention mums.* Sighing, she puts the phone away and goes to join her mum, who has chosen a fleecy rabbit onesie for Aunt Lynne and a koala one for Uncle David, who is Australian. They're only twenty-two pounds each, and Mum will also give them jars of home-made halva.

"I need a sugar hit," Mum announces when they get out of the shop. "Shall we get cake?"

Eleri stops herself from saying that cakes here will probably cost a fiver each, and they head down to the basement food halls. At the bottom of the escalators a crowd of schoolgirls are blocking their path, and when Mum says, "Excuse me," they look her up and down before grudgingly moving aside. As they pass, Mum completely ignores the suppressed titters and Eleri lowers her gaze.

The crowds are starting to disperse now and they find a free table at a central island selling freshly baked pretzels. They are six pounds each. Eleri says she could never eat a whole one and that she's really thirsty so can she just have a glass of tap water. Mum gets a coffee and they share a spice-dusted knot of warm dough that is so delicious Eleri ensures not a single grain of cinnamony sugar is left on the plate. To preserve the deliciousness in her mouth she doesn't drink the water. Mum finishes her coffee and heads to the toilet.

71

The shopping centre is emptying out, so it must be getting late. Is it past four? She takes out her phone. The message is waiting for her.

Door 4.

It is accompanied by an emoji of a koala.

Eleri frowns and looks around quickly, searching the faces of the shoppers streaming by for a familiar tangle of black curls.

But fifteen minutes ago Ras was playing with his cousin's pug, so how could he also be here watching them buying the koala onesie? She checks her feed again. His message was posted thirty minutes ago. Could he have made it here in time? She doesn't even know where he lives.

Her Snapmap is crowded with avatars, but she can't see Ras's. Beni is there, at his local park, but Calista is not. There was a talk at school about stalkers last year and quite a lot of them turned their locations off after that. She checks her own settings. Her location's off too, which means that the only way anyone would know she was here would be if they were actually following her in person.

"Ready?"

She jumps as her mum appears at her side.

"Ooh, someone's twitchy. Got some secrets there?"

"No." Eleri thrusts the phone back into her pocket and gets up to go.

*

It's not a koala, she decides when they get home. It's just a grey bear (maybe hinting at another cuddly toy). Sometimes emojis don't cross platforms perfectly. She can't remember what phone Ras has.

The light streaming out of a window on the fourth floor of Gibea Tower as they tramped across the grass was so obvious that Eleri kept waiting for Mum to notice, but she didn't, and now they are back in the flat Eleri is wondering how she can get back out there.

"You OK with green curry for supper?" Mum calls through from the kitchen. "I've got some ready meals in the freezer."

"Yeah, great," she calls back from the sofa. An idea occurs to her. "Have we got prawn crackers?"

"No, I don't think so."

"I've got a real craving for them."

"Go out and get some then, if you can be bothered." Mum hobbles in and hands Eleri her debit card.

"OK," Eleri says, feeling guilty. "I won't be long. I'll just go to the Nisa."

When she gets out of the lift, Eleri calls Calista on FaceTime.

"I can't believe you're doing this again!"

"Nothing bad's happened so far, has it?"

"He was lulling you into a false sense of security."

"He could have killed me the first day if he wanted to."

"What about that junkie Mr Roberts warned us about?"

"The homeless guy? He wouldn't be able to organize all this, and why would he want to?"

73

"No, I mean that he's been seen in the area again. I heard people talking about it after school on Friday. He went up to a girl in Murder Alley." This is the shortcut that runs to the tube station. "But then one of the upper six boys came along and scared him off. If he hadn't, he could have just pulled her through the gap in the fence and strangled her or something."

Eleri pauses, her arm outstretched to open the main door. How long has this guy been hanging about? Could he have had something to do with Nina's disappearance? Eleri went to Nina's house once and they took the shortcut to get there. But surely the police would have searched the wasteland on the other side of the alley.

"What are you waiting for?" Calista huffs. "Let's get this over with."

Crossing the grass, Eleri lets herself in through the splintered door and makes her way to the stairwell. The night is clear and steady moonlight illuminates the stairs all the way up to the fourth floor. She runs up, bursts through the door and takes the left corridor – the light blared shamelessly from the front of the building tonight. Surely someone will report it to the council in the end.

Her trainers squeak against the lino as she walks towards the light streaming from a door halfway down.

Sitting in the middle of the floor of flat 46 is a tin of Quality Street. It's sealed with tape around the edge so must be brand new.

"There's *your* Secret Santa sorted, then." Calista smirks. "You can regift it."

"Yeah…"

Is she disappointed? Maybe a bit. It's a fairly unimaginative gift. She checks herself — what a brat. So far he has given her an Elf on the Shelf, a forty-quid cuddly toy AND a box of chocolates. And who knows, maybe he's going to carry on with this all the way until Christmas, so he's allowed a no-brainer now and again.

Emerging into the chill night with the tin under her arm, she finds she isn't as breathless as normal, despite the extra two flights of stairs. She's starting to get used to this whole thing. Starting, actually, to enjoy it.

"Thanks for coming, Cal."

"Hmm. If there's another one tomorrow, FaceTime me again, or just call and I'll come over."

"OK."

"I heard from Mum, by the way. Freya's in hospital with pneumonia."

"Wow."

"I know, right." Her tone is flat.

"Hope she gets better before Christmas," Eleri says tentatively, not wanting to wish Freya well if Calista is still bitter.

"Yeah."

She hangs up and heads back towards the lights of Shiloh, planning her excuse for no prawn crackers. At the door she pauses and, looking back at the light still burning softly in the darkened tower, finds herself smiling.

Sunday December 5

"Where did you get this guy? He's cute."

Eleri looks up from her phone. Mum has put a pile of laundry on her desk and is holding the Elf on the Shelf at arm's length. The day is so overcast that Eleri has had to turn on her desk lamp, and in its warm light the little round face glows with cheer.

"Calista," she says.

"That's sweet." Her mum settles the doll back on the bookshelf. "What's she doing for Christmas? Will she be spending it with her mum?"

"I don't know. She might not want to leave Paul on his own."

"God, no." Mum grimaces. "I suppose we could invite them both here. It'll just be the two of us this year."

Eleri makes a face. Paul can't help being depressed but there's something about him that drains all the life and fun out of a room. Eleri can't imagine what it must be like actually living with him.

Her mum leans against the wardrobe, arms folded – lecture pose. "You have to be kind to people, El. He's having a really tough time at the moment."

"I know…"

"Don't you remember when you were little and you used to love going over to their house? He would set up assault courses in the garden and have Nerf gun battles with you. Once you asked him if he'd be your dad."

"I did not!"

"You did. He was a good man, and he still is, underneath it all. When people are depressed they aren't great to be around, but that's when they need you most."

Eleri sighs.

Her mum pushes herself upright. "I get it though, and it's our Christmas too."

As she heads out of the room Eleri calls after her. "When are we leaving for the cemetery?"

"No rush. I need to pick up my prescription first."

The cemetery is a tube, overground and bus ride away in East London, which was where Gran lived most of her life with Granddad Musa, who died of lung cancer when Eleri was nine. By the time they emerge into Liverpool Street station, the rain, which was a drizzle when they left home, has become a deluge. It thunders on the station roof and finds its way through cracks and holes to drip on the heads of the travellers and turn the floor to an ice rink. Mum buys a large bunch of pink and white lilies to put in the metal vase on Gran's grave.

This part of London was once the seat of industry and as the train chunters out of the station they pass warehouses with all their windows smashed and huge, brick sheds with rusting corrugated-iron roofs. Mum says nothing, only stares out at the bars of rain.

The bus stop is already crowded when they emerge from the station and they're forced to stand at the very edge of the shelter, half in the rain, so by the time the bus arrives, one side of Eleri's jacket is drenched. On the bus they manage to find a seat together but it's impossible to see out – the windows are steamed up, condensation streaming down them like tears.

Eleri wipes one with her sleeve. Red brake lights stretch as far as the eye can see. They will be sitting here for hours. She swallows her irritation. There is absolutely no point making this interminable journey to stand in the rain and look at a piece of granite, no point wasting money on flowers that will just wilt and decay and be dumped on the compost heap by the cemetery groundskeeper. *Dead is dead*, as Granddad Musa used to say. Gran wouldn't want them weeping over her grave. She isn't there. She isn't anywhere any more.

A screen on the back of the driver's booth switches between views from security cameras stationed at various points in the bus. Not all the passengers' faces are visible:

many of the women wear niqabs and burquas while others have hoods pulled far down, but the ones that are display the same misery and boredom Eleri feels.

She takes out her phone. According to Snap, Beni is up in town. Maybe he's choosing the new trainers he wants for Christmas. Beni's parents are quite rich. His mum works for the BBC and his dad is on the board of some charity. She checks Insta. Nothing from Ras, though the hockey girls appear to be ice-skating at the Natural History Museum. There are beautifully filtered photos of them laughing and holding each other up and sipping hot chocolate with marshmallows and cream. This depresses Eleri's mood even more. She's said no so many times to hanging out with them after school that they don't bother asking her any more, and though it's her own fault it still hurts.

A prickling sensation of being watched makes her glance up at the CCTV screen. Nothing much has changed, apart from a few of the older passengers seem to have fallen asleep.

The bus finally pulls into the stop outside the cemetery and a straggle of people get out, presumably all making their annual Christmas duty visit.

Mum struggles even to climb down off the bus – the weather does this to her sometimes – and Eleri waits while she stretches out her stiff leg in preparation for the trek to the grave.

The ranks of stones march away into the distance, dull grey beneath a dull grey sky. The only colour in the whole bleak landscape is from the dying petals of the bouquets rotting in tarnished vases, heads lolling, leaves turned to black slime.

They set off down the main artery that leads to Gran's section, the rain pitter-pattering on Eleri's hood and Mum's umbrella. The gravel path is one long puddle that immediately soaks her trainers and it would seem that "showerproof" doesn't mean "waterproof" because her jacket is soon drenched and she pulls in her stomach to keep it from brushing up against the damp chill of her T-shirt.

Before Gran died, Eleri used to like cemeteries, trying to spot the oldest grave, reading the names and the things people had chosen to say about their lost loved ones.

Loved by all. Together at last. Gone but not forgotten.

Now she just finds them depressing. There are dead toddlers and teenagers, young mums and dads who left little kids. And it turns out death has none of the romantic poignancy she used to imagine it did from watching films like *Romeo and Juliet* and *The Fault in Our Stars*. It's just absence, regret and guilt. Mum thinks she should have done more for Gran – visited more, had her live with them, taken her out of the home as soon as Covid hit.

They're passing a particularly elaborate marble edifice featuring scrolls and angels and an enamel portrait of a child with blonde bunches when suddenly she understands. They're not doing this for Gran, they're doing it for Mum. It's a kind of pilgrimage to appease her guilt. Death is worse for the survivors.

They come level with the chapel, a modern concrete box

with a little porch that they could stop and shelter in if it looked like the rain was going to ease any time soon. This was where they had the service for Gran, a handful of family and friends and a few of the nurses from the home, listening to the priest talk about how much Gran liked Argentine tango. It turned out he'd mixed her up with the next old lady – they were all dying so fast it was easy to get confused.

Rain pours from the eaves and gushes from the flooded gutters.

When they reach the right row they pick their way across the waterlogged grass to the simple rectangular stone of pink marble etched with a picture of two roses intertwined.

Musak Kirdar, 1941–2015. Beloved husband, dad and granddad.

Pearl Kirdar 1943–2021. Greatly missed but together at last.

While Mum tucks the flowers into the vase and spends ages arranging them to her satisfaction, Eleri slips her phone out of her pocket and checks the time. Two twenty-three. An hour and a half until the next message is due. The sun is already low in the western sky.

"Can you do the back and I'll do the front?" Mum's holding out a clump of wet wipes. Eleri takes them, trying not to roll her eyes, and sets about cleaning the back of the stone. This has become their ritual. Flower arranging, cleaning and weeding, though the weeds have stopped growing now that it's winter. Once that's done and Eleri is hoping they can finally go home, Mum takes out the box of mini baubles and begins hanging them on to the flowers.

Eleri shifts from foot to foot, making her trainers squelch. A few bedraggled crows watch mournfully from the bare branch of a nearby tree. The sound of an approaching bus makes her glance towards the road. Through the mist of rain she can make out the red blur of the bus, with its warm yellow windows. They come every half an hour, and because of the wet wipes nonsense they're going to miss this one. Then she sees something else. A sliver of darkness against the white porch of the chapel, as if someone is standing there, sheltering from the rain.

"Did I ever tell you about Lee Taylor?"

She turns back to her mum. "What?"

"He was in my class at primary school and he used to spit at my back as I walked home. He also called me horrible names but that was par for the course in those days. Ow!" A thorn has drawn a bead of blood from her thumb. She puts it in her mouth.

Eleri glances back at the chapel but the figure, if it was a figure, is gone.

"He lived in this lovely detached house with a proper front lawn and flower beds. They used to enter their hydrangeas for competitions. Anyway, I never told your gran, but one day I forgot to clean the spit off my jacket when I got in and she saw it."

"Was she angry?"

Mum's answer is a belly laugh. "Your granddad didn't want to make a fuss, so Gran went round to their house one night and sprayed the whole front lawn and all the flower beds with weedkiller. Within two weeks everything had turned brown and died. I had to try not to laugh every time I walked past." Hanging the last bauble on a rose leaf, she straightens up. "There you go, Mum." She pats the shoulder of the stone gently. "All dressed up for Christmas. Right, Eleri, shall we go?"

They make their very slow way back to the road, but when they get to the chapel there is no one there and the doors are closed.

The message comes through as they are climbing the steps out of the tube station.

```
Door 5.
```

This time there is no emoji.

Mum stops halfway up the last flight, leaning heavily on the banister, her face grey. Eleri jogs back down to help her, but she waves her off.

"Don't worry about me," Mum says. "You go on home. I don't want you standing about in the rain catching your death."

Eleri's about to protest, but then she changes her mind. If she runs it will take her less than five minutes to get back to the estate, and it will take Mum at least ten, maybe fifteen, so she has a clear window of five to seven minutes to be in and out of Gibea.

"OK. I'll run you a bath, then."

"Lovely, thanks." Mum smiles, though her eyes are crinkled with pain.

Eleri runs all the way, her steps only faltering when Gibea rises up in front of her, in apparent darkness. But then she notices a faint glow coming from the side of the building.

Today there is no moon to light the stairwell as she trudges up the ten flights to the fifth floor. Remembering the open lift shaft on this side of the building she turns her torch app on and follows its cold glow to flat 58.

The gift is very small, and this time it's wrapped in Christmas paper featuring what looks like an angel. She can only see its flowing hair and halo. There isn't time to open it now.

Back home Eleri has five minutes to hang up her coat, get the bath on, strip off her wet clothes and dive into her onesie before she hears the lift announce, "Floor thirteen."

She waits till her mum is safely ensconced in the bathroom before slipping the present out of her jacket pocket. The wet fabric has turned the Christmas wrapping paper soft and pulpy, blurring the features of the angel, and she really hopes the gift inside isn't damaged.

Carefully peeling off the paper, she discovers a small velvet box with a hinged lid.

She opens it and her breath catches.

It's a gold ring. But not the sort of gold that rubs to grey. She knows this because, easing it out of the slot in the cushion, she finds a hallmark on the inside of the band. And this makes her think that, just possibly, the large clear stone in the middle, standing at least half a centimetre from the bridge, might be a real diamond.

Monday December 6

At first break on Monday morning, Eleri, Calista and Beni head for the DT block: a prefab building at the edge of the sports pitches. They've looked online and, without taking the ring to a jeweller's, there's only one test they can do to see if the stone is real. Apparently if you rub a real diamond against sandpaper it doesn't get a scratch, whereas a fake one will be ruined.

To get there they have to pass Ray's shed. It's a long, low wooden building that the groundskeeper religiously creosotes every summer in a pair of faded shorts that show off his varicose-veined legs. A monosyllabic, wiry man in his sixties, Ray speaks to no one unless he is forced to, and then only in gruff monosyllables. A bushy grey beard conceals all his features apart from his eyes, which look out from behind large square bifocals, and his clothes are grubby and threadbare. The younger children refer to themselves as

Ray-prey, and though it's pretty par for the course that any adult male dealing with kids is accused of being a nonce, there is definitely something weird about the way Ray has put up curtains in the shed. He keeps them closed all the time, as if he's doing something in there he doesn't want anyone to see.

As they walk past the shed, slivers of light are visible through the cracks in the curtains and his shadow moves back and forth across them.

One of the rooms of the DT block is occupied by a small, scowling Year 8, using the 3D printer to produce mini Marvel figures, so they walk on to the next, at the far end of the building, looking out over the football pitches. Large tables fill the space, and beneath each Formica top are drawers that contain all manner of crafty things – scissors, glue guns, clamps, scalpels, etc. There must be some sandpaper somewhere.

Opening one, Eleri rummages through sawdust shavings and scraps of newspaper that waft a strong smell of old grease.

"New boy alert," Beni says. He is gazing out of the window at a gaggle of Year 11s scuffling over a neon-pink football. He gives a shrill squeak. "Oh my days, he just looked at me!"

"Ben!" Calista snaps. "This is serious. Help us here."

He sighs, and turns away reluctantly.

"Got some!" Calista holds up a burgundy-coloured roll. "It's pretty coarse, like bits of sugar. Do you think that's OK?"

Beni goes over to her. "It'll definitely show if it's real."

Eleri bites her lip. "What if it isn't? It's still a nice ring. I don't know if I want to ruin it."

"Oh, give it here." Calista snatches the box from her hand. "If it's a piece of crap, who cares?"

As she plucks the ring unceremoniously from its cushion, Beni tears off a strip of the sandpaper and smooths it out on the table. Now Calista puts the ring on her own finger and, before Eleri can stop her, she makes her hand into a fist and begins scraping the ring up and down the sandpaper. There is an ugly rasping sound and the ring leaves a smear of white.

Eleri winces.

Finally the paper tears.

"Stop, please," Eleri says as Calista moves to another section.

"Yeah, that should do it," Beni says, holding out his hand. Calista slides off the ring and he carries it over to the window. "We'll see better in the light."

Eleri scampers after him. The football pitch is empty now, as Beni holds the ring up to the wintery sunlight.

For a few seconds there is complete silence.

"Well, as my granny used to say, blow me..."

The stone glitters, white fire burning at its heart. As Beni turns it slowly, each tiny facet flashes, as unblemished as a pane of glass.

"Let me see." Calista snatches the ring.

"See?" Beni says. "Not a scratch. That, my darlings, is a real-life, bona fide diamond."

"How much would something like that cost?" Eleri breathes.

Beni takes out his phone, taps it, stares at the screen, then looks up at her. "About a grand."

Eleri gives a breathless laugh, but Calista is stony-faced. "You need to give it back." She hands the ring back to Eleri. "It's obviously stolen."

Eleri's face falls. Beni wrinkles his nose and sighs. "She's probably right, El. I mean, Ras's bike is a deathtrap, his shoes are scuffed to hell and his shirts are all too small: he's not exactly minted, is he?"

She lays the ring down on the worktop where it glints in the overhead lights. It's the most beautiful thing she's ever seen and, however briefly, it was hers.

At the end of the day Beni and Calista hang around the gates as Eleri trudges over to the bike racks. She's almost sorry to see that Ras hasn't gone yet, then she could avoid what is bound to be an awkward confrontation. He doesn't even bother with a lock: his rusty red bike just leans wonkily against the metal arch. The gash in the ancient saddle has got bigger since last year, the foam spilling out to expose the wooden base. She can remember the way the ragged plastic scratched her thigh when she rode on it last year, Ras sitting pillion behind her.

He had been taking her and Nina for a milkshake to make up for the detention. The MooBar was only a few hundred metres from school and they did over a hundred different flavours: Eleri's favourite being peanut butter and banana.

They met here, at the bike rack, and Ras offered to take turns with the two girls riding pillion. Nina looked dubious, so when they got out of the school gates he told Eleri to jump on and, amazingly, she did. They freewheeled down the pavement, with Nina jogging along beside them. His chest was warm under her arms and when a bus went past it blew his hair against her face.

After a few minutes, Nina pulled up to a panting halt. Steering into the kerb, Eleri said brightly, "Your turn, then!" and sprang off the bike so fast Ras almost toppled off backwards.

"I don't know. I'm probably too heavy."

"Course you're not," Ras said. "Hop up behind me."

Blushing, Nina climbed on. She wrapped her arms around him, burying her face in his Harrington jacket as he pulled away, wobbling slightly, the spoke beads clacking.

But it was like Nina wasn't used to the weight of her body. Almost immediately she seemed to be off balance, clutching at Ras to steady herself, and then the bike lurched sideways and she toppled off. Throwing out her arm, she landed jarringly and cried out in pain.

They wheeled her the half mile to the Minor Injuries Unit, Eleri holding her on the saddle while Ras steered, keeping up a steady stream of banter to keep Nina's mind off her rapidly swelling wrist. Eleri was surprised by how tough Nina was about the whole thing. She didn't cry at all. For some reason she had imagined that an overweight, nerdy girl would dissolve into tears at the drop of a hat. Which, she supposed, just went to show how prejudiced she was.

In the waiting room Ras went to the drinks machine and got them all cans, which wasn't as good as a milkshake but they clinked them and blamed him for all their troubles. It was then that Eleri noticed the scar running from the heel of Nina's other hand, up her forearm, to disappear into the sleeve of her coat. For a moment she thought it was a self-harm scar, but she'd seen plenty of those before and they weren't that thick – Nina's scar tissue was raised and purple – plus they didn't have little lines where stitches had been.

"Have you broken your wrist before?" she said.

Nina's smile vanished. Swapping the can to her other hand, she pulled the sleeve down over her hand and said nothing. Eleri glanced at Ras helplessly.

"Right," Ras announced. "Who bets me a fiver that I can't down this can in one without burping?"

Any awkwardness was forgotten as they watched him chug the drink, then grimace and squirm as he tried to hold in the inevitable burgeoning of wind. Failing miserably he soon let out a burp that ripped through the room, and then had to apologize to every scowling face that turned in their direction. Nina spluttered into her hand and Eleri said, "Is that a fiver for both of us or between us?" but before he could answer, the doctor called Nina through.

"Jesus," Eleri had murmured, when the door had closed behind her. "What was all that about?"

Ras stuck out his bottom lip and blew his hair out of his eyes. "Looked like it was a thing, didn't it?"

"Do you think someone did it to her?"

Ras shrugged. "If she doesn't want to tell us, there's not much we can do."

"Poor thing. And she's so nice."

"Yeah, she is. And really pretty."

Eleri blinked. "You think?"

"Of course. How could you not?"

"I dunno. It's just that most boys wouldn't see under the weight and the glasses and the hair."

"I…" he announced, leaning into her and batting his eyelashes, "am not most boys."

"Thank god," Eleri huffed. "Then we really would all be screwed."

Ras laughed. "You're funny."

"You sound surprised."

"I could never tell before, what with you being joined at the hip with that blonde girl."

"Calista. She's my best friend. We've known each other since we were four."

He shrugged. "Maybe you should give other people a try too."

Eleri could have got into a sulk then, but she made a conscious decision not to be offended and steered the conversation back to safer topics like teachers and work.

Nina returned within ten minutes, her arm encased in a beige wrist support. It wasn't broken, only sprained.

Ras offered to walk them both home. "I mean, it's the least I can do, given that everything in the whole entire world is my fault."

All the way to Nina's house they went on to list these calamities. The extinction of the dodo. The First World War. The birth of Hitler. The shrinking of Snickers bars. Ed Sheeran.

Nina lived in a sweet little red–brick terraced house, with net curtains and a burgundy-painted door, with a brass knocker in the shape of a hand. When she let herself in, a woman came bustling up the hall: diminutive and bespectacled with light brown skin and frizzy black hair flecked with grey. When she saw Nina's arm she cried out in heavily accented English: *What happened now?* To his credit, Ras owned up immediately and the woman peered at him curiously.

"You are new friends of Nina's?"

They said they were, and after that day the three of them *were* friends, at least until Nina disappeared and Ras stopped talking to her.

On the way back from Nina's, Eleri told him she lived with just her mum, and it turned out they had that in common.

"My parents split up when I was eight and my brother was twelve," he said. "Then my dad moved back to Chennai. What about yours? Is he close?"

Eleri hesitates. "I've never met my dad."

"Did he die or…?"

"I just never met him." She turned away, biting her lip. It was common enough to have divorced parents but she knew from experience that most people did *have* a dad, even if they didn't see them much.

For a while they walked on in silence and then Ras said, "My mum has some mental health problems." He said it quietly but without any apparent shame or embarrassment.

"I'm sorry, that must be hard."

"Sometimes."

Eleri took a deep breath. "My mum has cerebral palsy."

"What's that?"

She bit her lip. She'd kept it a secret all these years, with only Calista and Beni knowing. Would Ras tell his friends, would everyone start following her round the playground like they did at primary school, grunting and staggering and flapping their hands?

"It's OK," he said. "You don't have to say."

"No, it's fine. It happened when she was born. They didn't get her out in time and her brain was starved of oxygen. Her mind is fine but she has some physical problems. She shakes, and her left arm and leg don't work properly. It affects her voice too, so she sounds a bit weird sometimes." She tailed off.

"I guess you have to help out a lot at home then, right?"

"Yeah. I don't mind, though." This is a lie. No other teenager she knows cooks dinner every other night – more now that Mum's working – as well as doing the laundry and washing-up and hoovering. Half of the reason she doesn't know anyone – the half that isn't down to Calista – is that she can never just hang out after school. She has to get back and do her chores. If Mum hadn't resigned they would have more money: they could get takeaways now and again.

"I do," Ras said simply. "Sometimes I really resent her for being sick. I know it's not her fault, but I just wish we were like other families, going shopping and to the cinema and stuff, going on holiday." He looked at Eleri and shrugged. She felt a rush of gratitude.

"Me too, actually," she admitted, and it felt so good to tell the truth to someone who understood. "What's up with your mum?"

"She has schizophrenia. Sometimes she's too scared to get out of bed. She has delusions and hallucinations. Once she thought a bear was hibernating in our spare room and wouldn't let us go in in case we woke it up."

Eleri laughed, then slapped a hand over her mouth. "I'm so sorry, I didn't mean…"

But Ras just smiled. "It's OK. Me and my brother called him Maddington. We left a jar of marmalade outside the room and gradually ate it and she totally believed it was the bear. When she was better again she thought it was funny."

"She sounds really nice."

"She is when she's well. And as long as she takes her medication she's fine." He sighed. "I used to wish I had a different mum, but now I just think you get what you get and you have to make the best of it. Some people are really lucky and have these perfect lives with normal healthy

95

parents that love each other and they have plenty of money, but I don't think it's many people."

"Beni has that."

"The guy with the hair like Sideshow Bob? Is he your boyfriend?"

"No, just a mate. But he was bullied at primary school because of being gay, so it hasn't been perfect for him either."

"We're all warriors," Ras said, then he made a fierce face and kissed his biceps.

And then suddenly they had reached the estate. It felt too soon, and for a moment she couldn't bring herself to say goodbye.

"Thanks. For walking me back. It was nice." She added quickly, "Of you."

"My pleasure. Turns out Eleri Kirdar is all right. You should let her out more."

He saluted her with two fingers then turned his bike around. Eleri set off down the path, but stopped and looked back when he called her name.

"If you, er, ever get fed up with stuff, just, er, just message me." He scratched the back of his head. "I can cheer you up by telling you about the time Mum thought my teacher was actually an MI5 agent who was going to implant a tracking device into my brain."

She smiled. "Yeah, I'd like that."

"What?" He frowned, confused. "Me having a tracking device implanted in my brain?"

Eleri laughed and he saluted again then walked quickly away, jumping on his bike when he got to the road and riding away into the traffic.

Before that day she could never have imagined Ras Mandip speaking about things like love and care and duty, and the way he talked openly about his mum put her own embarrassment about her mum's condition to shame. Perhaps he wasn't the bad boy everyone thought he was: perhaps he might actually be a good person. She suspected, in fact, that he might even be a better person than her.

And now suddenly he is standing right in front of her, a little bit taller than last year, his jaw more angular, a faint dusting of stubble on his upper lip.

"Couldn't keep away from me, huh?"

He's wearing an enormous khaki parka with a hood that frames his face in whispery grey fur.

"Oh, hi." Her face ignites. She can only hope the blueish glow from the playground floodlights takes it down a tone or two.

He wheels his bike out from between the racks. "Want a lift home?"

"Actually, I'm…"

"Oh, it's *actually*, is it?" He leans on the saddle and folds his arms. "Come on, then. What have I done now?"

"I'm not being funny," she gabbles. "It's really nice and everything." *Nice?* "I mean, it's been fun. I've really enjoyed it, but I just can't…" She glances across to the bench. Beni's on his phone but Cal is scowling over at them. She takes a deep breath, draws the ring box out of her pocket and holds it out to him. "I just can't accept this."

She winces in preparation for his response. Judging by whatever got to him last year, he's obviously super touchy, so this rejection is bound to piss him off. She avoids his eyes as he takes the box from her hand and opens it.

There's a long pause in which she concentrates on not looking at him. A crowd of vapers has gathered just outside the gate, their faces hazy in the plumes of smoke that drift across the playground, bringing with it the sweet scents of vanilla and strawberry. Above them the sky has darkened to indigo and the first stars are popping out, like pinpricks in a velvet curtain. Finally he speaks.

"You don't think this is a bit soon? I mean, you're a great girl, but marriage, at our age?" He grins, exposing the twisted incisor that is so much nicer than a mouthful of veneers, like Tamara George and her friends have.

"I... I..." she stammers in confusion.

The grin fades. "Wait. Did you think this was from me?"

She stares. "Isn't it?"

"Er, no."

"You didn't leave it for me, in the tower?"

"What tower?"

"Oh my god," she mutters, the colour draining from her face.

"Where did you get this? It looks expensive."

"Th... There's been a misunderstanding. I... I'm really sorry." She's so mortified she can barely coordinate her body movements to snatch the ring back and hurry away to the bench.

"Eleri!" he calls after her.

"It wasn't him," she hisses when she gets there. "Come on, let's go."

"Seriously?" Beni says.

"Can we please go? Now!"

They flank her like an armed guard as she passes Ras on the way to the gates. She doesn't even glance at him, but she can feel his eyes on her all the way to the bus stop.

As the bus pulls away she feels sick and weak, like she's got flu.

"Of course he denied it," Calista snaps.

"Why would he do that?"

"Because he gets a kick out of mind games. What did I tell you? The guy's a psycho."

Eleri stares out of the window as the bus picks up speed, turning the lights of the shops to coloured smears.

"I get it that unstable people can be exciting, El, but you really don't want to get involved with him. If he gets a kick out of screwing with your head like this, then he's capable of anything. Forget him, honestly. He's not worth even thinking about." Calista lays a hand on her shoulder and gives it a gentle squeeze, but Eleri doesn't respond. She's angry and upset, and not only because of what just happened, but because deep down she knows that Calista is probably right.

They don't say much for the rest of the journey, but as Cal gets off she leans in to kiss Eleri, leaving her characteristic scent of cherry lip balm. It's a comfortingly familiar smell and it makes her feel the tiniest bit better.

When the bus pulls up at the estate, she sees that Gibea Tower is in complete darkness. She experiences a mixture of disappointment and relief. That brief conversation was all it took for Ras to give up. Calista is right: he isn't worth thinking about.

Crossing the road she sets off down the flickering path. The clear sky has turned the night bitterly cold and there's not a breath of wind. The stillness is almost uncanny, in fact, seeming to mute all sound as if an invisible blanket has been spread out across the estate. She's glad to pass through the doors of Shiloh and even gladder to see a young mum and her two little kids already waiting for the lift. A moment later it arrives and she holds the door open for the children to totter in before entering after them.

But as she turns to press the buttons, she sees she was wrong. Gibea is not in total darkness. On the side of the building that faces towards the railway line, a light is on.

She steps back out into the atrium and the doors slide closed behind her. Alone in the gloom, she breathes deeply.

Was Ras lying, like Calista said? It doesn't necessarily mean he's playing mind games with her. *Secret* Santa is the point. It's no fun if he admits it.

She takes her phone out of the pocket of her jacket. Two messages: one from Mum that says she's going to be late as they've asked her to cover the first part of someone's evening shift. And another that says: Door 6.

The game is back on.

Letting herself out of the building, she sets off across the grass towards the dark side of Gibea, but as she rounds the corner of the abandoned tower her steps falter. Someone is standing by the back door. The high window casts only the faintest glow and he is just a silhouette against the darkening sky, bulky in his parka. She smiles.

"Caught in the act!"

The figure turns and for a moment they regard one another, perfectly still. That's when she notices the smell in the air, unpleasant and sickly sweet. It takes her a moment to place it: human body odour mixed with alcohol. There is a rustle, followed by a clinking of bottles, and then he is coming towards her.

The smile dies on Eleri's lips because the gait is so unlike Ras's usual long-limbed lope. It's more of a lurch, a fast one, each step accompanied by a wet grunt.

She backs away and the figure lumbers into the light streaming from Shiloh. A man, horribly emaciated: the impression of bulk created by a sleeping bag wrapped around his hunched body. From the haggard face, with hollow eye sockets and cheeks, ragged stubble and lips encrusted with sores, he could be any age from twenty to ninety. His hair hangs in matted dreadlocks and his clothes are brown with filth. He clutches a thin blue carrier bag outlining the shape of a wine bottle. Spittle flies from his toothless mouth as he bellows incoherently, swinging the blue bag back as if to hurl it at her.

Too shocked even to scream, Eleri turns and sprints away, her panicked breath and the rush of blood in her ears drowning out the sounds of pursuit. Tearing her fob from her pocket, she slams it against Shiloh's entry panel and as soon as the door starts to open, thrusts her way through the sliver of a gap. But spinning round to slam the door closed again, she sees she is safe.

The man is on his hands and knees crawling about the grass. The empty bag lies beside him, sucking and billowing in the wind, and she can see that the handle has broken. His bloodshot eyes widen and he reaches for something then draws back his hand quickly. Eleri sees a slash of blood on his palm, but he doesn't seem to notice, reaching for the object again and lifting it into the light. It is the wine bottle, its base sheared off jaggedly, its contents presumably soaking into the grass.

Throwing back his head he gives a roar of rage and grief. Eleri runs to the lift.

Tuesday December 7

The light didn't go out all night. Eleri knows because she stayed awake all night and every hour or so she went to the window. Now she barely has the energy to raise her spoonful of Shreddies to her lips.

The homeless guy is definitely not her Secret Santa, she's certain of that. He's way too chaotic, and she's never seen him before so why would he take an interest in her? But the look in his red eyes, of rage and madness, really frightened her. What if he had managed to get hold of her? Without a sixth former to come to her rescue, he could have dragged her into the tower and … and then…

At least Cal and Ben would know where to start looking for her. Her mum wouldn't have been left in limbo, like Nina's mum was, never knowing what happened to her daughter.

Nina.

She swallows her mouthful with an audible gulp.

Nina's movements were always so slow and lumbering. She couldn't have sprinted away from him. He would easily have caught her, easily overpowered her. There was the supposed sighting of Nina boarding a train, but what if that wasn't actually Nina? What if Nina never left the area? What if her body was lying, buried or covered by undergrowth, in the wasteground next to Murder Alley?

When Eleri gets to school, she confides her fears to Ben and Cal in hushed tones at the back of the form room. Beni tries to dismiss them, but she can see the doubt in his eyes and Cal goes pale.

Eleri's so tired it's hard to concentrate in her lessons, and her wretched laptop crashes halfway through English for no apparent reason, so she'll have to complete the Powerpoint presentation on Macbeth when she gets home. By the time the bell rings for the end of school, she can barely put one foot in front of the other; plus she has to do the laundry and make dinner when she gets in, and on the bus she'll no doubt have to endure another lecture from Calista. After hearing about the homeless guy, even Beni was on a downer about the Secret Santa and agreed with Cal that she should block his number and never go back to Gibea.

And the problem is, Eleri knows they're right. It was just so nice to have a break from being sensible, to do something reckless and exciting for once.

When she gets to the stop, her bus is there and she's tempted to get on it rather than wait for Calista, but that would just cause a row, and she's too tired to deal with anything like that today.

Glancing back at the gates to check if Cal's coming, she sees Ras emerge, freewheeling on his bike as he chats to Kika. Eleri pulls her hood up and takes out her phone.

And right then, when she's scrolling through TikTok, the message comes through.

Door 7.

This time it's followed by an emoji of a milkshake.

She looks up sharply. Ras's bike is nowhere to be seen. She searches the groups of EHS kids, straggling along the street and crowding the convenience stores and takeaways, but he's gone. Or else he's hiding somewhere. For a moment she considers throwing caution (and pride) to the wind and DMing him, but fortunately, before she gets the chance, Calista arrives.

As soon as she gets off the bus, she sees the light, burning boldly from the seventh floor window of Gibea Tower. Averting her gaze, she crosses the road and walks purposefully towards Shiloh without a backward glance.

After loading the washing machine, chopping veg and putting chicken in to marinade, she finishes the PowerPoint at the kitchen table, saving her document every minute because the wretched machine cannot be relied upon. They got it "reconditioned" from a shop on the high street, but it's never really worked properly.

"Don't they work you hard enough at school that they have to make you slave in the evenings too?" Mum says when she gets in.

"We've got mocks in January," Eleri says, adding in her mind, *And it wouldn't be a problem if I didn't have a million chores to do.* As if reading her mind, Mum says, "I'll do dinner tonight."

"I've done all the prep."

"What's the plan?"

"Only stir-fry."

"OK, well, I'll cook it then. I'll just have a quick bath first."

She leans in and kisses Eleri on the top of the head, then shuffles out. Because of the cost, her mum only ever has an evening bath if she's in real pain.

Eleri grinds through the final slide, but after a few minutes Mum comes back in.

"Have you seen my Sinemet pills?"

"No."

"I picked them up on Sunday and I could swear I put them in the cabinet, but there's no sign of them." She glances at her watch. "Damn. The surgery's closed. Even if I order them tomorrow they'll take three days to get to Boots." Her voice has tightened a notch. Without the medication her shake can be bad. Will she even be able to work?

Eleri starts to get up. "I'll help you look."

"No, no, no, you've got homework to do. I've just put them somewhere and forgotten. I'll check my bag again."

She leaves the kitchen and Eleri goes back to her computer. As she thinks, her eyes move to the window again, and the light burning steadily in Gibea Tower. Then she goes very still. Putting the mug back down on the table, she slips her phone from the pocket of her blazer and looks back at the message. At the milkshake emoji.

Mum is in her room feeling about under the bed.

"I need to pop downstairs for a minute."

Her mum looks up. "Why?"

"An experiment on gravitational potential energy." Hopefully Mum wasn't paying attention to what was on her screen. "I need to drop a ball down the stairwell and time how long it takes to hit the floor."

"Oh, right, OK. Well, just look out for a white and brown packet, will you? It might have fallen out of my bag on the way in, though I can't see how because I always do up the zip."

Eleri winces as she watches her mum struggle to her feet. If she's wrong, it would be better to stay and help her look. But what if she's right?

It'll only take five minutes.

When she gets out of the lift, she sprints across the grass, skidding to a halt by the splintered door. She stares into the shadows beyond, listening hard. All is still and silent.

Is this madness? Has she put two and two together and made fifteen? Shouldn't she just go home, help Mum, finish the PowerPoint, cook the stir-fry, block the Secret Santa number and have an early night?

Yes, probably, to all of the above. The wind lifts her hair, but tonight it carries with it no stink of booze and dirty body, just the faint savoury scent of the kebab shop on the high road. Yesterday was just an unfortunate coincidence, wasn't it? She happened to time her visit with the moment that the homeless guy was looking for somewhere to shelter. But maybe he *did* find shelter, inside Gibea. Maybe he's there now.

She should go home. Of course she should.

She slips through the door.

It feels like a long way up tonight. Her footsteps are small in the cavernous stairwell, and yet somehow as loud as rifle shots, and when she's passing along the seventh-floor corridor she can't help but picture ghostly occupants of the flats, ears pressed to the door, eyes glittering in the dark.

This is the last time she will ever do this, but she needed to make sure.

There's the light. She picks up speed, and is almost running by the time she gets to flat 76.

In the middle of the floor lies a slim white box with a green stripe. The label reads *Sinemet*.

The Secret Santa took the pills that keep Mum's shake under control. Which means that unless he pickpocketed her or she dropped them on the way home from the pharmacy, he has actually been inside the flat.

A thought occurs to her that makes her whole body go cold. That was why he took her bag. To copy her door keys.

This is the first time the light has been on this side of

the building, and through the window Shiloh Tower glows cheerfully against the night sky. Eleri can make out the windows of their own flat. Her bedroom is in darkness, but the lights are on in the kitchen, and her mum's hazy shadow moves back and forth. With a pair of binoculars you would be able to see in quite clearly. She has never thought of that before, never imagined that she could be observed by anyone when she came back from the shower to get into her pyjamas, or dressing for school in the morning. Someone has been following her movements, that's clear from the message sent at the shopping centre. Could they have been watching her at home too?

Adrenaline surges the strength back into her legs. Bursting out into the cold night air, she doesn't stop running until she is safely back in the flat.

"You're sweating," Mum says when she goes to the kitchen for a glass of water. "Did you have to do the experiment a few times?"

"Yeah… Any luck with the pills?"

"No. I'll just have to try and get an emergency appointment tomorrow morning."

Going into the kitchen, Eleri gazes out at the yellow eye fixed on them from Gibea Tower, and pulls the blind. Then she goes to every other window with a view of Gibea, closing all the curtains until not a chink of darkness is visible. Finally she enters the bathroom.

Glancing at her pale reflection in the foxed mirror of the cabinet, her lip curls. She's been such an idiot. Why didn't she listen to Cal? She goes back to the kitchen holding out the box of pills. "Mu-uum," she sing-songs, attempting to sound amused. "They were literally on top of the cabinet."

"They weren't!"

"Just tucked back a bit. You're just too much of a short-arse to see."

Her mum shakes her head. "Early-onset Alzheimers, I tell you."

The rest of the evening is taken up with serving dinner, eating, washing up and then sitting down to watch *Stranger Things*. Eleri can't help but notice how big the on-screen friendship group is: Will, Dustin, Mike, Lucas, Max, Robin, Jonathan, Steve and Nancy. Imagine having all those people that will always be there for you, however weird you are, like Eleven, or quiet like Will, or stroppy like Max: one big quarrelsome, irritating, wonderful family. Glancing at her mum, she feels a stab of loneliness.

In bed later she opens the messages from the unknown number and, from the menu in the corner, selects *block contact*. The messages disappear with reassuring immediacy. Now all she has to do is get the keys back, then that will be it: game over.

"Don't stay up too late on that thing," Mum says, poking her head round the door. "You know it affects your sleep."

"I won't."

The elf grins at her from the shelf.

Wednesday December 8

"Just tell him if he doesn't you'll go to the police."

The three of them are sitting on the floor of the gym, their backs against the stack of musty crash mats. It's double games this morning — a "cross-country" run around the sports pitches that is bound to descend into chaos, with kids chasing each other, running backwards and generally doing their best to antagonize the teachers — so with luck no one will notice their absence.

"She's right," Beni says. "That's just not funny. Your mum would have really suffered."

"Beni!" Calista barks, her voice echoing around the cavernous space. "That isn't the point! He's broken into her house!"

"I dunno, maybe…" Eleri tips her head back against the mats and gazes up at the white ceiling tiles, cracked and pockmarked by the balls hurled up there with the specific aim of bringing the whole ceiling down. She can hear the distant shouting and laughter of the cross-countriers. The school atmosphere is light, with the approach of Christmas, but Eleri's heart is a lead lump in her chest. She was so excited about what was happening, and now everything's spoiled. Cal was right all along: Ras is a stalker.

And yet, isn't it a funny kind of stalker who completely ignores you for a whole year?

Calista breaks the unhappy silence. "If you won't, I will. That lot vape by Ray's shed, don't they?"

Eleri nods unhappily.

"We'll go at lunchtime, and if Ras tries to bullshit us that either he hasn't taken it, or that he's left it at home or whatever, we'll go to Mr Roberts."

Eleri is about to tell Calista to go easy on Ras – she doesn't want to wind him up – when they all freeze. They all heard it. On the other side of the gym doors: a high-pitched sound like someone's trainers squeaking against the parquet floor. Scrambling up, they dive into the gap between the mats and the wall, breathing heavily. Is it a teacher? Another kid looking for a quiet refuge? Either way it sounds like they've turned around and gone away again. Tentatively, Eleri peers out.

The door is open a crack.

The gym doors are weighted. They swing shut automatically. It would never hang there ajar like that, unless someone was holding it.

"There's someone there..." she breathes.

She is propelled sideways, her own trainers squealing as she stumbles out from their hiding place, to see Calista racing for the door.

"Hey! Psycho! We know you're there!"

Beni sets off after her and the pair of them arrive at the same time, throwing themselves at the door and sending it banging against the wall with the sound of a rifle shot.

There's no one there.

"Did you see him?" Eleri pants, catching her up, but her friends don't say anything. Their eyes are fixed on a point in the middle distance.

Eleri follows their gaze.

There, on the other side of the field, sitting on another boy's shoulders in order to joust an opponent with a fallen branch, is Ras Mandip.

To Eleri it seems impossible that Ras could have been spying on them – if that's what it was – but Calista is undeterred from the lunchtime confrontation.

"So it wasn't him this morning," she snaps, striding over the grass, her blazer swinging. "That doesn't change the fact that he copied your keys and you want them back. At least I assume you do? Unless of course you want that psycho creeping into your room one night?" Calista turns her flashing eyes on her and Eleri shakes her head.

As they near the shed, she can see the wisps of white vape smoke. She has the sudden urge to turn around and go back the way she came, but then Ras stumbles into view, laughing, as if he has been on the receiving end of a playful shove. He turns, catches sight of her and Calista, straightens up, and smiles.

"Hey, girls. Fancy a smoke?"

Calista walks right up to him. "Give Eleri her house keys back."

Ras stares. "I'm sorry, what?"

"You heard. The keys you copied. Give them back or she's going to the police."

Ras's friends wander into view, Kika, Teddy P and a couple of other boys.

"Keys? What keys?"

"The house keys that you took copies of when you stole her bag the other day."

"Her *bag*?"

"*Keys, what keys*?" Calista mimics, "*Bag, what bag*?"

The curtain at the window nearest to them twitches and Eleri catches a glimpse of a hulking figure behind it.

Ras looks past Cal, to Eleri. "Keep her under control, will you?"

Teddy P titters but Kika shoves her e-cig into her back pocket and folds her arms menacingly. "What's the problem?"

"The problem is that your friend here took Eleri's bag, stole her keys, copied them and then robbed her flat."

"Not robbed, exactly," Eleri murmurs helplessly, though she supposes that's what it was. The look on Ras's face, a mixture of bewilderment and anger, is making her feel sick.

"You calling Ras a thief?" Kika snaps.

Short and muscular, with hair that is always scraped back in tight, sculpted waves, Kika is a little bit scary. More than a little bit.

Before Calista can open her mouth and make the situation worse, Eleri mutters, "Come on, let's go."

Calista's lip curls in disgust. "You're right. He's a lying psycho. The police will get a warrant and search his shitty house."

Kika lunges at her, but Ras holds her back as Eleri pulls Calista away. But they haven't got far before he calls her name.

She turns. The curls of his hair fall about his shoulders, and his breath has turned to smoke in the chill air.

"I don't have your house keys, all right? I swear." The look on his face is so uncharacteristically serious he's almost a stranger.

For a moment they just stare at each other, until finally Eleri allows herself to be dragged away.

Cal is predictably enraged by the encounter and wants to march straight to the head's office, but somehow Eleri manages to persuade her that they will wait and see what happens. If the copied keys are magically returned to her bag or locker in the next few days, nothing more needs to be said – it was just an ill-judged prank and best forgotten.

That afternoon her thoughts are a tangle, but fortunately she doesn't have to concentrate much because they have one of their monthly life skills classes, this time focusing on healthy relationships. There's role play and a video depicting a coercive and controlling boyfriend and eventually Eleri drifts off, her attention only returning to the teacher when the girl beside her shoots up her hand so fast Eleri's pencil case flies off the table.

"Yes, Miriam, tell me another example of an unhealthy relationship."

"Co-dependency."

"Can you tell me what that is?"

"It's, like, a problem with boundaries and separation, where you have a really unhealthy relationship with someone you're close to."

"Good. Co-dependent people can be controlling, manipulative, dishonest: often due to low self-esteem. And this can often happen in romantic relationships where we feel as if we love that person so much we almost subjugate our own needs to theirs."

Eleri sighs and turns back to the window. No chance of a romantic relationship now.

When she gets to the bus stop later, Calista is already there – with Beni.

"Ben was desperate for a milkshake," Cal says. "So I said we'd go with him, if you want."

"Sure, yeah." She may as well take the opportunity as it's Mum's turn to cook.

"I'll just call my dad to let him know I'll be late," Cal says.

"Thought you might need cheering up," Beni says, squeezing her shoulder while Calista walks ahead.

"Thanks," she says, smiling weakly. How can she explain how she feels? It's not just that someone might have broken into her house and stolen her mum's pills, though that's horrible to think about. It's more what she's lost. Ras was like a little spark of light dancing at the peripheries of her grey and sensible life, and now it's been snuffed out – again.

"It's OK." Beni turns the squeeze into a side hug and kisses the top of her head. "I get it. My love life is just disappointment after disappointment. I should be used to it by now, but it always hurts."

Unable to reply, Eleri turns her head into Beni's chest.

"Dad's fine," Calista says, jogging back, her cheeks flushed by the cold. "He's out with some new mate."

"That's great." Blinking back her tears, Eleri joshes Cal on the shoulder. "He's starting to enjoy life again."

"I know!" Cal beams.

Eleri takes out her own phone. "I guess I should let my mum know too."

But when the screen lights up, she stops in the middle of the pavement, forcing a woman with a pram to make an abrupt detour. She glares at them as she passes.

"What?" Beni says. Eleri shows him the screen.

"Shit."

"Another one?" Calista snaps. "I thought you blocked the number?"

"I did."

"So, what, he's got another phone?"

"Must have." The three of them stare down at the message on the screen from an unknown number.

Door 8.

"Ignore it," Cal says finally.

"What if it's my keys?"

They look at each other.

"I have to find out."

"Come on," Beni says. "We'll go together."

The conversation continues on the bus.

"Even if it is your keys," Calista says. "You should still report him."

"They'll expel him if she does," Beni says.

"Serve him right. He should have been expelled years ago."

"I'm not sure it's Ras."

Calista looks at her.

"He just looked so surprised when we asked him about it. Like, genuinely shocked."

"Who else could it be?" Calista says. "It's definitely someone from school. This whole thing has a Secret Santa theme, and he deliberately *set out* to be your Secret Santa. Of course he's going to deny it, right? He's trying to freak you out."

"But why?"

Calista shrugs. "Because of whatever it was that upset him last year."

"But what *was* it?" Eleri cries in exasperation. "I don't even know!"

"There's nothing *to* know. Psychos like that flip out at the slightest thing."

They arrive at the estate to see a light burning steadily on the eighth floor of Gibea Tower, but this time there is no sense of excitement as they pass through the splintered door, no boisterous echoes hurled up the stairwell, just a tense silence broken only by their footsteps and increasingly laboured breathing as they ascend the sixteen flights to the eighth floor.

Is the quality of the silence different? Eleri wonders as they pass down the corridor towards the light. More watchful? They're almost at the door when Beni stops.

"Shh!"

She jumps and pulls up sharply.

"What?" Calista hisses.

But then they all hear it, a rapid whirring sound coming from the other side of the door.

"What is that?" Eleri breathes.

Beni stretches out an arm to hold them back, then slowly approaches the door to flat 83. He takes a deep breath, then pushes it open. They stare at his face, as his expression changes from trepidation to surprise, then he turns to them and smiles. The girls go to join him.

It's a mouse: its tail caught in a trap. The whirring sound is being caused by its feet sliding across the floor. Eleri cries out as Beni steps forward and picks it up, plucking the tail from the teeth of the trap. Then he turns it upside down to reveal four little plastic wheels.

"It's a wind-up toy."

Calista frowns. "Weird present. Is it supposed to mean something?"

"It means," Beni cries, jumping to his feet, "that someone has just wound it up! Come on, we can catch them!" He makes a run for the door, and they set off after him, hurtling down the darkened corridors and bursting out into the stairwell where Beni skids to a halt and puts his finger to his lips.

All is silent apart from the last clicks of the mouse's motor as it grinds to a halt.

They set off down the stairs, as soft-footed as they can to hear if anyone is going down ahead of them, but when they emerge from the building there is no sign of a figure hurrying away in any direction.

"Is there another way out of the building, another set of stairs?"

"I don't think so. There's only one in our block."

"So how did he get out?" Calista says.

Nobody answers her.

"That's it, then. He had his chance. Now you have to go to Mr Roberts, right?"

Beni looks pained but he doesn't disagree.

"Tomorrow morning. First thing. I'll come with you."

Eleri nods miserably.

With nothing more to be said, they hug goodbye and

Eleri walks back to Shiloh. She's about to swipe her fob when Cal calls after her. "Have you got a chain for your door?"

She turns back. "Yes, why?"

"Because he's still got your keys."

Thursday December 9

"It sou-ounds," Mr Roberts says slowly, opening his hands and smiling, "like a poorly judged prank."

Somehow, despite being the head of a school of over a thousand pupils, some of them challenging, some positively nightmarish, he is always cheerful. The school magazine is full of pictures of him beaming in a catering hair net, laughing as he is tackled into the mud by the school rugby star, or cracking up as he uses the Van de Graaff generator to absolutely no effect. Some of the kids are sure he's on happy pills, but Eleri's mum has been on antidepressants and it didn't make her particularly jolly.

Sitting beside Eleri on the sofa opposite Mr Roberts' desk, Calista folds her arms. "It's burglary and theft. Plus he has been putting Eleri in real danger."

"Yes, well, I must advise you not to go back to this

tower. Aside from anything else, there are obvious health and safety risks."

This from the man who tried to parkour down the front steps and broke his ankle.

"And you are certain it's Mr Mandip?"

"He deliberately arranged to get Eleri for his Secret Santa, so who else? He needs to be expelled."

"Now that's not something to throw about lightly, Miss Szajna. Exclusion can have a terrible legacy for young people." Last year Mr Roberts sent a message to all the parents to say that detention was being abolished in favour of "positive reinforcement" and advised them that bad behaviour should be rewarded with "love bombing". This generated a huge backlash and detentions were swiftly reintroduced, but even the nastiest of the parent militia can't bring themselves to call for his removal.

"So can stalking!"

Mr Roberts bites his lip, then he steeples his fingers and turns to Eleri. "It's wonderful of Miss Szajna to provide such support to her friend, but you are the victim, Eleri, and I am a great believer in victim-led justice. What do you feel Mr Mandip's fate should be?"

"Expulsion," Calista repeats.

"Perhaps a short suspension would send him the right message?" Mr Roberts suggests.

"Yeah, maybe suspension," Eleri says quietly. Her toes are scrunched up in her shoes. She wouldn't necessarily even have gone that far. She's not even a hundred per cent sure it *is* Ras.

"Right, well, I think you know me well enough to know that I may be harsh but I'm always fair. I will speak to our friend and the situation will, I'm sure, be resolved very quickly."

They both get up, but though Calista walks out of the office, Eleri lingers.

"Is there something else, Eleri?"

"That homeless guy, who went up to the Year Eight girls. I was wondering if maybe he had something to do with Nina's disappearance."

Mr Roberts pales. "Nina Mitri?"

"What if… What if he killed her and buried her in that wasteground by the alley?"

"The police searched that area last year. They found nothing."

This is the first time Mr Roberts has acknowledged that something really bad might have happened to Nina.

"I've already spoken to DI Everett about the rough sleeper. The man is from Scotland, and they believe he only came down in the summer. They're going to increase patrols in the area now."

"OK."

Eleri goes out to join Calista. She should feel better but she doesn't. When they say they've searched, what do they mean? A police officer doing a visual sweep looking for a body, or a proper fingertip forensic examination like on CSI programmes?

Did they dig?

By the time they get to the canteen some Year 7s have taken their table.

"What the actual...?" Calista mutters.

"It doesn't matter," Eleri says quickly. "They weren't to know."

"The new boy's sitting on his own," Beni says casually.

"There's a free one," Calista says, gesturing with her tray, and sets off towards the back of the room. Following her, they pass the table where the new boy is sitting, looking at his phone. The table by the tray racks is the least popular spot to eat lunch – the mingling aromas of uneaten food surround it in a disgusting miasma – so the new kids usually end up here, at least until they've made some friends. This boy seems to be finding it as difficult as Nina did.

The day after Eleri and Ras took Nina to A&E, Eleri had spotted her sitting alone by the trays and beckoned her over to their table. Calista wasn't there. It was around the time of her dad's suicide attempt and every break and lunchtime she would call home to check on him. When she finally did arrive and spotted Nina occupying the spare seat her face darkened. She'd said nothing for the whole lunch break, but Beni kept up a stream of inane chatter so Eleri was pretty sure Nina hadn't noticed. Cal would get used to Nina's presence in the end, probably even come to like her. Or so she'd thought at the time.

As they pass through the dining hall, no one so much as glances at them. They're not hated like the bitches or despised like the emos, they just don't seem to exist for the rest of the school body.

They haven't long sat down when the ear-splitting noise of a thousand pupils clacking cutlery on to a thousand plates falls momentarily silent. Eleri looks up to see Mrs Banwa has come into the canteen. The diminutive secretary casts her gaze over the tables, then sets off purposefully across the room, her huge hips swaying. For one horrible moment Eleri thinks she's heading for them, but she stops in front of Ras's table. Mrs Banwa can either be warm and maternal, with a laugh like a screech owl, or downright terrifying. The look on her face as she addresses Ras veers more towards the terrifying, but whatever his response is it makes her face split into a broad smile. She shakes her head, making the beads woven into her dreadlocks shimmer, and then Ras is up and the pair of them walk out of the canteen together, Ras's arm draped across her shoulders like a favourite auntie.

Eleri drops her fork and sinks her head into her hands. What has she done?

By the time school ends, the rumours are flying like poison darts: Ras has been expelled for smoking weed by the shed, for groping Mrs Banwa, for stealing Mr Roberts' car. It's striking to Eleri that absolutely none of the rumours mention her. Who could possibly imagine that Ras Mandip would have anything to do with invisible Eleri Kirdar?

She and Cal haven't been waiting long at the bus stop

when a car pulls up. The window slides down and a man's voice calls, "You ordered a cab, ladies?"

Eleri's chest tightens, but as she bends down for a glimpse of the driver, Cal claps her hands and laughs.

"Dad!"

"Got my licence back! Jump in and I'll give you a ride home!"

Grinning like a little girl, Calista jumps into the passenger seat. Eleri gets in behind her and Paul pulls out into the traffic.

"Oh my god, that's so good!" Cal beams.

"I know. I only applied two weeks ago, but it obviously didn't take long for them to decide I'm no longer a menace to other road users. But what do they know, eh?" He winks at his daughter then presses his foot to the accelerator, making the engine roar. The trio of teenage girls crossing in front of the car flinch, and Paul gives them an apologetic wave.

"How was school?" Paul asks, and unlike most children when greeted with this question, Calista doesn't grunt and shrug but launches into a description of the topics they're learning in history, oozing animated enthusiasm like a children's TV presenter.

Calista is so preoccupied with assuring her dad of what a great day she's had that she doesn't notice when Eleri slips out her phone. Doesn't register the sudden stillness in the back seat.

Door 9.

Ras has already been suspended, presumably with the threat of expulsion if the messages don't stop. Which means either he doesn't care, or the message isn't from him. Eleri tucks the phone back in her pocket. She doesn't want to ruin the happy atmosphere by mentioning it. Besides, if she told Paul he would go straight to her mum and the last thing Mum needs is more stress.

Paul drops her off at the beginning of the path and she waits until they are out of sight before turning to face the towers. The light is on the eastern side of Gibea: she can tell by the faint yellow halo around the side of the building, about a third of the way up. There are twenty-six floors in Gibea, the same as Shiloh. What did Beni say? *A real-life advent calendar.* If he's right, this might go on for another fifteen days, with each door getting higher and higher up the building, until the final gift on the twenty-fourth floor.

The top of the block is stark black against the orange-tinged dusk. She thinks of the charred skeleton of Grenfell cursing London's skyline. It haunted her dreams when they first moved here.

What if a fire started when she was twenty floors up in Gibea? The fire brigade wouldn't be in much of a hurry, thinking the tower was unoccupied, and even if they came, how would they rescue her? She's seen the footage of people jumping from the twin towers because no one could reach them and they'd rather fall than burn.

Closing her eyes, she takes some deep breaths. She will do this *once* more, in case it's her keys, and then she and the

Secret Santa are done. Opening them, she sets off down the flickering path.

Tonight's gift is a flat box wrapped in the angel paper.

She takes it back home to unwrap.

Lying inside, on a cloud of white tissue paper, is a small band encrusted with pink jewels and fastened with a buckle. A single round stone dangles from the centre. She slides it on to her wrist.

The hanging stone looks wrong, as if it's supposed to go around the neck, but it's too small even for a child. She takes it off and turns it over in her hands. The buckle reminds her of a dog collar and the back of the jewel is a blank circle of metal, as if to take an engraving. Is the Secret Santa calling her a bitch?

No, it's too small for a dog.

She gathers up the Secret Santa gifts from under her bed and lays them out on the carpet.

The Elf on the Shelf, the Quality Street, the octopus and the ring are just lovely gifts, for someone you really liked.

And then there are the strange ones: the mouse, and now this weird bracelet.

And of course the pills – that felt like a threat. Or a form of persuasion, perhaps: Mum wouldn't have died without them, it would just have been an inconvenience for a few days.

And yet the Secret Santa may have gone to the trouble of breaking into the flat to get them.

That's the creepy thing.

Well, if this is set to carry on for another fifteen days, perhaps by then she'll have figured it all out. Taking a pillowcase from the airing cupboard, Eleri puts the gifts inside, then stashes them back under the bed, then she goes to the kitchen to prepare dinner.

Friday December 10

Calista isn't at school the next day, which is a shame as it's Christmas lunch day. A lot of kids are wearing Christmas hats or jumpers, but Eleri has grown out of her only Christmas jumper – a boring reindeer with a red pom-pom for a nose – and she doesn't want to waste money on something that only gets worn once a year.

Beni has come in a knitted creation with a screen in the front showing a flickering log fire beneath the slogan, *Baby it's hot in here!* And as they make their way down to the canteen people chuckle and fist-bump him.

By the end of the year she's sure she'll be sick to the back teeth of turkey, but this first sight of steaming vats of gravy and glistening piles of roasties makes her mouth water. She gets the works, even the overcooked sprouts which look like they might crumple into fart-tasting sludge as soon as she bites down on them. At the end of the counter is a great trug tub of Christmas crackers and they each take one. Eleri's about to head over to their table but Beni has paused.

"With Calista so unfortunately indisposed," he says, side-eyeing her, "I suppose we could sit with my people today?"

She grins. "Why not?" She starts walking towards the raucous table by the windows.

But Beni doesn't follow. He's looking over at the trays where the new boy is sitting alone. "Actually…"

Eleri can't help smiling as she watches him clearly trying to pluck up the courage to speak to the new kid, pausing before he gets to the table to lay his tray down and pat his hair into place.

When the new boy looks up, El can understand exactly what Beni sees in him. His face has an almost ethereal handsomeness. At some words from Beni, he smiles, gets up and follows him to the drama table. Eleri gets there first, but before Beni and the new kid can sit in the free places beside her, they are taken up by a couple of girls. Beni gives her an apologetic look and leads the new boy to the other end of the table. As they go, Eleri sees the badge sewn on to his blazer: a Pride flag. She smiles. *Go, Beni.*

The drama girls are perfectly nice and say hello and everything, but they're already deep into a *he said/she said* conversation and it clearly doesn't occur to them to include her.

She pulls her own cracker and the gift plops into her gravy. It's a set of red plastic lips. The same gift she got last year.

Picking it out, she wipes it clean on the napkin and holds it for a moment in her palm.

This was what gave her the idea for Nina's present.

Like Ras said, Nina was so pretty "underneath it all". With a bit of make-up, a change of hairstyle and a nice dress she would be stunning. Eleri didn't even think about her faith, then. Didn't consider that her family, or even Nina herself, could find such a gift offensive. And maybe she hadn't. *Probably* she hadn't. It just felt like an uncomfortable coincidence that Eleri gave her the Secret Santa gift and the next day she went missing. It has played on her mind ever since.

The room is filled with the snaps of crackers being pulled and jokes being booed. Paper crowns that would be scorned at home are worn proudly as kids flick each other with yo-yos, play snap with tiny packs of playing cards and try to find out their romantic personalities from fortune fish curling in their palms.

Eleri is partway through her main course when the first sprout hits her, on the side of the head.

"Snitch!" yells a voice from Ras's table. Her heart sinks. Ducking down in her seat she forks up a cube of parsnip.

A potato strikes her arm, leaving a greasy mark on her blazer. Now there are cheers.

The next missile hits one of the drama girls in the back. She turns. "Hey, piss off!"

"She's a snitch!" the voice cries again. "Her lies got Ras suspended!"

"That's nothing to do with us! Cut it out."

"I'm really sorry," Eleri says, scrambling to her feet. Hurrying past Ras's table, she is concentrating so hard on looking straight ahead that she doesn't spot the foot that darts out to trip her. She goes sprawling, landing heavily amidst the food scraps and splashes of custard. Laughter echoes around the canteen, but someone takes pity on her because a moment later a pair of Dr Marten's appears between the chair legs. She reaches up gratefully, but no helping hand is proffered. Kika Aledari is standing perfectly still, fists at her sides, eyes cold. The jeering laughter continues as Eleri gets to her feet. Now she and Kika are eye to eye, but Kika isn't laughing. Her sharp features are screwed into a mask of hatred and for a second Eleri wonders if Kika might actually hit her.

"Leave Ras the hell alone," she hisses. "Or you'll have me to deal with."

Edging past, Eleri hurries out of the canteen and spends the rest of the lunch hour hiding in the girls' toilets, trying to get the worst of the stains off her clothes. By the time the bell goes, her shirt is soaking wet and her hair hangs in damp straggles from where she's rinsed gravy and sprout leaves out of it. But it's probably safe to say that, after five whole years at the school, Eleri has finally been noticed.

She and Calista are in the same science set, so she sits alone for the entire lesson, trying to figure out how to carry out the experiments while the other groups muck around and share whispered jokes. No one says a word to her for the entire two-hour lesson: even the teacher's eyes skim over her raised hand.

But hockey practice is on today, and after an hour pelting about in the fresh air and taking out her bad mood on the puck, she's feeling better. In the changing rooms afterwards she hears the girls discussing whether to go to McDonalds or MooBar.

Sitting on the slatted bench, folding her kit into her bag, she tries to pluck up some courage. Calista isn't here. She could hang out with her teammates for once. Eventually the girls start to leave, team captain Thea one of the last to stay, as she blowdries her long chestnut hair. Tall, slim and always cheerful, Thea is the pin-up of the school, but unfortunately for the boys she's dating a player at the West Ham Academy, so they haven't got a hope.

"Are you lot heading to MooBar?" Eleri says when Thea's finished, her voice sounding shriller than usual.

The captain smiles. "Yeah. Do you wanna come?"

"Is that OK?"

"Yeah, great. They've got a special seasonal flavour apparently. Christmas pudding. Sounds gross but I guess we've gotta give it a go."

To her ears, Eleri's laugh is cringingly obsequious, but Thea doesn't seem to notice, and the pair walk out together to join the gaggle of girls hanging around under the floodlights. However cold it is, they're always hot after training and the other girls drape their jackets over their shoulders, knotting them at the chest. Calista says it makes them look like wannabe cheerleaders, but Calista isn't here, so as they set off for the gates, Eleri pulls the jacket from around her waist and ties it around her shoulders too.

But tagging after the group who are deep in their individual conversations, she feels like a spare part. Some of the girls are checking their phones, so to avoid looking as pathetic as she feels, she does likewise.

Door 10.

Eleri almost hurls the phone on to the pavement. What the hell is wrong with him? Does he *want* to be expelled?

She almost turns around on the spot, but then Thea calls back to her: has Eleri ever been to the sushi bar on the high road? Eleri hasn't, but she knows full well Thea is just being nice and trying to include her, and is she really going to throw away this chance of bonding with her teammates?

She jogs up to join Thea and one of the goal defence girls, who is thinking of taking her mum out for sushi for her birthday, but her dad thinks raw fish is full of parasites.

At the cafe Eleri is the first to be served and after ordering her usual peanut butter and banana shake, she heads to the nearest empty table.

The MooBar is styled like an American diner, with blue and white tiled walls and individual booths with red leatherette benches. A moment later, Rebekah plonks herself down opposite. The six-foot girl with a bright orange crop is a brilliant goal attack and a generous passer, but merciless if you screw up. In matches at other schools, Eleri has cringed at the roastings Rebekah's inflicted on players she perceives to have thrown points away. That must be the reason she has never been made captain, because as a player she's better than Thea.

"To what do we owe this honour, then?" Rebekah says, arching an eyebrow.

"I just wanted to come. Is that OK?" That sounded more confrontational than she meant it to. Dipping her head, she sucks up a mouthful of the tooth-achingly sweet milkshake.

"Yeah, right. Your girlfriend's off sick, isn't she?"

"Calista? She isn't my girlfriend."

"Really?"

"We went to primary school together, that's all."

"Didn't they put you in different forms though, when you arrived?"

"Yeah…"

"That's why they split you up, you know, so you don't end up co-dependent."

"We're not co-dependent."

"Weren't you listening in life skills?" Rebekah smiles and shakes her head. "I used to feel really sorry for you."

Eleri bristles. "Er, why?"

"Cause all those times we asked you to hang out with us you clearly wanted to, but she wouldn't let you."

"It's not that she wouldn't *let* me."

"Look, I know how it feels, OK. My last relationship

was super controlling. I had to finish it in the end, for my own sanity. You're a nice girl, Eleri, but you're only half a person at the moment. Break away. Tell her you want to have some time apart. Find yourself."

Eleri's heart is pounding and the hand holding the milkshake is shaking. Rebekah feels *sorry* for her? She's *half a person*?

Thea sits down beside Rebekah. "Hey, sluts. I went for it. I got the Christmas pudding one and it's actually—"

"Sorry, I have to go… Sorry." Eleri gets up and stumbles clumsily out of the booth.

"Is everything OK?"

"I just realized I should have handed in an assignment."

"Wow, that's evil! Two days before the end of term? It's Mr bloody Scarf, right?"

"Yeah, it's… Thanks for inviting me. See you later."

As she heads for the door, she hears Rebekah's voice sing-songing after her, "Run run run; Calista's waiting."

Grabbing her hockey bag from the pile by the door, Eleri bursts out into the night, her heart pounding. A bitter wind lacerates her bare flesh and she pulls her jacket off her shoulders and puts it on. Marching blindly for the bus stop, she feels like she's going to cry.

When the bus arrives, she throws herself into a free seat at the back. Blinking rapidly, she directs her gaze out of the window so no one will be able to tell. The school comes into view, in darkness. But – she squints, cupping her hands against the glass to see better – not total darkness. A single splinter of orange light burns in the window of Ray's shed. Why would Ray still be there when it's far too dark to do any gardening? The bus turns a corner and the school passes out of sight.

Taking out her phone, she finds that Beni has called twice. She calls him back and he answers with a burst of noise. It sounds like he's out with friends again. She feels a stab of envy.

"Oh wait, wait," he says. "Let me go out of the room."

"Where are you?"

"Watching the match at Ewan's house."

Ewan is one of Beni's football mates. It took a lot of courage for Beni to try out for the football team, and for the first couple of years no one really talked to him, but now they're starting to include him more and more.

The sound recedes and when Beni speaks again his voice is echoey, like he's standing in a hallway. "What the hell happened at lunchtime? I tried to find you."

She tells him about the food throwing, about Kika's threat.

"She's scary," he says at the end. "You want to stay out of her way. Oh wait," he gasps. "You don't think..."

"What?"

"You don't think it could be her, do you, doing this? The Secret Santa thing."

"Kika? Why?"

"She's obviously totally protective of Ras. Maybe she decided to punish you for upsetting him last year."

139

"I didn't upset him!" But now another thought occurs to her. "You don't think maybe she's in love with him?"

"She looks queer to me."

Eleri snorts. "Homophobe."

"Not at all. Short hair, no make-up, piercings, DMs. Classic lesbian. Doesn't Cal do geography with her? Ask her what she thinks."

Eleri grunts.

"Why was she off today? Have you spoken to her?"

"No."

"You two haven't had a fight, have you?"

"No. It's just…"

"What?"

She tells him everything Rebekah said, about people pitying her, about her being half a person because of Calista. "I dunno, Ben." She sighs. "Maybe she's right. Remember what Cal was like with Nina last year? And then the other day, when she was funny about you inviting the new boy to sit with us."

"Hendrick Jameson," Beni preens. "I know his name now."

"I just think" – Eleri sighs – "maybe Cal *is* controlling."

The line goes quiet. "Hello? Ben? You still there?"

"Yes, I'm here." His voice sounds oddly guarded.

"What? If you've got something to say, just say it."

"I just think… I just think it takes two to tango, El. You and Cal have been in each other's pockets since primary school and I didn't see you complaining up until now.

Remember how she was when I started hanging out with the drama crew?"

Eleri frowns. "No."

"She used to call them all sorts of names, trying to put me off them, but I ignored her and went anyway, and she was fine in the end. You just have to stand up to her."

Eleri blinks in surprise. She'd always thought that Cal just didn't care about Ben as much as she did about her, but looking back to primary school, they were a tight little trio then. Could it be that Beni has just had the guts to step away and make a life for himself, and she hasn't?

"What was she going to do, anyway, dump me? Then who would she have? Look, I know she's being a pain at the moment, but she's having a tough time and she's been a good friend to us in the past: don't forget that."

"Yeah."

There's a sudden roar from the other end of the line, followed by booing and swearing.

"Shit, they've just scored. Better go. Message me later."

"OK."

She hangs up and stares vacantly out of the bus window until the passing scenery blurs into a smear of coloured lights. Then she closes her eyes and a guilty tear creeps out from between her eyelashes.

Cal is her best friend.

At primary school it was Cal who first offered her the hand of friendship when the other children kept their distance, put off by Mum's limp and her twisted arm. It was

Cal who invited her for play dates, even though Eleri never ever invited anyone back to hers. When other kids teased her Cal waded in, once losing a baby tooth in a fight.

When they arrived at Elsinore House, Eleri had been terrified of what would happen when the other kids found out about Mum's disability, that she would be teased or bullied, but Cal never breathed a word. And when it came to hanging out with the hockey girls, the first time she went to practice Eleri had *asked* Calista to wait for her, for moral support. It had become a habit after that, but how was that Cal's fault?

It wasn't. It isn't.

If Eleri doesn't like the way things are, then it's up to her to change them. And the first thing she's going to change is being at the beck and call of the Secret Santa. It ends now. She won't go round there this evening, and if he tries anything like the pills again, she really will call the police.

When she gets off the bus, a light is on around the side of Gibea, but she strides straight past and into Shiloh.

It's spaghetti bolognese tonight, which she can make with her eyes shut, so while she sets about chopping the onions, garlic and carrots, she decides to FaceTime Calista. It's already weird that she hasn't messaged to ask why Cal was off, but at least she has the excuse of the incident at lunch.

It takes a while for Calista to answer and when she does Eleri can see that her friend is still in bed. There's a croaky "hello" and a puffy, squinting face swims up to the camera.

"Wow, you look rough!" Eleri props the phone up against the microwave. "Are you sick? That sucks, just before Christmas. Hope you don't lose your sense of taste or you'll miss out on all the good stuff!" As she scrapes the veg into the frying pan, she wonders if the bonhomie sounds forced.

A pause.

"Not sick, no." Calista sniffs. "My mum doesn't want me for Christmas."

Eleri stops stirring.

"Steve's booked them a romantic trip to Paris."

"What about Freya?" Eleri asks weakly, unsure of how to try and soften this blow.

"She's going to her cousin's."

As quietly as possible, so Cal doesn't think she's taking this lightly, Eleri opens two cans of chopped tomatoes and slops them into the pan. What can she say? It must be horrible to be rejected like this by the person who's supposed to love you most in the whole world.

"It was Steve's fault though, right, not your mum's. He booked it."

"She could have said no."

"Maybe she didn't like to when he'd spent all that money."

The tomatoes start to bubble so she puts the lid on the pan and sits down at the kitchen table. Beside her she can feel the light pulsing from the tenth floor of Gibea Tower. It reflects in the black bead eyes of the elf, now perched on the shelf above the fridge. Mum has obviously decided it will be fun to pretend he's moving around the flat on his own.

Cal's face is swollen and blotched, as if she's been crying all day, and her eyes are just a sliver behind their puffy lids.

"Look, why don't I come round at the weekend and take you through the science homework?" Eleri says gently. "Accompanied by Nutella pancakes?"

Calista's face breaks into a wan smile. "Yeah, I'd like that. Thanks, El. Love you." She blows a frail kiss.

"Love you too." Eleri blows one back, blinking away the tears pricking behind her own eyelids.

"Can we have dinner in front of the TV?" Eleri says when her mum comes in from work. "There's a programme on iPlayer everyone was talking about at school."

This is a lie. No one talks about iPlayer shows, they all watch Netflix and Apple TV, but they don't have any subscriptions, and Eleri doesn't want Mum sitting at the kitchen table. The lights are high enough up the tower now that you don't have to be standing close to the window to see them.

While Eleri serves up, Mum tries to connect to the iPlayer app but, as usual, it's just endless buffering thanks to their trashy internet connection.

"Can you believe," she says, as they stare patiently at the revolving circle, "Cal's mum is going to Paris for Christmas so she can't have her. Isn't that so mean?"

Her mum says nothing.

"What?" Eleri says. "Don't you think it's mean?"

Her mum sighs. "You girls are getting older now. In a couple of years you'll be off to uni, and us parents, we'll have to try and build lives for ourselves that don't involve you."

Eleri makes a face. "You've got lives already."

"They've always revolved around you: your needs — meals and laundry, school, birthdays and holidays, getting you to and from all the places you want to go, making sure you get enough sleep, that you're not being bullied, that you have friends. You've been our number one priority all this time."

"Clearly not for Sally."

Her mum looks at her and puts down her fork. "Sally was unhappy with Paul for years. She stayed for Calista's sake. And then it got to the point that she was so unhappy she couldn't go on. She waited until Calista was fifteen, and I know it upset her when Sally left, but that's an age when you're starting to be more independent from your parents. She made the decision and I respect her for it. The alternative was more unhappiness and then a lonely, empty life when Calista left home."

Eventually the connection kicks in and the show begins, but the images on-screen wash over Eleri without leaving any impression. She was wrong to blame Cal, and now her mum thinks she's wrong to blame Sally too. But the thought that really troubles her is the last thing Mum said. When Eleri leaves for uni, which she has always hoped to do, her mum will be faced with just what Sally managed to avoid: a lonely, empty life. Stuck here in this flat all alone, exhausting herself with work and chores.

Her appetite gone, she slides the unfinished meal on to the table as unobtrusively as possible. Her mum is completely obsessed with eating disorders, and any time she doesn't eat everything on her plate Mum gets paranoid Eleri's developing anorexia.

Sitting back, her eye is caught by a flash of red in her peripheral vision. Turning, she sees a speck of light dancing on the back of Mum's head.

She frowns, then realizes what it is. Someone is shining a laser into the room. Glancing at the window in alarm she sees the faint thread of light stretching away into the darkness towards Gibea Tower.

It's not threatening or anything, just silly and annoying. Any second Mum is going to notice and then if she sees it's coming from Gibea she'll probably call the police, or at least the council, and then it will all come out.

An idea comes to her. It's not a great one but it'll have to do. With as little haste as she can muster she picks up her phone and starts scrolling.

"Thought you wanted to watch this?" Mum says.

"It's a bit boring though, isn't it?"

"I was enjoying it, but we can turn it off if—"

"Oh wait. I've got a message that a parcel's been delivered." She looks up innocently.

"It must be Isla's dresses."

"They must have left the package downstairs. I'll go down and check. Don't want it to be nicked."

"Lazy sods," her mum grumbles. "Though I suppose they only get about ten pence an hour. Off you go, then. Shall I pause this?"

"No, don't worry."

The gift waiting for her in flat 108 is a friendship bracelet, in contrasting shades of dark and light pink. She hasn't seen one of these since she was at primary school. Did the Secret Santa weave it especially for her?

But when she picks it up, it falls apart in her hand. At first she thinks it hasn't been tied, but then she sees that the middle of the band has been clumsily hacked through. It's unwearable.

Pink is for girls.

Could this mean that the Secret Santa is a girl?

And what about the severed band? Is the friendship somehow over? Broken? Is it referring to whatever happened between her and Ras last year?

Back in the flat, Eleri tells her mum that it must have been a spam email because there was no parcel in the pigeonholes. After this she has to endure her mum wittering on about cyber viruses and the dangers of opening emails if you're not sure who they're from, but at least it means she doesn't have to speak. Today has drained her, and at nine she announces that she's having an early night.

Tucking the bracelet into the pillowcase, she yanks the

curtains closed and gets into bed. But however tired she is, sleep eludes her. She hears Mum going to bed at eleven, and later still, when the traffic noise has died away, the haunting screams of the foxes as they prowl the high street fighting over scraps from the takeaway bins.

Saturday December 11

"Upsy-daisy, Sleeping Beauty."

Eleri lifts her groggy head from the pillow and peers out through half-closed lids.

"Wha—?"

"We're going out."

"Where?" She flops on to her back and rubs her eyes.

"A surprise adventure."

Eleri groans. "It's only nine."

"And we need to be there at eleven."

"I'm supposed to be going to Cal's."

"You can see her tomorrow. Come on, I want to leave in fifteen minutes."

The adventure involves two buses, though the distance itself isn't far: a couple of streets away from the Sainsbury's where Mum works. They disembark on a main road and set off down a side street, Mum navigating via Google maps.

The houses, grand Georgian stucco affairs, have seen better days, and most have been divided into flats with grimy windows and makeshift curtains created by sheets. They have to dodge piles of dog poo and crushed nitrous oxide canisters. Eleri doesn't know how much sleep she got last night, but she feels so tired her bones ache, and the wind buffeting her back feels like she's being shoved along by a bully.

"Here we are."

The house they stop in front of has a battered old Saab parked outside and an England flag plastered across an upper window. Eleri's heart sinks as they approach the front door, its dusty paintwork peeling off in strips. What the hell are they doing here?

"Oh, wait," Mum says, peering at the panel of buttons on the wall. "I think it's the basement flat."

They descend a flight of white painted concrete steps into the stairwell of 79A. The windows are clean down here, and there are plant pots arranged by a front door painted a cheerful shade of pale yellow. Eighties music is drifting out from behind the door and when the beat drops her mum does a little dance move, then she winks at Eleri and presses the doorbell. Eleri rolls her eyes.

The door is opened by a very tall, very thin man in jeans and a denim shirt. He might once have been handsome, but his face is now a mass of lines and his blonde hair has receded to flyaway wisps.

He beams. "Kerry?"

Mum beams back. "Yes. We've come for Lavender."

Lavender? They've come all this way to buy flowers?

"Come in. I'm Adam. I've just put the coffee machine on. Do you want one?"

"Ooh, go on then."

The flat has an ethnic feel, its stripped wood floors scattered with Turkish rugs and leather pouffes, its walls hung with an eclectic mix of art, from depictions of Hindu gods to framed concert posters. The big mirror above the fireplace is so mottled and tarnished that Eleri can barely see her own face. The place smells of brewing coffee and incense and something more pungent and animal.

"Take a seat. I'll be back in a sec."

They sit down on a wide tan leather sofa with split cushions and a faded patchwork quilt draped over its back. Mum is looking around appreciatively. "What a lovely flat. So light."

"Couldn't you have just gone to the garden centre rather than some stranger's flat?"

Mum smirks. "Wait and see."

"Right." Adam comes back in. "One perfectly made coffee, one can of Coke for the teenager — sorry if I'm stereotyping but it's the only liquid that passed my son's lips until he was old enough to drink beer. And one" — he stands back — "small, naughty kitten."

A ball of silver fluff swaggers into the room, its paws slipping a little on the polished floor. Mum squeals and reaches down and the kitten scampers over and sniffs her hand before scampering away to the nearest rug and attacking its tassels with minute claws.

"We're getting a cat?"

"We are." Mum's cheeks are pink.

"But we haven't got a garden."

"That's OK," Adam says, sitting on the arm of the sofa next to Mum and gazing benevolently at the little vandal ripping holes in his rug. "She's half Persian, so she'll be fine being a house cat."

Mum wrinkles her nose. "Flat cat, I'm afraid."

"No worries. Just get her a scratching post and some toys and she'll be happy as Larry. Won't you, Lav?"

The kitten pauses to look up at him with huge cornflower eyes.

"I name them all after flowers, but she's still really young, so you can rename her if you like."

"Maybe something Christmassy, El?" Mum turns to her. "What do you think? Cracker? Or Egg Nog?"

"Or Family Row," Adam suggests and both adults laugh.

"Is she your Christmas present, then?" he asks Eleri.

"No, she's mine!" Mum interjects before Eleri can reply. "Gotta have someone to talk to when this one gets a boyfriend. Or girlfriend."

Eleri rolls her eyes.

"Parents are dreadful, aren't they?" Adam says, his crinkly eyes crinkling even more. He's not that old, Eleri decides, but he's spent a lot of time in the sun.

"I'd been thinking about getting one for a while and

was just browsing Gumtree, and then I saw her face and that was it." Mum places her good hand on her chest and flutters her eyelashes.

"Not so easy to swipe left with a kitten, eh?"

"Oh, I wouldn't know about all that. I'm far too old-fashioned."

'Very wise," the man says. "It's the Wild West out there. Oh, for the good old days when you met people at the Friday disco."

"God yes. Did you grow up around here? Do you remember the one at the Ilford Pally?"

"Do I? I was there without fail every week."

"Oh wow, we must have met each other then!"

Eleri sighs. This is clearly going to take a while. She gets out her phone to message Cal that she won't be able to make it today and can she come tomorrow instead.

The kitten abandons the rug and struts over to wind itself around her feet, its tail somehow insinuating itself up inside her trouser bottoms.

The adults go on and on. More coffee is made and Mum is taken off to see the other kittens while Eleri looks at her phone and prods the kitten away by turns. When the adults wander back in, laughing at something, Eleri stares pointedly at her mother.

Her mum finally gets the message. "Right, well, I suppose we should be going."

"No problemo. I'll just get you the carrier.

He returns with a small plastic box with a cage door.

Lifting Lavender unceremoniously from the hearthstone where she is licking her behind, he plops her expertly inside and fastens the door. Lavender sets off a piteous yowling.

"Don't blame me for your mother's libidinous ways," he says, poking a finger through the grille and wincing as Lavender's needle teeth close on it. After he's withdrawn his hand the yowls go on, and now the kitten starts clawing at the bars of its cage.

"Shh … shh…" Mum croons. "It's OK, it won't be for long." But her words have no effect.

And then Adam begins to sing. *"Lavender's blue, dilly, dilly, Lavender's green. When I am king, dilly, dilly, you shall be queen."*

Miraculously, by the third verse of this, the creature quietens and sits down on its little bottom. The song seems to have the same effect on Mum who is gazing at Adam with doe eyes. At another pointed look from Eleri she seems to remember herself and gets out her purse. "Twenty pounds, wasn't it? And how much for the carrier?"

Adam scratches his head. "Actually the twenty was to cover the price of the carrier. It's hard to get homes for mongrels like these. I'm just grateful I managed to get families for most of them, otherwise I'd just have to keep them all and then the place would be even more of a pigsty."

"Well, thank you. She's worth a hundred times that." Mum holds out a twenty-pound note. But Adam doesn't reach for it.

"Or you could just pay me back with a coffee sometime?"

There's a pause that could be described as awkward.

"Oh. Yes, OK," Mum stammers eventually.

"You've got my number, so … um … give me a call. We could meet at the Pally."

Mum's laugh is way too loud and Eleri blushes on her behalf as they make an undignified rush for the door.

The kitten yowls all the way back to the bus stop. Sitting down on the red plastic seat, Mum holds the cage up in front of her and gazes affectionately at the furry little hooligan. "Now all she needs is a nice sparkly collar."

Eleri freezes in the act of checking the bus arrival time. A kitten collar. That's what was behind *Door Nine*.

They spend the rest of the day chasing the kitten around the house and cleaning up little black sausages of its poo, which Mum seems to find hilarious, especially considering the shortened version of the cat's name. It's a good distraction from the Secret Santa, and the message has been waiting for her for an hour before Eleri finally notices it.

The predictable `Door 11` is followed by an emoji of a key.

Finally. He's giving her door keys back.

She messages Calista.

> `About time,` the message pings back. `What`
> `a psycho, making you wait like that.`
> `Want to put me on FaceTime?`

155

        No, it's ok.

But looking out of the kitchen window, she wonders if she should have agreed to Cal's offer.

Dusk is falling and the crimson-streaked sky reflected in Gibea's windows gives the tower a lurid ghastliness, like a Hammer horror. For a moment Eleri thinks there is no light, but then she spots a faint glow at the back of the building, facing the railway line.

While Mum's preparing dinner, she lets herself quietly out of the flat.

Today's gift is the size and shape of a shoebox. It's wrapped in the usual paper, but with its bigger surface area she can see that the angel is standing outside the door of a house with a family inside. It must be Gabriel coming to tell Mary she's going to have the Baby Jesus.

Back in her room Eleri unwraps it and takes the lid off the Nike shoebox inside. This reveals a second, slightly smaller box. This continues for three more boxes, going down in size like a Russian doll until finally she draws out a matchbox.

She slides the cardboard drawer open upside down and the object in the box tumbles out to clink on the carpet, where it lies, glinting in the ceiling lights.

It is a key. But it's not hers.

Sunday December 12

"So whose is it?" Calista says.

They are sitting in her bright bedroom, easily the size of Eleri's living room at home. Cal's walls used to be covered with posters of Outer Banks and Billie Eilish, but last year she repainted the room dark grey and now there's just a full-length mirror and a single framed picture of a stone angel weeping over a grave. On the desk her MacBook scrolls through family photos, from holidays in Greece and Italy, and baby pictures of her with her mum.

"I have no idea. It's too small for a door so maybe a drawer or a box or something."

"A locker?"

"Maybe, but not one of ours." The school ones are secured with combination padlocks. You're supposed to change the number every week for security but nobody bothers.

"His bike lock?"

Eleri looks at the little brass key in her palm. It's too ornate for that.

"Either way, it's not your door keys, so you need to go to the police. This is harassment and stalking. *And* he threatened your mum."

Eleri murmurs her agreement, though she isn't sure how the Sinemet and laser pen could really constitute a threat.

"Not to mention the breaking and entering of a council-owned building and the theft of that ring. The guy's a psychopath. Next he'll be torturing animals, you wait."

Eleri frowns. "That's another thing: the kitten collar. How did he know we were getting a kitten?"

"Your mum said she'd been looking at Gumtree, right, so maybe he hacked into her computer?"

"But why?"

Calista circles her finger around her temple.

"I guess I just have to wait and see. So far he hasn't done anything actually dangerous."

"Yet."

They work quietly on some difficult titration equations, but after two poor nights' sleep Eleri's attention drifts. Calista has a dressing table as well as a desk: it's crowded with make-up and nail varnish and pots of creams and powders. Eleri's shelf in the bathroom is much the same, not that they ever have much chance to use any of it. The popular kids at school often have house parties and some even go to bars and clubs, but Eleri and Calista have never been invited. The only opportunity she had to dress up was last year, at the dance. And that was wasted because Ras didn't talk to her all night and the only person she danced with was Beni.

Her heart sinks as she thinks about this year's dance, three days away. This time she'll be positively disliked rather than just ignored. Will Ras's friends throw food at her? Spike her drink? Maybe she just won't bother going. Though Cal will be livid. She glances up at her friend. Cal is frowning down at the forest of figures filling her page.

Eleri realizes with a jolt that this time last year she was doing exactly the same thing: helping a friend with her chemistry homework. That time it was Nina, because of her sprained wrist.

Calista's house is a bit of a mess because Paul doesn't do much housework, but Nina's was immaculate; the cushions plumped and neatly arranged on the beige sofa, the pale carpets spotless, despite Nina having a brother who was only eight (he was on a play date when Eleri went round, which Nina assured her was a very good thing). Even the clothes on the airer by the patio doors were arranged neatly, little pairs of Marvel pants lined up like bunting beside EHS school shirts and paired socks.

Nina's room, when they went up there to work, was similarly characterless, which had struck Eleri as odd for a teenage girl: there were no clothes on the floor, no pastes and potions spilling out over every surface. The only furniture was a pine bed and an antique desk, so they sat on the floor to work, Eleri scribing for Nina. At one point she plucked up the courage to send Ras a picture, with the caption, `Look what u did`. He answered immediately, `I deny everything`, with a side-eye emoji, and after that the work was a bit more erratic as she and Ras batted messages back and forth, until Nina's mum called them down for lunch.

The chapatis and dahl were delicious, but sitting down at the round table by the French doors nobody said much, to the point that Eleri began to feel uncomfortable. Nina was different at home than she was at school, and her mum had an air of quiet watchfulness, her dark eyes tracking Nina's hand as she took more and more bread. And yet she made no comment. Looking from one to the other, Eleri wondered if there was something else going on, because after the first couple of chapatis Nina didn't seem to be enjoying them much. She ate laboriously, pausing now and again, as if weary of eating, before carrying on. And though her mum's gaze became more and more troubled, she didn't take the plate away, she just let her daughter overeat.

In the end, Eleri could stand the silence no longer.

"So are you looking forward to the Christmas dance?"

Nina looked up at her mum and her mum looked back, then she gave a very slight nod. But in response, Nina gave an almost imperceptible shake of her head. "I don't think I'll bother."

"Oh, go on," Eleri cried. "It'll be fun. Well, it won't, but it'll be less bad if you're there!"

Her mum's face softened then, a tentative smile playing on her lips. "Nina? You should go with your friend."

Nina looked at her mother, her lips pressed together.

"It'll be fun, I swear," Eleri urged.

"I'd have to get a new dress."

"Yes, of course."

After that the conversation died again and Nina carried on eating.

Eleri looked around the room. On the wall behind Nina was a large, framed landscape picture, and beside it, an illuminated paragraph of Arabic script. On the other side of the French doors was a small back garden, featureless but for a football in the middle of the lawn, and a shed. Through the window of the shed she could make out what looked like an easel. She looked back at the picture. The initials in the corner were JG.

"Who did the painting?" Eleri said. "It's really good."

There was a pause.

"My dad," Nina said finally.

"Did you ever find your travelcard, Nina?" her mum said quickly.

"No, not yet. I've ordered another one though, so it should be here in a few days. The bus driver's been good about it."

"Ah well, that is good." Mrs Mitri got up and started clearing the table. Eleri sprang up to help. The quicker the table was cleared, the quicker she could leave.

Had Nina's parents split up recently? Was that why she had to change schools?

As Nina's mum went back and forth to the kitchen, Eleri

noticed how careful and birdlike her movements were, as if she didn't want to be seen. Like her daughter. Two invisible women.

Her thoughts are interrupted by Calista hurling her pen down.

"Screw it! I'm just going to fail chemistry. Let's go and get some lunch."

Eleri follows her down but almost bumps into her when Cal stops abruptly on the last stair from the bottom. She follows Calista's eyeline to the coat hooks behind the door. Hanging between Paul, Calista and Eleri's jackets is a pale pink duffel coat.

There are voices coming from the living room.

Calista walks briskly down the hall and Eleri follows. The Szajna living room is considerably tidier than usual. Gone are the piles of laundry waiting to be sorted, the discarded takeaway boxes and drifts of unopened mail, and instead of dirty mugs and week-old newspapers, sitting on the coffee table is a large bunch of pink and yellow roses.

Paul is sitting on the sofa, his usual garb of stained joggers and Primark T-shirt replaced by a button-down shirt and chinos. He has shaved. Beside him sits a small, curvaceous woman with bobbed brown hair. Her bust fills out her tailored navy dress and when the girls walk in she tugs it down over her plump knees. They appear to have been sitting in silence, but now Paul smiles brightly.

"Oh, hi, girls. Jill popped over to say hello. Calista, this is Jill. Jill, Calista and her best friend, Eleri."

Eleri smiles and says hello. Is this the new "mate" Paul was with last week?

"Nice to meet you," the woman says brightly. "You've been doing homework I hear? Poor you."

Paul says, "We were wondering if you fancied a walk down to Pret for a cake and coffee."

"Sorry," Calista replies coldly. "We're going out."

Jill looks at Paul.

"OK, no problem. Where are you going?"

"The shops. For a dress for the dance."

"OK, then." Paul looks at Jill. "We'll just go on our own, shall we?"

"Sure," Jill says, with a palpable air of relief.

"That's great, isn't it?" Eleri says, as they walk down the driveway. "If your dad's got a girlfriend he'll be so much happier. You won't have to worry about him so much."

By way of response Calista yanks up the zip of her jacket and stabs her hands into the pockets. They get on the bus to the shopping centre nearby, a drab, soulless place that has lost most of its customers to Westfield. They wander around a shabby clothes store whose listless staff can't be bothered to refold the jumpers and tops that people have looked at, leaving them to lie in piles on the display tables, so that the place resembles a jumble sale. The only other customers are two women in burkas browsing the children's clothes. A brief scan of the partywear confirms there is nothing that could be worn to the dance without incurring ridicule.

They leave, and browse the make-up in a Superdrug that has seen better days.

Scanning the display, with its greasy mirror and blunt eyeliners, Eleri comes to the Maybelline section, and there is the very lipstick she bought for Nina last year. Red Revolution.

What the hell was she thinking? Overweight, frumpy Nina, who never wore a scrap of make-up or a remotely revealing or flattering item of clothing, and Eleri decides to get her a lipstick, in a colour Gran would have described as *slutty*. There were so many others: frosted caramels and soft damasks that would have flattered Nina's colouring without making such a massive statement. It had felt like fun at the time, choosing it. Calista didn't want to know, so Beni had come. He'd insisted it was a great idea: the colour would suit Nina's brown skin beautifully and it might give her more confidence.

But she can't blame Beni. It was her own decision.

Caught by a movement to her left, Eleri's heart sinks as she watches Calista slip a nail varnish up her sleeve. Calista started shoplifting in the months before her parents' marriage break-up, but Eleri had hoped the phase had passed.

"We're sixteen now," she mutters when they make it out of the shop without being collared by the security guard. "You'll end up with a criminal record."

But before Calista can reply, Eleri's phone trills.

This time the *Door 12* message is accompanied by a flame emoji.

The blood rushes to Eleri's face. Is he calling her hot? Then just as quickly it drains away. The Secret Santa is nothing other than literal.

"What?" Calista says, registering her expression.

"The cladding on Gibea is flammable. What if he's set it on fire?"

"Not your problem."

"I need to go back and check."

"You don't."

"I do. I'm sorry."

"Then I'm coming with you."

"You don't have to."

"My only other option is making small talk with *Jill*."

But when they arrive back at the estate, a circuit of the tower reveals no illumination.

"Maybe he hasn't got here yet."

"Let's go to yours and wait."

They cross the grass to Shiloh, but as Eleri is getting her fob out of her pocket, Calista grasps her arm. "Look." Eleri turns.

There is a very faint glow coming from a window on the twelfth floor of Gibea. A glow that is flickering. She was right. The Secret Santa has set the building on fire!

But then she frowns. The glow is limited to that one room, as if it's contained. In a bin or bucket perhaps? And with the whole building empty of inhabitation, there is no fuel that would allow a fire to take hold.

She sets off back across the grass, but Calista runs after her, pulling her back. "Are you out of your mind?"

Her friend's eyes are wide with horror, but Eleri feels perfectly calm. "Listen. For the past eleven days, someone has gone to great lengths to give me this series of gifts. Maybe it's Ras, maybe it's someone else, but whoever it is, they're doing it for a reason and I want to know what that is."

"How is going into a burning building going to help you do that?"

"I don't know. Maybe it won't."

Edging through the splintered door, she wonders if she'll have to do this alone, but then Calista comes in behind her and they make their way up the twenty-four flights of stairs to Door 12.

The flickering light is produced not by a fire in a bucket, but by a semicircle of fat altar candles, some already spilling puddles of wax on to the cement floor. They are arranged around a torn photograph.

"Who is that?" Calista says.

Eleri picks it up. A teenage girl smiles at the camera. Her dark hair is piled up on her head, with a few tendrils left loose to frame her face. And what a face. Eleri has never seen cheekbones like those, and yes, she is wearing make-up to enhance them, but her smoky eyes are heartstopping. Her neck is long and elegant, and in the simple black dress she could easily be a model. And yet this is not a professionally filtered shot, just a snap. In the background is a messy teenage bedroom, with posters on the walls and teddies piled up on the bed.

"Do you recognize her?" Calista murmurs.

"No." But she must be important because the Secret Santa has built this shrine for her. That's all it can be described as.

Then something catches her eye, a point of light on the girl's hand that is entwined in the hand of the missing person.

On her middle finger is a diamond ring.

Monday December 13

Calista comes back to the flat but they don't get much of a chance to talk about the new gift, because Mum comes home. She makes a big fuss of Cal, to the extent that Eleri starts to feel a little bit grumpy, and then Paul texts to say that he's ordering a takeaway for *the two of them*, so Cal heads home.

With Mum safely ensconced in the kitchen making dinner, Eleri goes to her room and lays out all the items from Gibea Tower on her bedroom floor. The first few are simply nice presents:

An Elf on the Shelf.

A cuddly octopus.

A tin of Quality Street.

A ring.

But the next three seem to be conveying some kind of meaning Eleri doesn't understand:

A wind-up mouse.

A kitten collar.

A broken friendship bracelet.

And then, the last two:

A key.

And now a photograph.

These feel more like – and there is surely only one word for it – like clues. There is only one purpose to a clue – to solve a mystery – and there is only one mystery in Eleri's life: Nina's disappearance.

Are these gifts all from Nina? If so, why the strange loaded messages in the middle? The kitten collar seems designed to unnerve her, showing as it does that she and Mum are being watched, but the other two are odd. The mouse was caught in a trap and the friendship bracelet is broken. This makes her uneasy but she's not sure why. Is *she* the one in a trap? The one who broke the friendship?

But she and Nina were friends until the day she went missing, so what is Nina, if it *is* Nina, trying to imply? Where has she been for a whole year? And why would she come back just to play mind games with Eleri?

After another bad night's sleep she wakes late and has to run for the bus. As it's rare for her and Calista to find themselves on the same bus in the morning, she brings a book to pass the time, but this morning her mind is too jumpy to focus, so she takes out her phone and scrolls through her Insta feed.

She's not really paying much attention and the make-up hacks and cookie recipes scroll by in a blur, but then a familiar face snaps her to attention.

Ras is standing by the Eurostar wearing a pair of Mickey Mouse ears. The comment beneath reads: suspension aint so bad!

He has tagged his location: Disneyland, Paris.

She hits his profile and scans his feed. Here is Ras queuing for rides, upside down on a roller coaster with his hair streaming behind him, watching the parade with a sappy look on his face, eating chips in a tacky themed restaurant, posing with Mickey and Pluto and the Little Mermaid who is planting a kiss on his cheek.

The time codes attest that he was there from Friday to Sunday. Which means that he couldn't have left the last three gifts.

If it really isn't Ras, then who is it?

But she doesn't get a chance to ponder this because suddenly they are at school and she stuffs the phone into her bag and stumbles off the bus.

She falls into step behind Ray, trudging through the school gates carrying a Tesco bag. The bag seems to be filled with frozen ready meals. A lot of the staff bring in their own lunches to avoid the canteen food, but to bring in frozen food at the beginning of the day? Has he got a freezer in the shed? What for? But before she has the chance to think on, Beni is bounding over to meet her.

*

170

Break time finds the three of them sitting on the scratchy carpet behind a bookcase in the library. It's a sunny day so most people are out in the playground, and the place is hushed.

"It has to be someone at school," Beni says. "And let's be honest, no one else really knows you exist."

Eleri sighs. "Kika does."

"Why would she be stalking you?" Beni says.

"Because she's jealous?"

"What, of him ignoring you?"

"He isn't any more."

"And that's weird in itself, don't you think?" Calista says. "It's like he suddenly started being nice to lull you into a false sense of security."

"I don't feel particularly secure," Eleri mutters.

"Say they *are* clues," Beni says softly. "Not from Nina, but from someone else."

"Like who?"

Beni's eyes are wide in the gloom. "From her killer."

In the silence that follows they can hear shouting and laughter from the playground as normal kids enjoy normal kid pursuits like playing football and laughing at TikTok videos. Being sociable suddenly sounds so easy and fun. Why has she avoided it for so long?

"Who says she's dead?" Calista says. "She probably just ran away."

"Or maybe someone took her, and these clues are supposed to lead us to her."

"In that case we need to take them to the police."

"Don't be stupid," Calista says sharply. "You'll be done for wasting their time."

Eleri blinks at her in surprise. A couple of days ago Calista was actively encouraging her to go to the police.

"These aren't clues, they're just some idiot playing with you."

Eleri nods, chastened.

Calista gets up. "I'll see you at lunchtime."

"What's with her?" Beni says as Calista marches out of the library, slamming the door behind her with such force that they can feel it through the floor.

"I guess she's worried about me."

"Let me see the photo again."

Eleri withdraws it from her pocket and Beni studies the beautiful girl. "What's wrong with her finger?"

He points and Eleri can see what he means. One of the girl's fingers is sticking out at a funny angle. But now that she looks closer, the finger is a different colour to the rest of her skin: pink instead of light brown.

Her breath catches.

It's not a finger. It's an octopus tentacle. Could it be that her pink cuddly octopus once belonged to this girl?

"Weird," Beni murmurs. Then he frowns and peers closer at the picture. "You know what, there's something familiar about her, don't you think?"

Eleri looks closer. "Maybe. Maybe she was in sixth form and left."

There's a moment's silence as they both gaze down at the half-familiar face, and then Eleri's heart gives a sudden plunge. "You don't think…" Her wide eyes meet Beni's. "That maybe *she* went missing too?"

"We'd have been told, wouldn't we?"

"I don't know. If she was eighteen that makes her an adult, so maybe the police don't care so much."

She remembers the chips in Ray's bag. As if he's got a freezer in the shed. And why would you need a freezer unless … unless there was something in that shed that needed feeding? When she tells Beni, his eyes turn dinner-plate round.

"Jesus. *Ray?* What, you think he might … what, be keeping someone prisoner? Wouldn't we hear screams or something?"

"Not if he's dug out some kind of bunker. He's got all that equipment, saws and spades and stuff."

Beni attempts a laugh but it tails off quickly. "You think *Ray* could be the Secret Santa, seriously?"

"I don't know, but he's definitely keeping something in the shed at night. Something that needs the lights to be left on, and to be fed."

Beni pales. "In that case, maybe this whole Secret Santa thing is some kind of elaborate build-up to an abduction?" His voice drops to a whisper. "*Your* abduction?"

"What should we do?" Eleri murmurs, sick with horror. "Go to the police?"

"On the evidence of a frozen lasagne? No. We wait til

he's gone home one night and then break in. I'll look up how to pick a padlock. There must be something online."

Eleri bites her lip. "I dunno, Ben…"

"Aw, come on. If we're wrong, then breaking into a shed isn't exactly the crime of the century. And if we're right…"

He leaves the sentence, with all it's horrible implications, hanging.

"How would we even get into the school grounds?" Eleri says, desperate for an excuse not to do this.

"The broken railings," Beni says.

In the autumn, a car driven by a guy who was under the influence, smashed into EHS's perimeter fence, and the broken balusters still haven't been fixed. Yellow tape has covered the gap ever since, and during the day teachers watch it like hawks to prevent any escape bids.

"I can't do it tonight, though," Beni goes on. "There's some TV awards do that I've said I'll go to with Mum, but how about tomorrow? We can say we're going to the cinema together. OK?"

Eleri nods weakly and gazes down at the girl in the photograph. The hairs on her arms stand on end, as if in fright. If this was *girl one*, and Nina was *girl two*, is Eleri *girl three*?

She didn't see Calista at lunch, after all.

As she entered the canteen Ras's table was more raucous than ever and, holding court at the centre of the table, like Jesus at the last supper, was Ras himself, a pair of Mickey

Mouse ears perched on his head. Eleri turned on her heel and spent the rest of the lunch hour doing her homework in the form room.

They all meet up after last bell instead, and walk out of the building together, Eleri promising Calista she won't go to Gibea Tower tonight, and this time actually meaning it.

"Heads up," Beni mutters before they have got halfway to the gates. "It's lover boy."

Before she's fully registered what he's said Eleri looks up and her stomach drops on to the playground tarmac.

"Hey," Ras says, his tone lacking its usual animation.

"Hey."

"Get lost," Calista snaps.

"It's OK," Eleri says quietly.

"That's me off, then," Beni says, and walks quickly away.

"She's not interested in what you've got to say." Calista is shooting iron filings from her eyes, but Ras just holds Eleri's gaze steadily as if Calista isn't even there.

"It's OK, Cal, you can go."

"What and leave you with this psycho?"

At the word, Ras flinches and Eleri feels a flash of anger towards her friend. "I said it's fine."

There's a loaded pause, then Cal says, "Call me later," and after a final, sharp look at Ras, she walks away.

"Come on, then," Eleri says when Calista is out of earshot, trying to sound as authoritative as possible. "Talk."

"Shall we go to Gino's?"

Gino's is a cafe opposite school. It serves anything under

the sun with chips and has a sign on the door saying *No Schoolchildren*. It's testament to the formidable ocean liner that is the cafe manager that the kids obey this directive. All of them except Ras apparently.

"It's OK. Paula loves me."

As they pass out of the gates and cross the road, Eleri is aware that there are eyes on them, and she can't help but feel grateful: whatever he has to say, just by walking beside her Ras has probably rescued her from a continuation of the canteen bullying.

Gino's is warm and low-lit, and they slide into a table near the counter. The place looks like it has been expertly styled in a vintage rockabilly pastiche but it genuinely hasn't been decorated in decades. The tables are Formica, the floors chequerboard and the walls hung with framed pictures torn from magazines featuring long-dead screen sirens. Paula comes out from behind the counter and seesaws up to them. Her hair is coiled into tight grey curls and you could rest a plate of food on her bosom. She pats Ras's cheek with a plump hand bedecked with gold rings. "You never tell me you got girlfriend!"

"She's not my girlfriend," Ras says. "She's my wife."

Paula gasps theatrically. "Run, my darling, he is nothing but trouble this one."

Eleri gives her a wan smile.

"Wha you wan, then?"

Ras looks at Eleri.

"Just a Coke, please."

"Same for me, Paula, and whatever you're having."

"Ha! You think I'm not sick of every fricking thing in this fricking place?"

"You're welcome." Ras grins as Paula tramps away, humming along to the radio.

"So," Eleri says after a pause, "how was Disneyland?"

"Yeah, good. It was a laugh. After all the shit with the school, my brother just decided we were gonna have some fun."

Eleri's face ignites and she looks down at the speckled pattern on the yellow Formica.

"That's, er, what I wanted to talk to you about. Obviously."

She nods.

"So what's going on, then? What is it exactly that you think I've been doing to you?"

She takes a deep breath. "I think I'm being stalked."

She tells him everything that has happened over the past twelve days: from the first few days when the messages from the Secret Santa felt exciting, and then the sinister turn that the gifts took: the pills, the laser, the broken bracelet and the kitten collar that implied he knew their movements. She doesn't mention the plan to search Ray's shed. The fewer people that know about that, the less likely it is they'll be expelled.

By the end, Ras's expression is grim. "And you thought this was me? Why?"

She cracks open the can of Coke that Paula brings over

177

and gulps half of it down to wet her dry throat. "Beni said he heard your friends say you'd picked me out of the box deliberately."

There is a pause and risking a glance at his face, Eleri sees to her amazement that Ras is blushing.

"I did, yeah." He raises his eyes to hers. "But it isn't me doing this, I swear."

His anxiety seems so genuine. And then, as if to prove his innocence once and for all, her phone buzzes.

Drawing it out of her pocket, she lays it down on the table, and touches the screen.

Door 13.

Ras stares at it for a moment, then he gets up, knocking the table so hard the salt and pepper mills fall over.

"This ends now. Come on."

The traffic is mercifully light and they arrive at Gibea just as the last sliver of a scarlet sun sinks behind the railway line.

"You've been doing this on your own for nearly two weeks?" he demands as they walk the flickering path to Gibea Tower.

"Mostly. Sometimes Beni or Cal come."

"I can't see a light." Ras's gaze is fixed on the black finger outlined against the dusk.

"Sometimes it's round the back."

She's relieved to be proved right: if there had been no

light he would think she was making the whole thing up to get him here. It's so high up, halfway to the top now, and they pause by the splintered door, their heads tipped back.

"Right, then," Ras says. "Let's do it."

They step through, into the dark.

When they get to the stairwell, Ras cups his hands around his mouth and bellows into the shadows: "Evening, arsehole!"

The echoes take a long time to die away.

"Come and say hello, why don't you? Or are you too scared now I'm here?"

Eleri waits, holding her breath: maybe this was what she should have done all along. But the silence unfolds itself again like a night-blooming flower.

As they climb the stairs, Ras keeps up a running commentary. "Third floor, dickwad...! Are you ready for us...? Fifth floor! You picked the wrong girl to mess with...! Ninth floor! Come out, why don't you?"

Tramping up behind him, Eleri imagines this is what it must feel like to have a dad. To be able to pass your problems along to someone stronger and braver than you to fix.

They emerge on to floor thirteen. *The Thirteenth Floor.* It sounds like the name of a horror film, Eleri thinks, and with a sudden lurch of her heart she wonders if the Secret Santa planned this to be the final day all along.

Ras opens the door and the tunnel of darkness stretches ahead of them. "Nina?" he calls out, softer now. "This isn't you, is it, honey?"

She's probably imagining the sudden change in atmosphere: a kind of thickening, so that she almost has to suck the air into her lungs.

"I know it isn't, right? Cos we were always your friends, me and El, weren't we?"

The building responds with a silence as dense as a collapsing star.

"If there's something we can do to help you, come and talk to us."

It can't be Nina. It would make no sense. And yet Ras seems to have conjured up her presence with his words, and now Eleri can see the lost girl in her mind's eye: a pale shape flitting in and out of the deserted rooms, looking for something, or someone. Her skin prickles.

"Come on."

They follow the light and as they approach the door of flat 136, Eleri sees something glinting in his hand. Ras has a knife.

"What are you doing?" she hisses, grasping his arm before he can get to the doorway.

"This isn't a game, Eleri. Whoever this is, they're trying to terrorize you. And at some point, they're gonna want to do more than just scare you."

She stares at him.

Ras steps over the threshold and starts back in horror. She hurries to his side and gasps.

Lying in the middle of the floor of flat 136 is a severed head.

Then her knees almost give way with relief.

Not a head. A Halloween mask. One of those silicon ones that just about hold their shape when you put them down. An ugly witch with a hooked nose, a chin covered in warts, and a grinning, grey-lipped mouth. There is something truly horrible about the empty eye sockets, and the effect is made even more unpleasant when Ras picks the mask up and wiggles his fingers through the holes, like worms.

"You'll have to do better than that to scare us!" he yells, striding to the door. "Now what say we have a little chat?" Then he walks out into the dark.

Alone in the lamplight, Eleri stares at the black rectangle of the doorway, waiting for him to reappear.

From somewhere deeper inside the building she hears a sing-song voice. "Come out, come out, wherever you are…"

A slamming door above or below her, the vibrations passing through the floor beneath her feet.

She walks to the threshold. "Ras?"

Running footsteps overhead.

She shrinks back, but with the light behind her she can be clearly seen, a frozen rabbit blinded by the dark.

"Ras!"

Her voice echoes back at her, mockingly. There is no sound now: no pattering footsteps, no slamming doors. Where is he?

She steps out into the hall. At the far end of the corridor she can make out the small window looking out across the railway line. Far away, orange lights glimmer: evidence that a normal, civilized world still exists, somewhere out of her reach. And then the lights are swallowed up. A figure has stepped across the window.

She fumbles with her phone, swiping so madly she passes the torch app and has to swipe back again.

Ras took his knife but she has no weapon, nothing to defend herself unless she hurls the phone and runs. She knows the layout of the building well enough to make it out in the dark, but he must know it better.

The torch app squeals to life and she raises the phone.

The figure coming towards her down the corridor is a very old man, and yet it doesn't have the gait of an old man: it moves rapidly. It will be on her in seconds.

She screams.

"Hey, it's OK!" Ras pulls off the mask, skidding to a halt a few paces away from her. "Sorry. I just wanted to scare him if I found him."

"D... Did you?"

He shakes his head.

It's faster going down than up and Eleri bursts gratefully out into the night air, tipping her head back to the canopy of stars spread out above her.

"Are you OK?" Ras touches her shoulder.

"Yeah, yeah, fine. I need to get home, though. Mum will be worried."

"Sure, OK."

"Thanks for coming."

"No problem. For once I agree with Calista. You shouldn't go back there. Whatever's going on, it's messed up." His face is serious but the mask dangling from his hand like flayed skin grins at her. She takes it from him, goosebumps passing up her arm like an infection at the touch of the cold, tacky rubber.

"I won't. I'll, um, see you tomorrow, then." She forces herself not to break into a run as she crosses the gap between the two towers, feeling his eyes on her back the whole way.

He swore that he wasn't the Secret Santa, but he put the mask on. He must have known it would scare her. As she dives through the door, slamming it shut and leaning against it to catch her breath, she realizes she's not sure she believes him.

Tuesday December 14

It's the day before the Christmas dance, the day the Secret Santa gifts are handed out. As the bell goes for break and the students all troop to the gym, Eleri keeps her gaze fixed straight ahead, away from the playing fields and Ray's shed. She hasn't even decided whether she'll go ahead with Beni's plan tonight. In the light of day it all seems ridiculous, but then Tamara and her friends go skipping by, all coltish legs and swinging hair, and the eyes of the boys follow them hungrily. If a paedophile wanted access to young girls, then wouldn't a school groundskeeper be the perfect job?

At the door she can't stop herself throwing a glance towards the sports pitches, and there's Ray, standing by the closed door of the shed, rolling a cigarette. He must feel her gaze because he suddenly looks up and their eyes lock.

Jerking her head back round, Eleri pushes through the

crowd, heart pounding, and passes through the gym doors to safety.

A glance around the room shows, to her relief, that Ras isn't there. Her thoughts have been flip-flopping all night. The thing with the mask was stupid, but Ras can be stupid. And she was with him when she got the message, so he couldn't have sent it, plus he was in Paris when the last three gifts appeared. And yet he deliberately picked her – he admitted it – and his behaviour towards her over the past year has been weird to say the least.

There's a holiday atmosphere in the gym, as if school has broken up already, and she passes the chattering groups to join Calista and Beni. She didn't tell them about last night's gift and neither of them asks. Beni keeps looking over at Hendrick, standing alone near the front, and Calista is wrapped up in her own bad mood.

The names are called out one by one and people open their packages of sweets and toiletries and toys. Some givers have made a real effort, some have just put a name sticker on a bag of Haribo. One joker put a square of burger cheese in a Tiffany box. Soon sets of wind-up teeth are chattering across the floor and pull-back racing cars are smacking people in the ankles.

Kika's name is called and Eleri watches her go up to collect a small box wrapped in pink paper.

More names are announced and she's so busy listening for her own that she doesn't notice Kika's reaction when she opens the gift, but when she glances across to the group again, mainly to check if Ras has arrived, she sees Kika gazing down at something small and glinting in her palm. When she looks up, her eyes are shining with tears. Eleri follows her gaze to the other side of the room. Rebekah is leaning against the monkey bars, smiling softly. Pressing her lips together, Kika slips the gift into the breast pocket of her shirt and turns away.

Suddenly it's clear to Eleri. The relationship Rebekah was describing in MooBar, the controlling one: it was with Kika.

Which means Kika isn't in love with Ras.

Which means Kika definitely isn't her Secret Santa.

Calista trudges up to the front of the room and is handed her package by the smiling Miss Merrion.

"Aren't you going to open it?" Beni says when she comes back, the gift held in her limp grasp.

"What's the point? It'll just be a bag of Haribos."

Beni snatches the parcel. "It isn't. It feels squishy."

Calista sighs, taking it back and untying the ribbon. The wrapping is cackhanded, the pattern pulled away in white strips where the giver has stuck and restuck the Sellotape. She opens it dismally.

Inside is a jade-green beanie topped with a pink fur bobble.

"That's cashmere," Beni says.

Eleri smiles. "Somebody likes you."

Cal looks up, her cheeks pink with pleasure. "Was it one of you two?"

186

"Nope."

"No, sorry. Put it on."

The colours work beautifully against Cal's straw-coloured hair and cornflower eyes.

"Who was it?" she asks, seemingly unable to move her fingers from the soft band around her forehead.

They cast their gazes around the room, and Eleri spots a face turned in their direction.

"Look at Harry Falconio," Eleri breathes.

She doesn't know much about Harry. Average looking, average height, a nice smile, which is playing tentatively on his lips as he holds Calista's astonished gaze.

"Smile," Beni hisses.

And for once Calista does what she's told.

After an hour or so the gym starts to empty. The drama group is one of the last to leave, followed by Ras's crew, until eventually there are only a handful of people yet to receive their gift. Eventually Beni's name is called.

He brings back the tin of Quality Street Eleri wrapped in a hurry last night and sits back down.

"Hmm." Beni taps his chin with his finger. "Now I wonder what this could be…"

As he sets about opening it, Eleri feels ashamed. Yes, she had a lot on her mind, but she should have made more of an effort.

"Someone's been at this!" he cries, when the coloured tin is revealed. "They've broken the original seal and Sellotaped it back up. The purple ones better not be all gone!"

He picks at the Sellotape, peels it away and opens the lid.

For a long moment there is just silence as they all look down at the dark soil filling the tin to the brim.

"Maybe there's something buried in it," Beni says, and starts to dig with his fingers.

"Don't!" warns Eleri.

He looks up at her.

"I got it from the tower. I just decided to regift it. I'm so, so sorry, Ben."

"Seriously? In that case I have to see…"

Eleri holds her breath as he pushes his hand deeper into the earth, braced for a sudden scream, for blood, for severed fingers. There couldn't be anything alive in there. She's had it under her bed for over a week, she'd have heard a scrabbling…

Finally Beni withdraws his hand, brushing the soil off on his trousers. "Nothing."

"Let me chuck it in the bin." Eleri tries to take the tin from him, but he pushes her hand away.

"Wait. It must mean something."

"A tin of mud?" Calista snaps. "What could it possibly *mean*?"

"I don't think these presents were chosen randomly." He replaces the lid. "Right, I'm coming home with you. We're going to examine every single gift and try to figure out some kind of meaning or connection with it all. I'll meet you by the gates at the end of school."

"Not me," Calista says. "Like I've told you a million

times, this is bullshit and you're just encouraging whoever's doing it. Ignore them and they'll stop."

Beni shrugs. "Maybe El doesn't want them to stop."

"I do," Eleri says quickly.

"But if you're being sent this stuff for a reason, aren't you curious what it is?"

"I guess it depends on the reason."

"This is ridiculous." Snatching the cashmere hat off her head, Calista gets to her feet and storms out. On the other side of the room, Harry Falconio's face falls.

Beni sighs and shakes his head. "She needs to get on the happy pills. Right, well, I said I'd meet Hendrick for a kickabout." He stands up. "Coming to cheerlead me?"

"I might just stay to the end," Eleri says. "Just to see."

"If Ras got you something after all?"

"If he did, wouldn't that tell us something?"

"Want me to wait with you?"

She shakes her head quickly.

"OK, well, thanks for my mud." He shakes the tin. "And I'll see you later."

He gives her a glancing kiss on the forehead and then is gone.

Eleri waits until the end, until tiny Alexander Keplan receives his gift – Miss Merrion pulling it out from under the table. It's the biggest teddy Eleri has ever seen in her life, even taller than Alex himself, and he drags it away, smiling.

"Nothing for you then, Eleri?" the teacher calls as she starts gathering up the drifts of discarded wrapping paper.

"It's OK," Eleri replies. Though she ought to help clear up, she doesn't want to get into a conversation or she might end up telling Miss Merrion everything, and that would kick off a whole world of trouble. To her relief the bell goes, so she says goodbye and hurries out of the gym.

The corridor is completely deserted now and she can hear the distant voices of students making their way to class. Heading for the exit, she rifles in her bag to check she's got the right books for the next lessons.

But as she comes level with the equipment cupboard, the door creaks open, an arm shoots out and she is dragged into the darkness. She tries to scream but a hand is slapped over her mouth. Kicking out and thrashing, she struggles to get away.

"Jesus! Will you just… It's me, OK!"

With a twist she is free and hurls a wild punch in the direction of the voice. It makes contact and there is a grunt followed by a clatter. She shoves the door open and light streams in.

Ras has fallen against the shelves at the back of the cupboard, knocking a pile of plastic cones on to the floor.

"What the actual…?" Eleri pants, half relieved, half furious.

Ras clicks his jaw from side to side, wincing. "I didn't want to give it to you in front of everyone."

She folds her arms. "Give me what?"

Picking up a red cone that has fallen on the floor, he puts it on his head and with a half-hearted "ho ho ho", draws a green canister from his pocket.

"My Secret Santa gift. "I went round to my uncle's last night – he's a fed – and ... borrowed it. It's pepper spray."

Eleri closes the door and takes the canister. The label reads *Advanced Incapacitant*.

"Hopefully you won't need it. Hopefully it's just someone messing around. But I was thinking. It's all very well me saying not to go, but if this shithead does something again, threatens your family or whatever, then I know you're gonna, and I just want to make sure you're safe when you do."

Ras being so serious about this makes it all feel very real and very scary.

"They're totally illegal unless you're police, so don't mention it to anyone and keep it hidden, yeah?"

She nods, manages a strained "thanks", then turns to leave.

"Eleri."

She turns back.

"Are you going to the dance tomorrow?"

"I guess."

"Good. Well, I guess I'll see you there, then."

While she's waiting for Beni on the bench her phone rings. It's Mum.

"I'm just on my break." She sounds breathless and Eleri's throat tightens. Has one of the shitty customers said something to her again?

"Are you OK?"

"Yeah. I just wanted to see if you'd mind if I went out tonight."

"With work people?"

There's a pause. "With Adam actually."

"Adam?"

"Kitten man."

"Oh … right."

"Just for a drink or two at the Rising Sun. It's on the high street, by the pound shop."

"Sure, no problem." This means Eleri won't have to use the cinema lie if she goes back to school with Beni.

"We're meeting at six so I'll definitely be back by nine."

"OK, see you later."

Beni arrives at the bus stop puffing after an energetic kickabout under the floodlights. On the bus he talks enthusiastically about how he's learned how to pick a padlock in an online tutorial, in preparation for their shed raid, and she doesn't tell him that she's having second thoughts about the whole thing. The traffic is bad and it's approaching five by the time they disembark and make their way across the grass, towards the light burning on the fourteenth floor of Gibea Tower.

Tonight's gift is a postcard from *Beautiful Wales*. It features four interlocked pictures: a forest, a bay, a castle and a field of daffodils. There's no writing on the other side, no address and no stamp.

Eleri slips it into her bag and they make a quick exit. As they emerge around the side of the building, she spots her mum, halfway down the flickering path. She must have popped home to change and is tottering along in black kitten heels and skinny jeans that emphasize the inward bend of her left knee. Eleri's heart sinks, but there's no point Mum trying to hide her disability from Adam: if he's an arsehole that judges people on that sort of thing, it's best she finds out now. They wait until she has crossed the road and disappeared behind the traffic, before running across the gap between the buildings and letting themselves into Shiloh.

The flat smells of hairspray and perfume and a note written in her mum's characteristically crabbed hand informs her that there's a microwavable lasagne in the fridge.

Eleri grabs a packet of Hobnobs, then she and Beni retreat to her bedroom. As she drags it out from under her bed, the pillowcase brings with it a colony of dust bunnies and hairballs. She empties it out on her rug. It's like a memory game. *I went to the shops and I bought a...*

Cuddly octopus.

Diamond ring.

Wind-up mouse.

Kitten collar.

Broken friendship bracelet.

Key.

Photo.

Postcard.

Beni adds his tin of Quality Street to the pile while Eleri

fetches the elf from its new position on top of the bathroom cabinet.

"There must be a connection," he murmurs, scanning the eclectic assortment. "We just need to think about it…"

Eleri looks and she thinks, but her eyes see nothing new and her mind is blank.

The kitten barges through the door, yowling for attention. When Eleri ignores it, it marches across the display, toppling the elf on to its back before plonking itself down on the photograph, thin tail flicking, paws framing the upper part of the girl's face.

"Get *off*," Eleri mutters, jabbing it with her finger.

After tumbling melodramatically on to its back, the kitten rights itself, fixes her with a look of reproach then marches away, rump swinging.

When Eleri turns back to the arrangement of gifts she sees that Beni has picked up the photograph and is frowning at it.

"What?"

He arranges his fingers to cover up the same portion of the photograph that the kitten's paws did. "Look."

She shuffles to his side, and her breath catches.

The way he has framed the image, concentrating just on the girl's eyes, it's completely obvious.

"Remind you of anyone?" Beni murmurs.

She looks at him. His eyes glitter with excitement, but her heart feels like a lump of ice in her chest.

It's Nina.

*

"Could be a cousin or a sister or something?"

They are lying on her bed, ploughing through the packet of Hobnobs, Eleri because she's a bag of nerves and Beni because, well, presumably just because he likes them, as he certainly doesn't seem stressed. In fact he is positively thrumming with excitement.

"Maybe," Eleri replies, but somehow she's certain that the girl in the picture is Nina. If only because of how different that Nina was from their Nina – as different as it was possible to be. Like it was deliberate.

"It doesn't make any difference, though. We should still check out the shed."

"But if this is Nina, then there's only one missing girl," she says, brushing crumbs off her tie. "Not two. And the police said there was that sighting at Paddington station."

"Alleged sighting. I honestly don't see the problem. Your mum's out, so it's not like she's going to worry. We go back to school, let ourselves into the shed, have a look round and check there's no false floorboards or, y'know, cages with girls chained up in them, then go. I can reattach the padlock so Ray will never know we were there."

Eleri sighs unhappily.

"Come on, El, it's not just the frozen meals, is it?" Beni's face his serious now. "Ray's clearly got something to hide. Otherwise why would he have put those curtains up? Why is the door to the shed always closed, even if he's just popping outside? The guy's a creep and it seems to me that someone should have spotted that and questioned him last year."

Eleri groans, covering her face with her hands.

"If Nina *is* in there," Beni's voice is quiet now, "and we don't go, then we might miss the chance to save her life."

"OK." Eleri takes her hands away from her face. "Let's go."

The bus is quiet and she sinks low in the seat so that the CCTV doesn't pick up her appearance. But as they get nearer to school her worry about getting caught breaking in is superceded by a more visceral fear.

Ray is hiding something. Something he's feeding. Could that something be a human being? And if so, wouldn't he have some kind of warning system or booby trap to prevent others discovering it?

They get off the bus and skirt the perimeter of the railing until they come to the section with the broken balusters. Beni prises open up a gap in the tape and, with furtive glances behind them, they clamber through.

Walking through the oddly silent grounds, Eleri can't shake the feeling that they are being observed. By the Secret Santa? Is he watching them blunder into the lair of a madman? Did he plan this all along?

No, she spotted the ready meals by chance. There might be zero connection between Ray and the Secret Santa. And yet there is. The connection is Nina.

"No lights," Beni whispers.

He's right. The shed is a black boat adrift in a sea of darkness. Her chest relaxes a little. There's no one in there.

"Ready?"

Eleri nods and they set off. Leaving the lights of the road, their eyes gradually adjust to the darkness of the deserted school. Passing out of the shelter of the main building, the wind increases. Dead leaves scurry across the grass, evidence of the losing battle Ray fights every winter. It's hard enough to gather piles and then load them into the huge building sacks that a smaller man would never be able to lug about, let alone when teenagers take such pleasure in kicking the piles down or throwing great handfuls at one another. No wonder he hates them all.

As they approach the door of the shed, the trees whisper to one another, their branches leaning in to watch Beni light up his phone torch, then take out a fat strip of wire.

"Shit," he mutters. "No padlock. It's just a normal lock."

At first Eleri is flooded with relief. There's nothing they can do about this, so they may as well head home. But then her anger bristles – with herself. That kind of cowardice is so typical of her. Beni was right when he said this might be their chance, however tenuous, to save Nina. Well, for once she won't be a coward.

She shines her phone torch around the edge of the door while Beni pats the windows, feeling for a loose pane. There are no signs of any of the screws that must fasten the lock to the inside of the door, otherwise they could tap them through and the lock would fall out.

Then she realizes something. For the screws not to be visible they must be shorter than the depth of the wood, and she can see from the windowpane that this is no more than a centimetre or so thick. If they push hard enough the lock will simply pull away from the door.

She leans against it and, sure enough, a splintering sound cuts through the silence. Understanding immediately, Beni joins her and they both apply their full weight to the shed door.

Suddenly they are through, stumbling over the threshold into a pitch-black interior that smells of creosote and grass cuttings. Regaining his balance, Beni starts picking his way between the looming skeletons of the groundskeeper's equipment – the lawnmower and leaf blower, the wheelbarrow and hedgecutter – lifting empty sacks that might cover a body, his torch beam skittering across the floor in search of trapdoors.

But Eleri's eye has been caught by something Beni hasn't noticed. A rippling line of light to their left. She frowns at the strange phenomenon, then suddenly understands. The light is coming from beneath a curtain that divides the room in half. Before she can articulate this to Beni, the curtain is whipped back and Ray the groundskeeper is barrelling towards them, an axe raised above his head.

With a scream, Eleri turns and bolts for the door, but Beni has had the same idea and they crash into each other. Ricocheting away, Eleri hits the shed wall, but Beni tumbles backwards over the lawnmower and lands heavily among bags of compost. Eleri thrusts an arm down to yank him up, braced for the blow of the axe. They should never have come here. They are both going to die.

But Beni does not take her hand. His gaze is occupied by something over her shoulder, and yet he doesn't look scared. Pulling himself up on the handle of the mower, he continues to look past Eleri, his face warm in the glow of a lamp.

Eleri turns.

Ray has put down the axe and is shuffling back into the room beyond the curtain. He sits heavily on a creaking chair pulled up to one of the trestle tables they use in the canteen. Over his usual outdoor attire of heavy lumberjack shirt and cargo trousers, he has on a fluffy dressing gown and his feet are encased in filthy Homer Simpson slippers. On top of the sour BO smell that always hovers around Ray is a deeper stink, and Eleri's nose wrinkles at the sight of a plastic bucket in the corner, covered with a folded newspaper. In another corner of the room, a microwave sits on top of a small fridge freezer plugged into a socket in the wall.

On the table a glass beaker is filled with a gold liquid. Ray raises it to his lips and drains it. Then he says, "I suppose you're going to report me."

Beni moves past her into the room.

There are no windows in this part of the shed, that's why they didn't spot the light. With the curtain for insulation, and a gas fire, it must be the warmest part of the building. Only two bars of the fire are lit, presumably for economy, as there are certainly no signs that the occupant of this place can afford luxuries.

Laid out on two pallets behind where Ray is sitting are a sleeping bag and a single pillow. Beside this makeshift bed is a framed picture of a smiling young couple, yellowed with age. They are standing in the sea and the man has his trousers rolled up while the woman's dress is tucked into her knickers.

Eleri shivers. The heater and insulation can only do so much to combat the cold rolling up through the floorboards. Ray has walked dead leaves in and the draught makes them curl and flip like fortune fish.

There's no sign of a cage, or a basement dungeon.

"You live here?" Beni says softly. "Alone?"

Ray sighs and puts down his glass. "I had a wife. Heather. She died. I weren't too good on my own. Couldn't get my head together. Missed some rent payments and got thrown out. Din't have nowhere else to go."

He looks defeated. Up close Eleri can see there is nothing intimidating about the groundskeeper. His broad shoulders and heavy head disguise the fact that he is actually emaciated, the patches of skin visible around his beard yellow as old paperback pages.

"I ain't got no money, if that's what you're after." His expression turns defiant. "But if you report me to Mr Roberts, I'll tell him how you broke in 'ere."

"We're not here to steal from you, and we're not going to report you," Beni says. In the corner of the room is a padded gardener's stool. Flipping it, he pulls it up to the table and sits down. "But you can't stay here."

"I ain't doing no one any harm."

"I mean for your own sake. It's not got really cold yet, but in January and February you'll freeze to death."

"Good," Ray says. Then he seems to notice Eleri for the first time. "If you ain't here to rob, then why *are* you here?"

Beni takes a deep breath. "We were looking for Nina Mitri."

"Who?"

They take it in turns to recount the tale, which now sounds completely ridiculous. When they eventually stammer to an embarrassed halt, Ray says, "So lemme get this straight, you fought I had that girl in a dungeon under the shed, and was feeding her ready meals?" He gives a wheezy laugh.

Eleri mutters that it was clearly a mistake and that the police must have been right about the sighting at the station. It's time to leave this poor man in peace. Besides, the smell from the bucket is making her nauseous. Then Ray speaks again.

"I saw her once, you know. At the bottom of the field." He points a skeletal arm in the direction of the line of trees that mark the boundary of the school grounds. "I was up here and I figured she hadn't heard the bell. Was gonna take the tractor down and tell her when this … person comes out of the trees."

"Person?" Eleri says.

"A boy, or a man, I think. I was a fair distance and he had a hood up, so I couldn't be sure, but that's what it looked like."

"A man," Beni echoes, looking up at Eleri.

"Thought he might be her fella. Decided to give 'em some privacy, pretend I hadn't seen 'em. Next thing I knew, she was gone."

"Did you ever tell the police?"

Ray gives a small shake of his head.

"But it could have been important," Eleri says.

"They would of come here, thrown me out. I'd of lost my job. Heather's buried in the cemetery up the road. What if they moved me miles away? I woon't of bin able to visit her or nothing."

"How long before Nina disappeared did you see this?" Beni says.

Ray shrugs.

Eleri looks helplessly at Beni. Can they do anything with this information that won't get Ray into trouble? It's not as if he's a great witness: from a distance of a good two hundred metres, Ray *might* have seen Nina talking to someone that *might* have been male.

"Here." Beni slides a twenty-pound note across the table. "Get yourself something hot for dinner."

Ray doesn't take it. Nodding down at the empty glass, he mutters, "That stuff warms me up."

"Spend it on whatever you like," Beni says.

Ray pockets the money, muttering, "Cheers."

Walking away from the shed back to the bus stop, Beni says, "Shall I call it anonymously into that number they gave us last year? I can't see that it'll be news to them, though. Surely Nina's parents would know if she had a boyfriend."

"Yeah," Eleri murmurs, but she's not so sure. When she visited the little red-brick house, Nina and her mother were reluctant to speak about her father. Maybe you wouldn't confide something like that, not if you were scared how someone would react.

All the way home on the bus, Eleri thinks about Ray, alone in the cold and dark after losing the only person who loved him. And then she thinks about her mum, in a bright pub, in her best clothes, with a guy she fancies, and offers up a quick prayer, to whoever's listening, that the date goes well.

Wednesday December 15

Mum comes home at half past eleven, in a good mood. Eleri can hear her humming as she emerges from the lift. It seems to take ages for her to reach the door of the flat, as if she needs to take regular pauses, and for a moment Eleri's worried she overdid it. But when Mum lets herself in, phone in hand, grinning, Eleri decides the pauses were probably to text Kitten Man.

If her mum had asked her there and then what she was doing sitting alone in the dark, Eleri might have told her, but instead she just enthuses about her date and what a *fascinating* guy Adam is. Apparently he was kidnapped in Nigeria but escaped after paying a guard off with his jeans, and then had to run away naked through the bush. Supposedly he also once helped a zebra give birth and pitched a tent on a nest of bullet ants. Mum hadn't laughed so much in years, and the pub was brilliant. They should go there for a ploughman's one weekend.

Eleri tries her best to smile, but it doesn't matter that it's unconvincing, because her mum's too tipsy to notice. She makes herself some toast and stands by the kitchen window to eat it, gazing across at Gibea Tower with a smile playing on her lips.

For the fourth night in a row Eleri doesn't sleep much.

Ray might have had nothing to do with Nina's disappearance, but someone must know what happened to her. The Secret Santa?

Sometimes the Secret Santa seems to be trying to give her a message, as if it might really be Nina attempting to communicate with her. But other times the gifts have felt malicious – and she's not sure what she's done to deserve this. She was never mean to Nina. The only thing she ever got wrong was that damn lipstick. She and Beni had thought Nina needed help to bring out her natural beauty, but if the photograph really is Nina, she knew perfectly well how to make the best of herself.

The Nina Eleri knew wasn't really the type to have a boyfriend, but what about *that* Nina?

And what made her put on all that weight, change her style, stop wearing make-up, don those ugly glasses?

Because someone didn't like the way she was before, and maybe didn't like the lipstick?

Someone who didn't like it so much, in fact, that they gave Eleri a tin full of *soil*? The symbolism seems horribly clear in the midnight silence. The soil represents a grave. *Her* grave?

This isn't just a game any more, and she's no longer curious about what's going to happen on the twenty-fourth. She's scared.

Mum is still half drunk the next morning, or maybe she's just happy. Either way, she got up early to make batter, so Eleri can have her favourite Nutella pancakes for breakfast, and so when Eleri gets up, too tired to have any appetite, she feels obliged to eat. She ploughs through the pancakes, staring with glazed eyes at the news playing from the TV up on the wall.

"Ooh," Mum says as Eleri forces down another mouthful. "Where's that naughty elf gone?"

"In my room."

"He likes to get around, doesn't he?"

After a while the national news ends and the local news begins. The camera cuts from the presenter to the face of a young man with faded blue eyes.

"A man discovered badly injured in a local park has been named as Alexander MacDonald."

He has slim features and a slight wince, as if the photographer has just said something that distressed him and he's trying to hide it.

"Police say he was badly beaten, but is now conscious and making good progress, though he can remember nothing of the attack."

Eleri leans forward, frowning at the screen.

"They are appealing for witnesses to the assault which occurred on December sixth, but advise the public not to approach anyone they suspect of involvement as the individual could be unstable and extremely dangerous."

"Can you believe Isla's dresses only arrived yesterday?" Mum says. "I was getting really worried because Aunty Lynne said she sent them over a week ago, first class. I've hung them in your wardrobe."

"Kay."

"Is Calista coming here to get ready again?"

"Mmm."

"In that case you'll need to cater for her too. Do something easy and filling, like macaroni cheese. I'm on late tonight, so you'll have left by the time I get home."

Her mum says something else, but Eleri doesn't register what it is, because suddenly she knows where she's seen Alexander MacDonald before. Kneeling on the grass, his sandy hair clumped into filthy dreadlocks, his blue eyes bloodshot and wild as he bellowed in grief over his broken bottle.

"Butter fingers!" Mum laughs, as the pancake slides out of Eleri's hands.

Eleri arrives at school to see Beni emerging from Ray's shed. Catching up with her, he explains that he's told his dad about Ray's plight, and his dad has promised to talk to his contacts in Shelter and see what they can do for him. He also sent Beni in with a huge food parcel for Ray, including a bottle of whisky.

"I've got a present for you too." Beni opens his bag and takes out a small black cube.

"What's that?"

"One of the digital cameras the BBC uses for documentary shoots. It has to be small so the monkeys don't see it."

"You told your mum?"

"Of course not! She's got loads of this crap at home. She'll never notice it's gone."

Eleri is almost disappointed.

"Set it up in the stairwell. You can tape it under the banister so it's out of sight. When you turn it on, the feed will come straight through to my phone. We'll be able to see who the Secret Santa really is."

Eleri takes the tiny camera, though when it comes down to it, she's not sure she really wants to know. "I won't be back in time today. I'll have to do it tomorrow."

In assembly Mrs Halfapple informs the school that the rough sleeper who had been harassing some of the female pupils has been taken to hospital after receiving a vicious beating. From there he would be taken back to Scotland where he would receive *all the help he needs*.

As if the children care about him getting help. Some of the girls might be relieved that he's off the streets, but everyone else is disappointed that this source of excitement has been taken away. Eleri isn't sure if she's glad or disappointed.

Alexander MacDonald only came to London in the summer, so he couldn't have abducted Nina last year, and now that Ray is out of the picture too, they are back to square one as to who might have taken her (if she was taken) and the identity of the Secret Santa. Maybe the camera will tell them.

The school day passes quickly, and the atmosphere in the classrooms and corridors is charged with excitement. It's not that there's any expectation that the party will be cool or fun, but something usually happens that provides gossip fodder for the next six months. Last year Miss Merrion was seen snogging the DJ and there was a fight between two Year 13 boys over a Year 12 girl who had said she would go with both of them.

Over lunch, Beni tells Calista proudly about the camera plan. He's a big fan of Netflix crime series where amateur sleuths somehow end up catching serial killers just by exchanging a few Facebook messages. Eleri has started to think it's time they just hand it all over to the police and says so, expecting Calista to agree with her, but when Beni shows her the image he took of the photograph, Cal doesn't even believe it's Nina.

What Beni is failing to take into account, Eleri thinks, is that the photograph is not their discovery at all. It was revealed to them by the Secret Santa, who might be one of the amateur sleuths himself, in which case he must think that Eleri was somehow involved in Nina's disappearance or – and this thought makes her hands go cold – he might be a killer who has chosen Eleri as his next victim.

*

The light is on on the fifteenth floor of Gibea Tower as Eleri and Calista walk down the flickering path at dusk to get ready for the party.

"Ignore it," Calista says.

Eleri hesitates, but in the end she follows her friend towards the warm glow of Shiloh.

Calista, for once, is in a good mood, after Harry Falconio Snapped her to say he was looking forward to seeing her at the dance, and she chats happily as they make the macaroni cheese.

Sitting at the kitchen table to eat it, Eleri can see, from the corner of her eye, the little light burning in the tower.

When everything's put away, they head to her room, where the kitten is sprawled, fast asleep on her pillow, leaving drifts of grey gossamer that will make Eleri sneeze all night.

She sits down at the dressing table stool and Cal sets about trying to arrange her unruly mop into some semblance of elegance. Cal knows exactly how much Frizz Ease to use, how many grips and slides to ensure that halfway through the night Eleri's hairstyle doesn't suddenly explode like popcorn, and Eleri knows that you have to use half a can of spray on Cal's sleek, fine hair or it will drop into lank rats' tails. As Cal primps and teases, making exaggeratedly horrified faces as every curl springs free of its moorings, Eleri gets a sense of déjà vu. This is what Calista used to be like, before her parents broke up. All her spikiness was directed towards making people laugh back then: it only became mean when her mum left.

"There," Cal says finally. "Knockout." She rests her hands on Eleri's shoulders as they both gaze into the mirror. Eleri is pleased by the result. Her gaze moves to Calista's face and she sees, to her surprise, that Cal's eyes are shining with tears.

"What?" she says.

"Nothing." Cal turns away, scrubbing her eye with her sleeve.

Now it's Eleri's turn to be hairdresser. She uses the straighteners to create soft curls, pinning them at Cal's temples with little jewelled grips, the flecks of blue glass perfectly complementing the honey tones in her best friend's hair.

After that they do their make-up, squashed together on the dressing-table stool.

"Look at us," Calista says when they've finished. "We grew up."

Eleri smiles at their reflection. They look like reverse images of one another. Snow White and Rose Red, as Sally used to call them. Bound together by friendship so close it was almost sisterhood.

Yes, that's exactly what it is. They are more like sisters than friends. Sisters fight and get sick of each other, but the bond never breaks.

Gazing at the more attractive version of her normal self, Eleri remembers the photograph of Nina. Calista promised to have a closer look. She gets up and pulls out the pillowcase from under the bed. Looking at the picture again, Eleri can't believe she was ever uncertain. This is Nina, definitely. Or else a twin sister.

She brings the picture back to the dressing table.

"So what do you think?"

Calista just looks at it down her nose.

"It's Nina, isn't it?" Eleri insists.

The corners of Calista's mouth bend down. "How should I know?"

"I'm sure it is. So's Beni. I'm going to speak to the police about it. Maybe if the camera works out we might even have a suspect for them."

"Are you out of your mind?" Calista spins round to face her. "They'll prosecute you for wasting police time."

"Why? It might be important."

"It's not important, it's bullshit!"

"What is?"

"The whole thing!" Cal jumps to her feet, knocking the stool over. The kitten jerks awake and scrambles off the bed.

"You know what, I was actually looking forward to this stupid party, but you had to ruin it!"

Eleri's mouth drops open.

"You're just loving all this, aren't you? Finally being the centre of attention. It doesn't matter what everyone else it going through, we all have to drop everything and pretend to be interested in this nonsense."

Anger courses through Eleri at the sheer unfairness of this. "Hang on a minute. Me and Beni have supported you for what *you're going through* for two years now. What about the other day, when you were upset about your mum not having you for Christmas? I was on the phone to you for— Hey, where are you going?"

Cal has picked up her bag and slung it over her shoulder. "I'll make my own way to the party."

"But you haven't even got dressed!"

"I'll do it at school."

Eleri stares as Calista sweeps out of the bedroom and a moment later the front door slams so hard the floor vibrates.

Half an hour later she's lying on the sofa, in her pyjamas and full make-up – slightly smeared around the eyes – when she gets a message.

As well as the usual one – Door 15 – there's another. From Ras.

Where r u?

Don't feel 2 gd, she replies.

This isn't a lie. The argument with Calista has left her feeling nauseous.

Shut up! Get down here now. I cant dance to ABBA alone.

Eleri hesitates before replying. Will Calista have gone to the party, as she said? In which case, she might have calmed

213

down. They can talk about things. They've both been under a lot of pressure, but it mustn't affect their friendship.

Plus Ras is there. And he has been waiting for her.

She taps out a reply.

```
K will take pill. See u in 30 mins.
```

Hurrying to her room she yanks open the wardrobe and grabs the first of Isla's dresses in its white polythene sheath: full-length, teal, covered in sequins, and so long that it will trail behind her like a mermaid's tail. If she tried to dance she'd end up in a tangled heap on the floor.

Stripping the polythene from the second dress, her heart sinks. It's a strappy red full-skirted number, with a line of cute fabric-coloured buttons running down the back, but there's no point even trying it on. This one is full-length too.

Sighing, she flops down on the bed to text Ras that the pills haven't worked. This was probably her last chance with him. Tamara George is bound to look fantastic in whatever designer dress Daddy picked her up from Harrods, and though Cal says she's shallow, she really isn't that bad. If Ras has a couple of glasses of spiked punch and Tamara's flirting with him, he's not going to say no.

And why should he? They are much better suited: two popular gorgeous kids at either end of the wealth spectrum. There's romance to it. If this was a prom they'd make the perfect king and queen.

Up on the shelf, the elf is smirking at her, thin legs spread wide to expose his stripy crotch. Picking up a balled school sock from the floor, she hurls it at the smug rouged face.

But, then again, maybe he's right to sneer: pathetic Eleri creeping away to hide in the background again, then boohooing because someone else takes her boy.

She shouldn't complain her life is boring if she avoids every opportunity to make it more exciting.

She gets out of bed.

The red dress, it turns out, has adjustable straps that, with the heels she's borrowing off Mum, means that when she stands up straight, it just avoids skimming the floor.

Looking in the mirror, she finds to her surprise that she looks OK. More than OK. The dress is cut on the bias and the fabric clings in all the right places, giving her the hourglass figure her mum always insists she has.

After freshening up her smudged eye make-up, Eleri is ready to leave. Running down the flickering path with her skirt gathered in her fists and a white faux-fur gilet about her shoulders, she feels like Cinderella, and enjoys the surprised glances of pedestrians who pause to give her a clear path to her pumpkin coach that has just pulled up at the stop.

Sliding into a window seat, the glass makes a perfect mirror against the darkness outside. She smiles. For perhaps the first time in her life she's happy with her appearance.

But as the bus's engine kicks in, the lights momentarily flicker out. Her eyes pull into focus and she sees, just for a moment, before they come back on and the bus moves away, a yellow eye burning in a fifteenth-floor window of Gibea Tower.

As she passes through the school gates, ghostly carousel music weaves through the night air. Coloured signs loom out of the darkness, lit by flaming torches pushed into the flower beds lining the path to the gym.

Beware of the tigers!
Fly through the air with the greatest of ease!
Send in the clowns!

Walking around the main building, a sharp rustling sound from a doorway makes her heart jump into her throat, but as she comes level with the entrance she can see it's just a couple making out.

The shorter figure, in a black suit that renders it almost invisible against the night, turns to look at her. It's Kika, her eyes blank and intoxicated. The one behind her is Rebekah, in a gold dress that catches and splinters the torchlight. She smiles dreamily, and Eleri hurries on.

The sports pitches stretch away to the jagged line of the trees, stark black against the orange-tinged night, where Nina met her hooded visitor. Ray's shed floats on a lake of darkness, a faint glow visible at the curtained windows. She hopes the whisky will keep him warm through the night.

A billowing canopy of red and yellow stripes, decked with fairy lights, has transformed the entrance to the gym, as if it has decided to throw off the dull grey of its daily grind and reveal its glamorous drag-queen soul. Ducking under the canopy, Eleri passes through the open outer doors.

The atrium, normally plastered with photographs and certificates of jock achievements, has been decorated with vintage posters advertising *Silas the Strongman, the Psychic Twins* and *the Amazing Bearded Lady* (beneath which someone has scrawled – *Mrs Halfapple*). A distorting mirror hangs on the wall and as she walks past it her head bulges and shrinks alarmingly.

Up close, the carousel music has taken on a hysterical, almost panicked quality, as if the players are going rapidly mad. Is this what they'll be expected to dance to?

The atrium is well lit but the room beyond is darker, so as she approaches the inner glass doors all she can see is herself, in her blood-red gown that fits so well it seems to stream down her body.

Pushing the doors open, she walks into a wall of heat and noise.

Along with the discordant music, shouting and laughter, the ringing of a bell reverberates in the gym's cavernous interior. Ceiling lights revolve queasily, from red to purple to sickly green, making it seem as if the room is changing shape, and there are occasional flashes of blinding white. The air is thick with the smell of spilled drinks, sickly sweet and sour at the same time. For a moment Eleri can only stand, swaying on her heels, as her dazzled eyes adjust.

A clown comes at her gibbering and grinning, and

she flinches as he whips a bunch of silk flowers from his voluminous sleeve, the sharp plastic stamens scratching her chin as he jabs it at her.

"Leave the poor child alone, Mr Hake!"

The handsome art teacher, who has morphed into something positively chilling, capers away and Eleri turns to smile gratefully at her rescuer who had the voice of Mrs Banwa. But the secretary's friendly face has been replaced by a gaping, fang-lined jaw beneath a pair of cruel, glassy eyes. With a muffled growl, the rotund tiger slinks away, spinning its tail.

Eleri starts to make out individual groups gathered around booths and fairground games.

The ringing is coming from a test-your-strength machine, crowded with jocks and popular girls. A photobooth is positioned against the left-hand wall beside a box of props. Flashes explode through the flimsy curtain, leaving an after-image on Eleri's retinas of familiar schoolmates transformed into strangers by feather boas and bowler hats and fake beards.

Lingering awkwardly at the margins of the fun, as usual, she considers turning around to leave, but then someone is coming towards her. At first she thinks it's one of the teachers but another flash goes off, illuminating the figure's face, and she stares in astonishment. It is Ras, transformed.

Gone is the straggly hair: he has had it cut to the length of the grown-out skin fade, leaving a little more length on top that falls in tousled curls on to his forehead. His suit is teal coloured and where most of the other boys have teamed theirs with white shirts and ties, Ras's shirt is black and buttoned up to his neck. He has no tie, and the only other concession to his ordinary scruffiness are the pair of somewhat threadbare Converses emerging from the bottom of his trousers. She takes all this in in one glance, but her eyes must have lingered because when she looks back at his face he is smiling. The ceiling lights scroll to green and his eyes flash emerald.

He says hello and she says it back, then from somewhere he produces a glass of crimson liquid accessorized with a slice of orange and a cinnamon stick.

"This is the school version." He jerks his head towards a makeshift bar that has been erected next to the monkey bars, being manned by a chemistry teacher. "But we can go off piste, if you like?"

He opens his jacket, presumably to show her a bottle of some spirit hidden in the inner pocket, but her attention is distracted. Whoever said he was ripped was right. Under the slim-fitting shirt she can make out every line of his chest and stomach muscles. A flush of desire heats her skin from her ankles to her neck. She grabs the drink and downs it in one.

"On second thoughts, maybe we'll stick to the school version…"

There's a burst of screaming feedback and Mr Roberts' voice comes over the tannoy.

"My fellow Elsinore Housers, welcome to the EHS Big Top!"

A stage has been constructed at the far end of the gym and he is standing at a microphone in front of a wide mixing desk.

There's a good-natured roar of approval and some whistles. Mr Roberts is dressed as a circus strongman in a pair of fitted black cycling shorts with a band of faux-leopard fur draped across his pasty chest. Beneath his nose is a drooping moustache as big and furry as Lavender, and his weights – clearly two black balloons tied to a stick – are balanced nonchalantly on his shoulder.

"Apologies for the late arrival of our DJ," he continues. "His elephant got caught in traffic."

The thin, dark-skinned man behind the desk scowls from the shadows of his hood.

"But now the festivities can commence, so eat, drink (non alcoholically, please) and be merry, and LET'S SHOW THIS TOWN HOW TO PARTY!"

The riotous cheering merges into the opening bars of the first song as Mr Roberts punches his weights into the air and leaps off the stage.

"The DJ's famous apparently," Ras shouts over the throbbing beat. "He's a cousin of one of the teachers so they got him at a discounted rate."

"Cool," Eleri says weakly. The power of speech seems to have deserted her. Thank god he hasn't commented on her appearance, or she might just dissolve into a hot puddle of self-consciousness.

She looks around the groups, trying to spot Calista, but there's no sign of her. Then a waving hand catches her attention: it's Beni, standing with the new boy. He points at her, waggling his forefinger up and down as if to take in her whole body, then slaps his cheeks in exaggerated amazement. She smiles.

"It would be totally cringe to dance to the first song, wouldn't it?"

She turns back to Ras. "Er, yes."

"Especially when there's no one else on the dance floor?"

It's true. People just hover around the edges of a red square of carpet in front of the speakers, looking bored.

"Everyone would laugh and point," Ras goes on. "And we'd be *so* embarrassed. We definitely shouldn't, right?"

"Definit—"

She yelps as he grabs her hands and yanks her towards the carpeted square.

Digging her stilettos into the parquet, she snatches her hand back in genuine horror.

"Why not?" he says mildly.

"We'd look totally stupid."

"Why, because we're not trying to pretend to be too cool for school?"

On the periphery of the dance floor, boys scowl and nod to the beat while the girls sway their sparkling shoulders or twirl beringed fingers.

"My mum always said, dance while you're still young enough not to pee yourself."

"I don't want to, honestly." Her mood has sunk. How could she have ever thought anything might happen between them? They are so different. He's fun and spontaneous and confident, and she isn't any of those things.

Ignoring her, Ras takes her hand again and after a brief hesitation she allows herself to be led through the straggling crowd. "The trick is not to try and be sexy or cool... Excuse us... Thank you, Jojo, looking lovely... Just let yourself go. That's what we all want to do really, right?"

She feels eyes on her as they pass among their peers. After a lifetime spent trying to stay under the radar, it's an uncomfortable sensation, but Ras's hand is warm and strong in hers and when she stumbles over an abandoned stiletto and instinctively clutches it tighter, he squeezes back.

But the border of the dance floor, marked out in a harsh line of black gaffer tape to avoid trip hazards, is like the edge of a cliff. She just cannot make herself take the plunge.

"Maybe later."

He hesitates, then shrugs and walks out on to the carpet. For a moment he just stands there very still, listening intently. No one is laughing or jeering or pointing. Some of the girls – including Tamara – have stopped twirling their fingers and are watching him with faint smiles on their contoured faces. Then he starts to move. First his head and upper body, then his torso, then finally his legs. Every muscle seems connected to the rhythm of the music, flowing with it like he's part of the sound wave. He closes his eyes, spreads his arms, tips his head back and smiles.

She is stricken with envy and desire. *For* him, yes, but

also to *be* him. If only she could let go like that, surrender to the bliss of the music, forget the world.

A gaggle of boys rush the dance floor and throw themselves at him, and in a moment it has become a mosh pit. Ras is shouting something, grinning as his mates bounce around him.

Eleri steps back into the shadows. She has lost him. Tamara and her friends sashay on to the carpet and start to dance, casting smoky gazes at the oblivious boys.

Suddenly she is enveloped in a clumsy hug. "My queen!"

Beni smells of alcohol and slurs that Hendrick has brought in a bottle of tequila. Apparently he's gone to the canteen to try and source some salt and lemon for slammers, and would Eleri like to come and join them?

Eleri thanks him but declines. She is not yet ready to move from this spot, however pitiful it is to be standing there like the aforementioned lemon, waiting to see if Ras will deign to speak to her again once he's finished having fun with his fun friends.

Beni doesn't seem to mind and wobbles away, punching the air and mouthing along to the song. She watches him wistfully. Life seems to work out well for people like Beni: he fancies someone, they turn out to be gay, and they like him back. There's a sort of sunshine about him that seems to attract light and happiness. He expects the world to be fun, and so it is, while Eleri peers at life from between her fingers, wondering what it's going to throw at her next.

The song ends and another comes on, a rapper with

a gentle London-accented voice, telling himself to dry his eyes because his girl isn't coming back. Ras's friends peel away, leaving him standing there, panting, his cheeks glistening. But as the floor empties he makes no move to follow his friends. Instead he holds out his hand to Eleri.

She hesitates. People will stare, if not with hostility then with derision. Look at Ras taking pity on the invisible girl. The girl who doesn't exist. Better to stay invisible than risk being seen and laughed at.

His palm is cupped as if waiting for something to fall from the sky.

And then she thinks of Beni, smiling into the sunshine, waiting for life's next gift to drop into his lap. She steps over the gaffer tape and takes Ras's hand. He smiles and they come together, her free hand on his shoulder, his palm on the small of her back. At first her body is stiff and wooden but as they begin to sway to the yearning melody, she softens into him. She can feel the heat of his stomach and chest radiating into hers. Their heads touch and his breath trickles across her earlobe. She closes her eyes and lets the music carry them both away.

The song ends too quickly. She doesn't want to separate from him, and he seems to feel the same, because his hand remains on her back and his eyes are looking right into hers.

At first it's practically impossible to hold his gaze, but she forces herself, and then it's not so bad, and then it's the most natural thing in the world. He leans forward and her heart slams so hard against her ribs she's amazed he doesn't feel it through his jacket and shirt, but instead of kissing her he just rests his forehead against hers.

"I'm sorry," he murmurs.

She pulls away. "Why?"

"I was a real dick to you this year."

"No … you weren't … you…" She tails off.

"I was. I had some stuff going on, and I got the wrong end of the stick about something."

A knot in her chest loosens. So she wasn't imagining it.

"About what?"

She breathes in as he sighs, inhaling the sweet taste of fruit punch on his breath.

"The party last year. I feel like such a dick." He squeezes his eyes closed so tightly his eyelashes shrink down to a normal length. "I heard you talking at the lockers the other day and you said you hadn't got an invitation last year, so I realized it must have been someone else who sent me that reply. The invite must have fallen out of your locker when you opened it or something."

"Reply?" she echoes.

"Nobody owned up to it, but I guess it was one of the guys. Teddy P probably. Little shit. I can't believe I thought it was you."

"Wait, you left an invitation to the dance in my locker last year and someone sent a reply saying no?"

"*In your dreams, psycho*, to be precise."

"But … but I never wrote that. I never even got the invite."

"Like I said, it was probably Ted."

225

"Yeah," she murmurs.

But she knows this isn't true. There is one person who knows her locker code, one person who calls Ras a psycho.

"Are you OK?" Ras says. "It's hot in here. Do you want some water?"

"Yes," she murmurs. "Actually. Please."

They weave through the dancers and back over the gaffer tape to the cooler shadows, coming to stand in front of a huge cut-out of Pennywise the clown, which doesn't seem entirely in keeping with the jolly circus theme.

"Looks like there's a bit of a queue," he says, craning over the crowds. "You OK to wait?"

"Yeah, fine."

"Want me to get you a seat?"

"No, no. I'll be fine."

"OK." He makes to move away but she grabs his arm and he turns back, his eyes searching her face.

"I would have said yes."

He holds her gaze a moment, then takes her hand and leads her behind Pennywise.

Her first kiss is nowhere near as bad as she feared. They don't bang noses or clash teeth. He doesn't try to push his tongue into her mouth or grope her breasts. It's soft and lovely and gives her such a head rush that she has to put her arms around him to stay upright. After a while he pulls away and murmurs, "OK?"

She nods.

"I've been worried about you. With that Secret Santa shit. Is it still going on?"

"Yeah."

"Has anything else happened? Like has he tried to contact you or meet up?"

"No, it's just the gifts, but Beni's given me a camera to set up in the stairwell. We might catch him in the act. I'll do it tomorrow morning in the daylight," she adds hastily, when he starts to look worried.

"OK, good. So what did you get yesterday?"

"Just a postcard. There was no address or writing on it."

"Did you carry the pepper spray when you went to get it?"

"No," she admits, then, at his expression, adds hastily, "I will next time. The camera might tell us who it is."

"As soon as you find out, I want to know."

She nods. "Can we not talk about this any more? I'd rather just try and forget it for tonight."

"I think I can help with that." He kisses her again. "Want that drink of water?"

Not trusting her voice, she nods and he smiles and walks away.

Smoothing down the front of her dress and re-clipping her hair, she comes out from behind the killer clown and immediately spots, on the other side of the dance floor, Calista standing with Harry Falconio. He's speaking animatedly to her as she listens dully, occasionally nodding or offering up a strained smile.

She must feel Eleri's gaze, because she looks up and immediately stiffens. For a long moment the two girls just stare at one another across the dance floor. There's something in Calista's expression, at first Eleri thinks it might be relief — she must have been waiting all year for Eleri to find out what she did — but it's more like an appeal. Does she want Eleri to confront her? And do what? Forgive her? Demand an explanation?

Eleri's expression hardens. She has stuck with Calista through thick and thin, made excuses for her, tolerated her negativity and spite, allowed other friendships to come to nothing out of some misguided sense of loyalty.

No, she does not want an explanation and she certainly won't be offering forgiveness.

She opens her mouth. *I know what you did.*

Calista sags, as if the air has been let out of her abdomen.

She says something to Harry, who looks about himself furtively before withdrawing a flat bottle of clear liquid from his inside pocket. Calista takes it and has a long swig, glugging the liquid down until Harry laughs nervously and extracts it from her.

Then Eleri becomes aware that beneath the music a hush has fallen on the room.

A stillness is passing through the crowd, like the icy breath of the Snow Queen freezing people in the act of drinking or laughing or talking. Every gaze seems to be directed towards the main doors of the gym and now she can feel the chill of the outside air. She pulls her gilet tighter across her shoulders.

Mr Roberts moves past her, walking quickly, peeling off his moustache as he goes, and as the crowd parts Eleri gets a clear view through to the doors.

A middle-aged man and woman are standing there, in dark suits and coats, their expressions grave.

Eleri has seen this woman before, here at school, on almost the same day exactly one year ago. She stood on the stage in the main hall and said that if any student had information about the disappearance of Nina Mitri they were to call the police in complete confidence.

Now she's back.

And if it was good news, the woman's face wouldn't look like that.

The whisking sound her skirt makes as she climbs the stairs of Gibea Tower sounds like the sharpening of a knife.

The dance ended quickly, the lights coming on like the floodlights of a prison, making the girls shrink away and cover their faces.

She passes floor six.

Unforeseen circumstances, Mr Roberts said. Someone had given him a jacket, but blinking into the light, his bald head glinting, he looked like a newborn baby who wished very much to return to the warm safe place he had just emerged from.

Floor twelve.

Everyone had to go home. There was a rush for the door and when she got outside Eleri went straight to the bus stop.

She didn't want to speak to anyone, not Ras or Beni and certainly not Calista: the evening's revelation about what she did last year was bad enough, but Eleri knew that the police had come to impart something far worse, and she didn't want to hear a hundred breathless theories about what that might be. She just wanted to be home, but when she got to the estate she found she couldn't walk past that light. Not now.

Floor fifteen.

Abruptly she stops climbing, staring into the darkness of the stairwell. Nina vanished on the day of the dance. December 15th.

Today.

Her heart hammers. Did Nina receive gifts in the run-up to that day? Will it be Eleri's photo left in an abandoned tower block for some bewildered girl to find next year?

She slips off her shoes, ready to run. Barefoot she can be down and out of the building in less than a minute. She could call the police and tell them everything that's been going on, and they will find him. It will all be over.

But she doesn't run. Instead she closes her eyes and exhales deeply.

The Secret Santa chose her for a reason and she has to know what it was.

Picking up one of the shoes, she grips the toe part so that the stiletto heel protrudes like a blade, then grimly passes through the door that leads to the fifteenth floor.

She stands in the middle of flat 156 for several long

minutes, just gazing down at the small rectangle of blue plastic in her hand.

It's a travelcard. Could it be the one Nina lost? It looks brand new, so maybe it's the one she said she ordered when Eleri went over to do homework. Intercepted somehow by the Secret Santa. But how? The card would have been posted through the letter box, so someone would have had to break in to get hold of it.

Unless they had a key.

That day she went to help Nina with her homework, mother and daughter changed the subject when Eleri asked who had done the landscape painting. Nina had dropped her head and averted her eyes, rubbing the wrist with the scar running down it as she answered.

My dad.

Thursday December 16

As the last of the Year 7s file into the school hall, taking their places on hastily laid-out chairs at the back, a hush settles on the room. There are no coughs, suppressed giggles or deliberately magnified farts. Every face is directed to the stage where the woman in the suit is standing with Mr Roberts, Mrs Halfapple and the head of pastoral care, Hannah Scaler, who they all call Hannah-rexia, because so many of her charges are struggling with the condition.

Eleri sits in the fifth row with Beni and the rest of her year group. In all the drama of last night, she almost forgot about setting up the camera this morning, and nearly missed the bus when she had to run back to the flat to get Sellotape, but it's in place now, taped under the banister in the Gibea stairwell, out of sight unless you're really looking, and the feed is coming through to Beni's phone.

There's been no sign of Calista all morning. Beni thinks he saw her throwing up on the headmaster's lawn last night as they all filed out of the party, her hair being held up by Harry Falconio, but she hasn't responded to any of his texts and Eleri can't bring herself to make contact.

Mr Roberts steps forward.

"Good morning, everyone." Uncharacteristically he does not wait for them to reply before continuing. "Detective Inspector Everett has been kind enough to give up her time today to come and speak to you all."

He pauses and takes a deep breath.

"Nina Mitri joined EHS last September and though she was only here for a few months, I know she made some good friends. What Detective Everett has to tell you will be particularly hard on them." His gaze searches the faces and settles on Eleri. He smiles sadly and she is suddenly overwhelmed by the feeling that she will burst into tears. A thousand pairs of eyes fix on her and when Beni's hand closes over hers she clutches it tightly.

"I would ask that if you have any questions regarding the events of last night and this morning, that you please speak to your form tutor. A counsellor will be available for the rest of the day for any pupil who feels they would benefit from it, and there will be a helpline available should you need support over the holiday. I'll now hand over to DI Everett."

As the police officer steps forward the silence takes on weight and form. Eleri can feel its palms pressing on her chest, squeezing the air out of her lungs.

"Good morning," Everett says briskly. There are lines around her mouth and eyes, as if, in some other place and time, she is quick to laugh. In her smart white shirt tucked neatly into black trousers she is a uniform monitor's dream.

"I am sorry to have to tell you, but yesterday morning a woman jogging in woodland near Cardigan Bay in Wales came upon human remains."

Eleri looks at Beni, who returns her gaze, eyes round. Wales. Like the postcard.

"An identification was made last night by a family member," the detective goes on. "The remains were that of Nina Mitri, who went missing from her home on December fifteenth last year."

She waits for the ripple of shock to pass over the room.

"Obviously this is a tragic end to our investigation, and specialist officers are comforting the family. The media may approach you for comment but I would ask that you refer them all to Mr Roberts or myself, as conjecture and rumour will not help anyone. If you have any information at all that you think might assist us in our enquiries, then please phone the incident number."

Mrs Halfapple holds up a piece of paper with a phone number on it. A few people tap it into their phones.

"Thank you, and I wish you all an enjoyable and restful Christmas." The police officer steps back.

"No questions please, Darren," Mr Roberts says to a boy thrusting his hand into the air, but Darren ignores him.

"How did she die?"

"Darren!" snaps Mrs Halfapple.

"The remains are now in the hands of the coroner, so we will know more after her report."

"Was she murdered?"

And there it is, that ecstatic murmur of scandal. To most of the school this death is only fodder for gossip and faked distress: girls will hug, Insta stories will be updated with candles. There will be few who seek the services of the counsellor. No one really gave a damn about Nina except Eleri, Ras and Miss Merrion. The young teacher is sitting in the front row, occasionally dabbing at the corner of her eye with her sleeve.

After being informed – to groans – that the school day will proceed as normal, they file out, year group by year group. Out in the corridor Eleri takes deep, gasping inhalations, as if she has been holding her breath the entire time she was in the hall.

Sure enough, girls are crying down their phones, informing parents who will no doubt find some way to blame everything on the school. When Eleri pushes past them none of them even registers her. They wouldn't know or care that Nina was actually, genuinely, her friend.

Further on, a large group fills the corridor and she dips her head to pass by unnoticed. They are boys, so there's no distress, either faked or genuine, just a callous glee.

"Definitely murder," one of them says. "If she'd killed herself or died of cold then they'd've found her sooner, so I reckon he must have buried her."

"She was probably dug up by dogs or something," another nasal voice says. "Do you reckon she was rotten?"

"When the bacteria in your gut starts to eat you, it produces all this gas, so she'd have blown up like a balloon."

"Not that you'd notice, though, right? Haha."

"*Shut up!*" Ten surprised faces turn in her direction. One of them is Ras. For a moment there is a stunned silence.

"You were supposed to be her friend," Eleri says to him.

"It was just a bad joke, El," Ras murmurs. "You know what this lot are like."

"I do know, yeah. And now maybe I know what *you're* like too."

She walks away rapidly.

"El!"

"Forget her, mate," says Teddy P's voice behind her. "You made your point: be nice to the girl with the disabled mum. Now forget it."

Eleri doesn't hear any more. As she gets to the stairwell at the end of the corridor, she breaks into a run and doesn't stop until she reaches the sanctuary of the form room.

As it turns out, there was no point going to lessons. She can't concentrate on the film Mr Scarf puts on for them, and when she does force herself to focus, the images of the Germans in the siege of Stalingrad, their expressions haunted or just resigned to death make her think about an open grave in the middle of a dark wood. The loneliness of it, the desolation, the despair. Blinking back tears, she glances at the clock for the twentieth time.

When the bell for the end of school finally rings, there are still cheers and screeching chairs and racing footsteps, but the last-day hilarity is definitely more muted than usual.

Beni is waiting for her at the school gates. "You OK?"

Eleri nods, laden down with holiday homework.

"It's coming up to four, so we need to watch the feed. I thought we could do it on the bus. I'll take you home, cos, well, it's been a difficult day."

She looks at him. At his kind, concerned face. Behind him, groups that he is definitely welcome in are planning trips to cafes and chicken shops. They call to one another, jump on each other's backs, blast music through portable speakers. And yet here he is because she needs him.

"Do you think she was murdered?"

"I don't know, El. I really don't."

As the bus creeps through the gathering dusk, the two of them huddle together on the back seat staring intently at Beni's phone screen.

She positioned the camera well, considering how distracted she was, and there's a good view of the first flight of stairs lit by the dying rays of the afternoon sun. Around them the bus is jumping with the general boisterousness of the end of term: shouting and laughter and tinny music blasting from phone speakers, but they are sealed off from it, in a little bubble of tension. After long minutes of nothing, she rubs her tired eyes, wondering if the feed has simply frozen. A commotion a few seats in front of them attracts her attention and she watches as two boys try to mess up each other's carefully styled hair.

Then Beni grips her arm.

On-screen the quality of the light has shifted, as if someone has opened a door somewhere out of shot.

"Look…" Beni breathes.

Eleri can only stare as every hair on her arm rises up.

Are they about to find out the identity of the Secret Santa? Or even, she swallows hard, the identity of Nina's killer?

And then the screen goes black.

Has the camera failed at this critical point? Or did the Secret Santa discover it? Beni swears under his breath and is moving his hand to the screen when the feed returns.

A single eye is staring at them.

With a cry of fright Beni hurls his phone away from him.

A younger girl snatches it from the floor and it is passed jeeringly from hand to hand, until the extremity of Beni's rage cows them into returning it.

By then the screen has gone black again and a message informs them that the feed has been interrupted. Whatever Beni does, he can't seem to get it back.

"So much for that, then," he mutters. "Hope Mum doesn't need it for the monkeys. I guess he must have seen you setting it up."

"Yeah…" Eleri murmurs. Doesn't Beni understand how creepy that is – the Secret Santa is watching her from first thing in the morning?

When they get off at the estate, Eleri is stunned to see a light on the sixteenth floor of Gibea Tower.

Beni comes to stand beside her. His shirt and jacket are flapping in the biting wind and his lips are thin and blue. "Shit..."

"Three quid." Beni finishes counting the ten pence pieces piled on the cement floor of flat 161 like a cairn over a body. "It has to be some kind of clue."

"A clue to what?" Eleri pulls her arms tight around her body. Up here the wind is louder, howling like a pack of wolves circling the building.

"I don't know." He gathers up the coins. "I need to see the other gifts."

They head back the way they came, casting a cursory search of the stairwell as they go, though the only sign the camera was ever there is a scrap of Sellotape under the banister.

Back in the flat, Eleri pulls out the pillowcase from under her bed and empties it on the floor.

As Beni rakes through the gifts she can't get the image of that eye out of her mind. It felt like a gleeful attempt to frighten her: almost childish, almost *Ras*-ish. But Ras's eyes are blue and this one was dark. At least she thought it was. In the dusk it was hard to tell.

"I'd forgotten about this." Beni picks up the little brass key with its head looped into the shape of a Celtic knot. "When it wasn't yours we didn't give it any thought. It looks to me like it's the key to a cabinet or a drawer. You went round to Nina's house last year, right?"

"Yeah, why?"

"Did you see anything it might fit?"

"I can't remember."

"We should go back there."

"Why?"

"To find out what's in whatever drawer this key opens. It might tell us something about her disappearance. Though I suppose if it's in their house, then her parents would already know about it."

When she doesn't reply Beni looks up at her. "What?"

Friday December 17

On the first day of the holiday, when she can lie in as long as she likes, Eleri wakes at four, jerking violently from her pillow as if someone lying beneath her has given her a sudden shove. It takes interminable hours for the sun to come up to the level of her bedroom window, and all the while she can sense the presence of the pillow buried beneath her bed, the gifts protruding through the cotton fabric like broken bones under skin.

Sure that her mum would guess at once that something is wrong, she waits until she hears the front door close before getting out of bed. The lino is ice cold on her bare feet as she goes to the kitchen window and follows her mum's halting progress down the path to the bus stop. From up here she looks tiny and vulnerable.

On the kitchen counter is a cheery note next to a pack of pains au chocolat.

Morning sleepyhead! Got you a treat for your first day off! Enjoy your rest, you deserve it xxx

The note makes her feel sick with guilt. She has hidden things from her mum in the past, the things she knows will upset her – the bullying, the shame, the resentment – but nothing like this.

She takes the pastries out of the oven before they've properly heated and the strips of chocolate running down the centre are still hard and tasteless, then ploughs grimly through them, forcing the claggy dough down her throat and washing it down with a glass of water. She suspects she'll need energy for what the day has in store for her.

She's been standing at the corner of the terrace of little red-brick houses for twenty minutes when Beni finally strolls up, swinging a Tesco carrier bag. Under the steel-grey sky, the crossroads forms a perfect wind tunnel, sending the already low temperature plummeting even further. Her feet, in aerated trainers, have gone completely numb and her bum aches from sitting on a low wall that seems to be constructed of bricks of ice. She doesn't return his smile.

"Sorry I'm late. I had an idea." He raises the carrier bag. "Cakes! It's a Muslim tradition that after a death people pay their respects to the family by bringing food and stuff. I figured Mrs Mitri will have to plate them up in the kitchen, so we'll have a few minutes to see if the key fits any of the drawers."

"Unless her brother's there."

Beni's face falls.

She gets up. "Come on, let's go. I'm freezing."

Maybe it's just the weather – last time she came it was a crisp bright day – but the house seems to have sunk into itself, hunching in the shadows, the curtained windows like closed eyes. Eleri has a moment of doubt. They shouldn't be intruding on Mrs Mitri's grief, but before she can stop him Beni is already at the front door.

The synthesized chimes of the doorbell are incongruously cheerful, echoing down the silent street like a dreadful faux pas. For a few blessed minutes Eleri thinks there will be no answer, but then a crack appears between the door and the frame, the chain pulled across it.

"Mrs Mitri," Beni says gently. "My name's Benedict Brown, and this is Eleri, who I think you know. We were good friends of Nina's and we just came to pay our respects."

The door closes and then opens. Like her house, Mrs Mitri too appears to have shrunk. And in the year since Eleri last saw her she has become an old lady. Standing on the mat in a shapeless tunic and leggings, her brown hair white from the scalp to the ears, like a strange dip dye, she blinks from behind her glasses, as if in the early stages of dementia.

"I brought some cakes," Beni says. "They were Nina's favourite, I think."

Mrs Mitri looks down at the bag, then up at Beni's face, searching it for meaning. Then, without a word, she steps back to allow them into the house.

An overwhelming sense of the wrongness of all this almost paralyses Eleri, but Mrs Mitri is waiting and eventually she forces her legs to move. The door closes and they are submerged in the gloom.

This time there are no scents of spice and warm bread, only a must of damp and rubbish that has been left too long. The only sounds are the slow ticking of a clock somewhere and the hum of a fridge. If there is a little boy here he is unnaturally silent.

Mrs Mitri shuffles up the hall towards the living-room door, with Beni following, but Eleri pauses, her eyes drifting up to the dusty bars of daylight falling from the window at the top of the stairs. She can picture Nina's room quite clearly: the bed, the desk, the beige carpet, the window looking out across a neat lawn with pots of lavender and rosemary.

And then a figure appears at the top of the stairs. She starts back.

With the light behind, it's impossible to make out any features, only a shape, tall and wide and thick-necked. The outline of a bald head forms a smooth circle of black against the grey-lit window.

The man comes down the stairs, slowly and purposefully.

"Who are you?" The voice is deep and heavily accented.

"E... Eleri Kirdar. I was a friend of ... of Nina's." Saying her name feels like a blasphemy.

His shadow swells as he descends the stairs and now the light from the little window above the front door falls on his face. His nose is broad and flat, as if it has been broken in the past. His sagging jowls are covered with stubble and though his skin is brown, it has a grey tinge to it, like mince that has gone off. His eyes are dark. Like the eye that stared down the camera at her. And yet, where that eye was clean and clear and glinting with malice, this man's eyes are dull, heavy-lidded and expressionless, the whites threaded with burst blood vessels.

Brushing past her, he turns down the hallway to disappear through the door Beni and Mrs Mitri went through, leaving a miasma of unwashed clothes and stale breath in his wake.

Eleri exhales and leans heavily against the wall.

This must be Nina's dad. The man who painted the picture, the one whose mention made both Nina and her mother clam up. This time last year, when Nina disappeared, he wasn't in the house. In fact, Eleri can't remember seeing any sign of a man's presence – no coats or shoes out on the hallstand, no men's laundry on the airer. So when did he come back? And why?

She wants to turn and walk straight back out of the door again, but she can't leave Beni.

Mrs Mitri is sitting on the sofa, her elbows propped on her knees, one hand shielding her eyes as if she's staring into the sun, while Beni murmurs quietly beside her. Eleri catches words like "wonderful", "creative", "such a good friend" but Mrs Mitri doesn't seem to be listening.

Mr Mitri is.

He glares suspiciously at Beni, his fists balled on the chair's arms, his chest rising and falling.

"Beni," she mutters. "I think this is a bad time. We should go."

At the sound of Eleri's voice, Mrs Mitri looks up. Her face clears and she manages a watery smile. "Eleri? I did not recognize you. How lovely to see you. Jimmy…" she addresses the man in the chair. "This is a friend of Nina's."

Eleri turns to face him, trying not to wince at his expression. "I'm so sorry for your loss, Mr Mitri. We all miss Nina very much."

He flinches, then gives a curt nod.

She turns back. "Beni, let's—"

"Stay, children, do," Mrs Mitri says with an air of desperation. "Sit down, Eleri. Let me make some tea and put these cakes on a tray." She gets up and hobbles to the kitchen, pausing at the doorway.

"Jimmy, can you help me get the cake stand down?"

With a grunt, the man gets up from the armchair and follows his wife into the kitchen. There are the sounds of cupboards being opened and closed and cutlery clattering.

"Over there!" Beni hisses, and she follows his finger to a cabinet against the wall by the door. It's a beautiful piece of furniture, inlaid with mother of pearl flowers and leaves. The lock looks like it might be solid gold.

Eleri snatches the key from her pocket and hurries over. It doesn't fit.

In the kitchen the kettle boils and there is a clink of mugs clashing together.

"Try that one!"

A dresser against the back wall has a number of drawers and cupboards, all with little keyholes. Dashing across the room, she sets about trying them one by one. None is a fit and in one of the drawers the key gets stuck. As she waggles frantically, the sounds from the kitchen stop.

"Hold the door for me," Mrs Mitri says.

Adrenalized by panic, Eleri gives one final twist and the key releases with a snapping sound. Has the shaft broken off? She doesn't have the chance to check before the living-room door begins to open and she bolts back to the sofa.

As Beni does a sterling job of keeping up a conversation with Mrs Mitri, Eleri marvels at his acting ability. She's always thought of Beni as a good and trustworthy friend but watching him lie so smoothly, relating Nina anecdotes that never happened, gives her a shiver of unease.

She puts it to the back of her mind. She can't let what's happening make her doubt everyone she cares for. Beni is her friend and he's doing all this for Nina. But as he folds Mrs Mitri's thin hand in his own, patting it with gentle concern, she turns away.

And jumps violently.

Mr Mitri is watching her.

"Eleri?" Mrs Mitri says. "Are you all right, sweetheart?"

"Yes, I…"

She glances at Beni for help and he flicks his eyes to the ceiling. *What does he mean?*

Suddenly she knows.

"I just need the toilet, if that's OK."

"Of course. Upstairs and down the landing to the end. You probably remember."

She can feel Mr Mitri's dark eyes on her back as she gets up and walks out of the room.

She hasn't got long. After climbing the stairs, she walks with heavy steps to the bathroom at the end, closes the door loudly, then tiptoes back to Nina's bedroom.

In the threshold she hesitates. The bed is made, without a single wrinkle in the powder-blue duvet cover. A three-legged stool is pulled up to the desk where Nina's books and pens are neatly laid out, but without Nina here to give it life the room is completely characterless, as if arranged by a prop manager on a TV show to look like a teenager's bedroom. Except that it doesn't. Where are the posters and photographs? The messy pots of cosmetics? The discarded underwear and dirty mugs? No, this is *not* a normal teenager's bedroom.

As she steps over the threshold, making the dust motes spin, she takes the key from her pocket. To her relief the shaft has not snapped, though the teeth seem to have twisted a little away from the head. Will it still fit? She shakes her head. Who's she kidding? They're never going to find what this thing fits.

But the desk, an elegant antique mahogany affair, does look promising and the drawer does have a keyhole.

She sits down on the stool, avoiding her own reflection in the mirror. Last year she sat here, taking dictation for Nina reclining on the bed behind her, and she still has the sensation of someone watching her. What if she looks in the mirror to see Nina standing behind her?

Averting her gaze from the mirror, she slips the key into the lock.

It fits!

Her heart is in her mouth as she eases the drawer open.

Disappointment floods her.

Whatever might have been in here has been removed, and the drawer is empty.

She should get back downstairs. But first, to be sure nothing is hidden in the dark recesses, she slides her hand inside and feels around.

Something scratches the back of her hand.

There is something taped to the top of the drawer.

It comes away with a little tearing sound.

Another key: this one modern, flat stainless steel. She's about to screw up the tape that held it when she notices something written on it.

UB 4161.

A dragging sound behind her makes her freeze. Her heads snaps to the mirror, eyes widening in horror.

A hand is stretching from beneath the bed, the fingers clawing the carpet as it drags out the rest of its body: a thin arm, a black head, bony shoulders.

Her heart starts beating again.

It's just a little boy. He gets to his feet, regarding her silently. His black hair has been left to grow out and the fringe hangs down in front of his eyes, so that all she can see is the glint of his pupils. It's gone midday but he's still in his pyjamas. The Hulk bursts out of his chest, the tendons of his green neck bulging as he bellows in fury.

Nina's little brother.

"I... I was just..." she stammers.

The boy raises his finger to his lips and pads out of the room.

When she gets back to the living room, Beni looks up at her in obvious relief. Mrs Mitri is dabbing at her eyes with a tissue and there's a rhythmic scratching sound as Mr Mitri picks at the fabric of the armchair with a fingernail.

"I think we should go now, Ben."

Mrs Mitri pockets her hankie and arranges her face into a wan smile. "Thank you for thinking of us, children. And of Nina. I am glad she had you, at the end."

Eleri sees then that whatever his motives for coming here were, Beni is genuinely moved. Rising from the sofa, he turns his head away and blinks back tears.

Mrs Mitri stands too, looking up at him. Then she pats his broad chest and tries to thank him, but her face twists in grief.

Beni pulls her into his body, enfolding her in his big arms, pressing her little head against the solidity of his chest, as if she is a child and he is a strong parent who knows all the answers and can promise that everything will be OK.

Mr Mitri looks away.

They don't speak until they have turned the corner and left the sad straggle of terraced houses behind. A rundown chicken shop on the corner is open and looks warm, so they go inside, ordering coffees from the tired looking young man behind the counter, before sliding into one of the white plastic tables at the back.

"So?" Beni says, his face still pinched with emotion. "Anything?"

She shows him the new key.

He frowns at it and turns it over in his hand. Then she remembers the tape, unfurling it on the table.

"What do you think the numbers mean?"

His eyes snap to hers, shining with excitement. "They could be for a security box!"

"What about the letters? UB. Could they be a name? The initials of whoever abducted her? U's a pretty unusual first name initial. Ursula, maybe? Or something foreign."

"Maybe…" But Beni doesn't sound convinced, and now he takes out his phone and opens up the internet. He taps *security box number London* into the search bar.

There are thousands of entries and he scrolls down them slowly. Then he stops.

One of the entries reads: *"How can I access my security*

box?" It is taken from the website of a bank called Urban Bank.

They look at one another.

There are three branches of Urban Bank in London but only one of them offers the security box service. With half an hour before the bank is due to close, Beni orders them an Uber and they arrive with minutes to spare.

The consummate actor, he strolls in and walks straight up to the information desk by the door where a young Asian woman sits primly, an expectant smile on her face. "Here to access my security box."

"In the basement, sir," she says, gesturing, and they set off towards the stairs.

Box number 4161 is tucked into a wall of slim metal bricks in a low-lit room. Fortunately they are the only visitors. Sliding the box out, they take it to a table in the corner. Eleri looks at Beni, then slides the key into the lock. It feels like a kind of miracle when there is a quiet click and the lid pops.

The first items are three more photographs of the beautiful girl in the picture left by the Secret Santa.

"See, it's her," Eleri says softly. "It has to be or why would she have kept them?"

The girl in the picture is happy, beautiful, confident, as she poses for the photographer, making silly faces, flipping her middle finger, licking her lips in a parody of sexiness. Eleri experiences a twinge of relief to see that this Nina is wearing full make-up.

Beni takes the last photo out of the box to reveal an ID issued by a school called Drinkwater Grove, for someone called Nalina Gamal.

"Nalina Gamal?" he says. "It's not her."

Eleri frowns, but then she points at something in the background of one of the discarded photos.

"Look. That's the same desk that was in her room. It has to be her."

The girl's amber eyes dance with amusement as if delighted to have tricked Eleri so well.

"So she changed her name? Why?"

Eleri picks up the school ID. "Do you remember that kid from primary school, Morgan Causeley?"

"The blinker?"

"Remember how he wasn't supposed to be in any school photos in case his dad saw and worked out where he was? He told me once he'd changed his surname too. It used to be Fudge. I remember cos we laughed about it."

"Like a witness protection thing?" Beni murmurs. "She was hiding from someone?"

Their eyes meet but Eleri doesn't answer him.

Beneath the ID are cinema tickets, concert wristbands, Valentine cards, cute hand-drawn cartoons, pressed coins from museums, art postcards.

It occurs to Eleri that these are romantic keepsakes. This is confirmed by the final item in the box: a polaroid photograph of a couple kissing. The girl leans against a tree and the back of the boy's head obscures her face, though

253

from the hair and figure Eleri guesses it's Nina. *Nalina*. The boy has twisted his arm back to take the picture and above Nina's head someone has carved initials into the tree: NG & JH.

Nalina Gamal and her boyfriend, JH.

"Shit…" Beni breathes. "So she had, like, a whole secret life? Do you think it was this guy that Ray saw her meeting with at the end of the football pitches? It's always the boyfriend, right? Maybe it's him that killed her."

"Or," Eleri says, "maybe someone found out about the relationship, and decided they didn't like it."

"Mr Mitri?" Beni says.

"He wasn't there last time I went to the house. Like, there was no sign of him living there at all."

"What if she changed her name and her school and her appearance to get away from him?"

"And then he found her."

"You said she had a scar on her wrist. Maybe he did it…"

"And then maybe he did something worse."

Beni takes out his phone and lays it down on the table so that she has a clear view of the screen. Opening the internet app, he taps *Jimmy Mitri* into the search bar.

There are no results. Eleri isn't sure whether she's relieved or disappointed.

"That doesn't mean anything, though," Beni says. "Just because they didn't report it, doesn't mean he wasn't abusing them… What?"

Eleri has snatched the phone from the table, because

254

she's just remembered the initials on the landscape painting. JG.

She types a new name into the address bar: *Jimmy Gamal*.

Down here the phone takes a long time to make the connection and neither of them breathes as the blue caterpillar in the top corner crawls to the other side.

Finally a result pings up.

Planning officer pleads guilty to assault.

They click through to the article. The victim isn't named "for legal reasons" but according to the journalist, "character witnesses described Gamal as a devout Muslim and said that his behaviour was completely out of character".

"When he finds out about Nina's boyfriend he assaults her," Beni mutters, leaning across the table as a man descends the stairs. "Breaking her wrist. Nina and her mum try to get away, start a new life, but he finds them. Then last Christmas he sees the lipstick you got her and loses his shit again, thinking she's back seeing her boyfriend?"

"What about the CCTV footage showing her getting on a train on her own?" Eleri says with an air of desperation, clutching at anything that will take the blame for this off her shoulders.

"Maybe she was running away because she knew he'd found her. And he caught up with her…"

In the silence, the only sound is the clink of the man's key as he accesses his own box.

"You have to go to the police now, El."

"But the Secret Santa can't be him. Why would he drop clues to his own guilt?"

Beni shrugs. "That's for them to find out."

The police station is a squat red-brick building between the tube station and the leisure centre.

A dingy reception area is lined on two sides with blue plastic chairs pocked with cigarette burns, and a pile of leaflets about domestic abuse sits on a table beside them. There's an internal door, splintered at the base as if someone has kicked it, and on the other side of a panel of Plexiglas is a counter, unmanned when they enter. The place smells of vomit.

Beni strides straight up to the counter and presses a buzzer. Several minutes later an overweight, prematurely bald young man in a tight-fitting police uniform appears through a door behind the desk.

He looks them up and down with a weary expression. "You can report non-emergency crimes online or by calling 101."

"DI Everett came to our school and said that if we had information about Nina Mitri's disappearance we should get in touch," Beni says.

The young police officer asks for their names, before waddling back the way he came. Ten minutes later, Everett opens the door to the waiting area.

"Eleri? Benedict? Come through, please."

They are led down a hallway of closed doors into an interview room. There's no two-way glass, no CCTV, no recording devices, just a plastic table and four chairs like the ones stacked in teetering towers in the school hall. They all sit.

"So what can I do for you?"

Eleri glances at Beni. How on earth is she supposed to begin? But it turns out that she doesn't have to. Beni does it for her.

"We think Nina Mitri's dad had something to do with her disappearance."

Everett folds her arms, leaning back in the chair. "Ok-a-ay. So what gives you this idea?" She clearly thinks they've been watching too many true-crime docuseries. There's no way to justify their allegation without admitting what's been happening with the Secret Santa, so Eleri takes a deep breath, and begins.

"I've been getting these messages…"

The story takes some explaining, and the DI makes her stop regularly to repeat or clarify something. Eleri can feel the DI's disapproval as she asks why Eleri carried on going back to Gibea when she had no idea who was leaving the gifts or why, so Eleri feels she has to explain about the pills too.

"They broke into your property?" DI Everett sits forward.

Feeling the need to play down the drama, Eleri adds, "Though I guess they could have got them from the pharmacy or online."

The DI nods and sits back. "It's possible. Why didn't you contact us when your bag was first stolen?"

"I didn't think you'd be interested, with other stuff going on."

"My job," Everett says, "is to protect members of the public. That's you. Now this might all just be a bad-taste prank from someone with a crush or a grudge. Or it might be that this person is stalking you."

Eleri's skin prickles. She has heard stalking described as *murder in slow motion*.

"Now when it comes to stalking, we like to use the rule of four: fixated, obsessive, unwanted, repeated. So how many of those do you feel you have been experiencing?"

She thinks for a moment. "I guess the last two."

"You've had some unsolicited text messages and unwanted gifts, but no abusive messages, or actual threats? You haven't been followed or been subject to any unwanted sexual advances?"

"No."

But *has* she been followed? It certainly felt that way at the shopping centre, and maybe even at the cemetery, though she can't be sure.

"It may be, as I say, that this is a prank taken too far. Teenagers don't always make the most sensible choices, particularly teenage boys who have a crush on you."

Eleri blushes.

Beni says, "Show her the stuff…"

He's right. They didn't come here about the Secret Santa, they came for Nina.

Eleri takes the security box out of her backpack and opens the lid.

"This stuff belongs to Nina, but from a while ago

obviously, because she didn't look like this when we knew her." She takes a picture of the slim, made-up version of Nina, and holds it up for the detective to see. Everett nods.

"There's one of her with a boy too." Beni shows it.

This time Everett looks more interested, taking the picture and scrutinizing the hooded figure.

"She clearly wanted to hide the relationship from someone. Tell her about the first time you visited her house, El."

"It's just that her dad wasn't there then, and when I asked if he painted a picture on the wall, they acted really ... weird." She tails off. Is this all sounding way too tenuous?

"And the lipstick," Beni mutters.

Eleri blushes. "Oh. I, er... I gave Nina a Secret Santa present of a lipstick and I thought maybe her dad had got upset about it..."

Beni's on a roll now: "... thinking she was some Western slut who deserved to be punished for, like, dishonouring him or something. Like he did before, when he broke her wrist! Tell her, El."

"What's this?" Everett asks, turning to Eleri.

"Nina had a bike accident and I went to A&E with her and saw a scar on her arm like she'd broken it before."

"And you think this was Mr Gamal, because...?"

It occurs to Eleri that the DI refers to Nina's dad as *Mr Gamal*, as if she's familiar with him. Is he a suspect already? What else do the police know?

"Because Nina and her mum were clearly trying to hide

from him, and he acted really hostile when we went round to the house today! And now he's stalking Eleri, because he blames her for what happened!"

DI Everett is frowning again. "So this "Secret Santa" has been communicating with you, you think, about Nina? Have there been any other gifts that are related to her?"

"Her travelcard, I think."

"How did you access this security box?"

Eleri looks at Beni. "I found the key in a locked drawer in her bedroom. The Secret Santa had given me a key to it."

"And why didn't you mention what you'd found to her parents?"

"Because her dad was acting so suspicious!" Beni cries. "*He's* the one you should be interrogating, not us! He's been done for assault before! We read it online."

Now the police officer's face is closed. Perhaps she doesn't appreciate being told how to do her job.

"There was also a ring," Eleri says quickly, "that we thought might be Nina's. And a soft toy that was in one of the photos."

Everett nods and gives a tight smile. "OK, well, there's a lot to unpack here, so I think you'll need to leave it with me."

"What are you going to do?" Beni demands.

"We have several lines of investigation."

"You need to arrest Jimmy Gamal!"

"I appreciate your time, but any investigation and arrest will be a matter for me and my team to decide. In the meantime, Eleri, you need to promise me that you will not go back to Gibea Tower, whatever message you receive. There's a good chance this is all the work of a hoaxer – they tend to creep out of the woodwork whenever a high-profile crime is committed – but it's better to be safe than sorry."

Eleri nods.

"And if anything else happens, please call me right away."

"Totally useless," Beni rages, when they get back out on the street. "*A matter for me and my team.* Why didn't they find the box, then? And I don't reckon she knew about JH either."

Eleri murmurs in agreement, but really she's just glad that the responsibility has been taken out of her hands. Hurrying along behind him as he strides up the high road, she pulls her jacket tighter. The sun never gets very high at this time of year and it's already slipped down behind even the low-rise shops lining the street.

"We should put this on social."

"Beni, no!" She grabs his arm.

The idea of hordes of people turning up at Gibea Tower, and what the subsequent response of the Secret Santa might be, horrifies her. "Please! Promise me you won't!"

Beni sighs. "Fine. Jesus, it's freezing, isn't it? Let's go home."

They head to the bus stop but have to stand outside the shelter, which is filled with old people and mothers with pushchairs and grizzling toddlers. Right behind the stop is a minicab firm. Eleri gazes wistfully inside, wishing they had the money for a cab. Overweight drivers nurse mugs of coffee, gazing listlessly at the tiny TV playing in the corner of the room.

"We should call Cal," Beni says, hopping from foot to foot to keep warm. "Tell her what's been going on. She said we shouldn't go to the police, didn't she?"

Eleri says nothing.

"Have you heard if she's any better?"

She shrugs.

"That is some hangover."

"Mmm."

Beni stops hopping and stares pointedly at her. "Ahem?"

"What?" She glances at him, then looks away quickly.

"What's wrong with you?"

Eleri rolls her eyes to the ceiling and sighs. "She did something – at least I'm pretty sure she did – to screw up things between me and Ras."

After she's told him, Beni gapes. "What. A. Bitch! So *that's* why he was pissy with you?"

"I guess."

A bus pulls in but it's not theirs. A few of the oldies peel away, dragging their shopping trolleys overflowing with fruit and veg from the market.

"That girl needs therapy. She's kept you like a bloody pet for the past god knows how many years and just when finally it looks like—"

"Shh!" Eleri holds her hand up.

"What?"

She doesn't reply. All her attention is fixed on the TV in the minicab office, because on-screen is a picture of Nina. Moving closer she can hear the crackly voice of the newsreader.

'... investigating the disappearance of schoolgirl Nina Mitri have taken her father in for questioning."

On the bus she sees that a message has already come through: Door 17. But the police have Jimmy Gamal now and it feels so good to be able to ignore it without fearing what the Secret Santa will do in retaliation.

As she gets off, the last feeble rays of the sun are draining away, leaving a grainy monochrome dusk, like the static on an old TV.

As soon as she gets in, Eleri changes into her onesie and slippers, but the cold has seeped into her bones, so she drags her duvet to the sofa to watch TV until Mum gets home. She scans back and forth through the news channels but there are no more mentions of Jimmy Gamal's arrest.

When Mum returns, she is quiet and at dinner the clinking of cutlery in the silence sets Eleri's nerves on edge. Though she isn't in the mood for a conversation, she speaks just to break it.

"How was your day?"

"Fine. Busy."

"Christmas shoppers?"

"Yeah, and I ... had to make some calls."

"Who to?"

Her mum pauses before answering, chewing her mouthful deliberately before swallowing and laying down her fork. "I've decided to take AWP to tribunal for constructive dismissal."

Eleri freezes, her own fork halfway to her mouth.

"Adam introduced me to his lawyer friend."

"Mum. You ended up on antidepressants because of the stress of working for that place, and now you want to start it all up again!"

"Exactly! They beat me down until I was too weak to fight for my rights, but why should they get away with what they did to me?"

"How much is a lawyer going to cost anyway?"

"Adam thinks we can win."

"*We?* When did Adam become part of this family?"

"Eleri, come on."

"Mum, seriously. Now? Just before Christmas?"

"You only have three months in which to—"

"Great, so that's Christmas ruined." She throws her fork down and gets to her feet.

"Hey!"

"No, Mum. You were well out of that place, you said so yourself, and now you're raking it all up again. Don't you know how hard it was for me when you were depressed? I mean it's hard anyway, right? Most sixteen-year-olds don't have to do the stuff I have to do, and on top of that to have to look after you too?"

Her mum is staring at her.

"It's not fair that you just go and make this decision when it's going to affect me as well! Is Adam gonna be there when you're too depressed to get out of bed? Is he going to cook and clean and make you take your medication while trying to get on with schoolwork, all the while terrified you're going to kill yourself? It's hard enough at the best of times, Mum, you know?"

For a moment it seems that her mum has stopped breathing, but then she takes a huge, gasping breath.

"You're right. It's not fair." Her face is white. "It's not fair that some shit doctor didn't read your grandmother's charts right, that they left me in distress so long I got brain damage. That I grew up being that kid no one wanted to be friends with, that people pointed and laughed at in the street."

"Mum—"

"That when I was a teenager I felt so goddamn ugly and undesirable that I went with the first boy who showed me any interest – your prick of a father."

Now it's Eleri's turn to stare. Her mum has never said anything disparaging about her dad before. She thought they were in love.

"But, *miracle of miracles*, that grubby little fumble in the back of a Ford Fiesta made you. You, my perfect, wonderful daughter. And no, it's not fair that though that child has brought you the most intense joy of your life, the mere fact of your existence is burdensome to them, and every day they wish they had a *normal* mum who did all the cooking and cleaning so they could hang out with their friends or spend all day on YouTube, or whatever it is that other teenagers do."

"I didn't mean—"

"It turns out that most of these unfairnesses you can do sweet FA about, Eleri. You just have to bend over and let them shaft you. But the one where they change your job description so that you can't actually *do* your job any more and you lose your career – that one. *That one*, you *can* do something about. So yes, I could forget it and accept the shitty hand I've been dealt yet again, keep my head down like I've always done, try not to be noticed, but actually, this time, I'm going to stand up and make a fucking noise, OK? And if that bothers you, Eleri, then I'm very sorry. About that, and about everything else I've inflicted on you over the years. You're excused the washing-up, you can go to your room and watch YouTube."

"Mum, I don't—"

"I said *GO TO YOUR ROOM*!"

Eleri does as she's told, slamming the door behind her and falling against it as her heart slams in her chest. Her brain feels like a scribble of thick black marker pen. She and her mum used to talk about everything, but now she's been confiding in Adam instead, taking his advice, as if his opinion is more important than what her own daughter thinks. But hasn't Eleri been doing the same with the Secret Santa? The closeness she thought she had with Mum was clearly an illusion, just like her friendship with Cal. All the things she thought would be there forever, unchanging, are falling apart.

She goes over to the window for some air, cracking open the upper pane the few centimetres that they are permitted, in case someone tries to throw themselves out. From here she can see Gibea Tower, unrelieved black against the static sky. There is no light.

It's over. They have got the right man. Jimmy Gamal murdered his own daughter.

She sinks on to the bed and cries.

Saturday December 18

She sleeps fitfully, half an hour here or there, jerking awake from half-remembered nightmares. The last one leaves her so agitated that she gives in and gets up. The heating doesn't come on until six and as she pads through the silent flat, her breath billows ahead of her like a phantom. On the coffee table is an empty bottle of wine. Her stomach sinks. Did Mum cry herself to sleep too?

The kitten is slumbering in the indentation her mum's weight has left on the sofa cushion. Somehow it has managed to claw down part of the throw and used it to cover itself.

To warm herself up, Eleri goes to the kitchen and puts the kettle on, then wanders to the window and gazes out at the gathering dawn.

Frowning, she leans closer to the glass. The sliver of gold at the edge of Gibea Tower could simply be a street light, or the first rays of the morning sun bouncing off a window.

The kettle boils and she takes the mug of sweet tea to the living room where the kitten is waking up with a stretch that exposes its downy belly. She blows on the tea, trying to ignore the pulsing sensation at the back of her skull, which is in a direct line with the kitchen window.

But it's no good. She has to know.

How can Gibea Tower still be standing, she thinks, as she emerges into the chill morning, after so many years of neglect? Why haven't its bones crumbled, its floors pancaked as it collapses to dust and rubble? Instead its skull grins out over the city, as if taking pleasure in reminding the populace of what can happen in tower blocks: a black and silent memento mori.

She walks a little way down the path until she has a clear view of the front of the tower. It's bitterly cold and her bare feet are already numb, but still she pauses a moment, looking out over the oddly deserted high road, before turning back.

A light burns on the eighteenth floor.

She goes straight home and back to bed, where she lies, wide awake and shivering until she hears Mum leave for work. Then she picks up her phone.

It takes a surprisingly short amount of time for her call to be redirected to the right place.

"Eleri?" DI Everett says earnestly. "Has something happened?"

"Another light came on, in the tower."

"You didn't go over there?"

"No, but you arrested Jimmy Gamal yesterday, didn't you? So it can't be him."

There's a pause, then Everett says, "We released Jimmy last night. It wasn't an arrest, we just wanted to speak to him about his movements."

"So the Secret Santa *could* be him."

"No. No, I don't think so."

"How do you know? He could have—"

"He was only released from prison two days ago."

Eleri sits up sharply. "He was in prison?"

"Jimmy was gaoled for assault. He was incarcerated when his daughter went missing *and* when you began receiving these messages, so no, Eleri, on both counts Jimmy could not have been involved. On Thursday he was released on compassionate grounds after the discovery of his daughter's body, to be with his wife and surviving son. Understandably he is distressed and angry at what's happened, which probably explains his behaviour when you saw him."

"Then ... who do *you* think killed Nina? Could it be the boy in the photo? JH?"

This time the pause is a long one.

"Look, it's going to come out soon enough anyway, though I'd ask that you keep this to yourself for the moment. Evidence points to the fact that Nina took her own life."

Eleri's hand tightens on the phone.

"The burial came later. In which case, the only crime

270

committed is the prevention of a lawful burial. We may never find out who did that. Though it was clearly someone who didn't think about the anguish it would cause the family, never knowing what happened to her."

"So you're not going to investigate?"

"It's true that the investigation has been taken down a notch. Two people were killed in a drive-by shooting yesterday, and I only have limited resources I'm afraid."

"And what about my Secret Santa? He's obviously got something to do with what happened to Nina. Aren't you going to try and find him?"

Everett sighs. "Eleri, you're not listening. Nina's death was suicide. As I said yesterday, if you feel in any way threatened by this prankster, then you must call me back straight away. The chances are that when you stop reacting he or she will lose interest. Now I have to go."

In the background Eleri can hear footsteps and then the sudden noise of a busy office.

"Wait," she says quickly. "Was he in prison for assaulting Nina? If he was due to be released, maybe she killed herself because she was terrified of what he'd do when he found her?"

Everett sighs. "Jimmy didn't assault Nina. He assaulted one of the teachers at her last school. So badly the guy ended up in an induced coma."

"And now he's back on the street?" Eleri cries. "After doing that?"

"I must go. I'm sorry."

After the call, Eleri gets up and goes to the window, trying to process what she's been told. Jimmy Gamal didn't assault Nina, or murder her. No one did. She gazes down at the shadowy figures moving up and down the path, hoods raised against the cold, hands dug deep into pockets. Is one of them Jimmy Gamal, out to get revenge for his daughter's death, somehow pinning the blame for it on Eleri? *Could* she have done anything to stop Nina doing what she did? Is that what he blames her for? Of all the students at EHS it was Eleri that offered Nina the hand of friendship, so maybe that did make her responsible somehow. Maybe she could have done more.

Gibea Tower glares at her, the sliver of its yellow eye still just about visible in the winter sunlight.

Grabbing her coat from the hook by the door, she lets herself out of the flat.

Beni's mum is pleased to see her. They used to have play dates at primary school, but it's been months since she last visited his home. As she crosses the threshold and inhales the characteristic smell of the place, she instantly relaxes. She's always liked this house. Beni's mum, Sonja, is an art director, so instead of the beige and stripped wood that most people seem to fill their homes with, their house is done up with vibrant colours and patterns. The rug in the living room – Beni calls it the puke rug – is a dizzying swirl of oranges and browns, which should be gross, but isn't alongside the sixties furniture – tall, cylindrical shelving units in multicoloured plastic, a sideboard scattered with gaudy blown-glass ashtrays and a lava lamp. There are way too many plants, and she has to push through spiky leaves to get to the black leather sofa.

"I'll just give him a shout, Bells."

El's Bells is what Sonja used to call her, and it makes Eleri smile as the woman, who never seems to age, strolls out of the room in a trail of multicoloured chiffon.

A few minutes later Beni comes in in his jacket and cap. "Hey. Everything OK?"

"I just needed to get out of the house. But you're obviously on your way out..."

"I can go later. Let me just..." He takes out his phone and taps out a message. "Come up."

"You two want anything to eat?" Sonja calls from the kitchen doorway as they climb the stairs. "Carrot sticks and houmous or something?"

"We're not five, Mother!" Beni calls back. "If we want something, I'll make it."

"*Woooo!*" Sonja calls back, but she's smiling as she returns to the kitchen.

Beni's room is as characterful as the rest of the house, the walls covered in wood panelling so it looks a bit like a sauna, and the floor scattered with neon-coloured sheepskins. His Japanese-style bed was taken from a BBC shoot, and he likes to brag that Harry Styles's naked body once graced it.

"So who were you meeting?" Eleri says as Beni strips off

his jacket, hurls his cap expertly on to a hook on the back of his door and throws himself on to the bed.

"Only Hendrick." His tone is casual.

"Wow. Are you guys, like, *together* now?" She sits down beside him.

"Not yet. But, you know…"

"Have you hooked up?"

"No!" He laughs. "We've just been hanging out. I can't tell if he fancies me or not, to be honest."

"Course he does. You're smoking hot."

"Yeah, right. Anyway, more importantly, *you* look like shit. What's been going on?"

He is suitably outraged when she tells him about the release of Jimmy Gamal, and the subsequent light that has appeared on the eighteenth floor of Gibea.

"For fuck's sake, it's obviously him, then. What are they gonna do, wait till he's murdered you, like he did his kid?"

"They think Nina killed herself. And when she went missing he was in prison."

Beni stares, for once lost for words.

"Everett said he assaulted one of the teachers at her last school."

Jumping up from the bed, Beni grabs his laptop from his desk, and brings it back to the bed. Opening it up, he searches: *teacher assault Drinkwater School*.

The first article is the one they've already seen, where the victim isn't named, but there are a couple more hits with the word *assault* crossed out.

Beni opens an article from a local paper, about a teacher given an award for his work with young people. A young man with cropped blonde hair grins from the picture. His shirt is taut across a chest and biceps that have clearly taken some dedication in the gym. His teeth are perfectly even and glowing white. The article is just as glowing, as are the comments below.

Mr Newham is the BEST.

So glad he's better.

Without him I would have def failed science.

Remember his karaoke at the school fair? LMAO.

There is only one exception, slipped in between a comment about how many press-ups Mr Newham can do and how cute his pug is. A single word: *paedophile.* The author is anonymous.

Eleri draws Beni's attention to it.

"Yeah, well, trolls love to call teachers nonces."

"But it doesn't say nonce."

"Nonce, paedo. Same thing."

He's right, the meaning is the same, but there's something more considered in the post than a simple throwaway slur. They have even spelled the word correctly.

She scans back through the comments. They are all from girls.

"Google him," she says.

The search finds several results. The first is the same local newspaper that reported his award, this time the headline reads: *Teacher accusation dismissed.*

The snippet beneath begins: *An accusation of sexual assault against a popular local teacher has been dismissed after fellow teachers and pupils alike gathered to support...*

But it's the article below that catches Eleri's eye.

Two-year sentence for vicious attack on popular teacher.

Eleri opens it. According to the article, the teacher had been put into an induced coma as a precaution and was now recovering at home with his wife and baby. This time the teacher was named: *Kobe Newham*. As was the attacker: *Jimmy Gamal*.

They look at one another.

"Maybe this was the guy Nina was having a relationship with? And Jimmy went ballistic about it."

Eleri shakes her head. "In the photo by the tree the man had dark hair and he was smaller. Like a student, you know? It says there was a sexual assault accusation. Maybe it was on Nina and that's the reason her dad attacked this Mr Newham."

"It might say." He goes back and starts scrolling through the hits, then pauses as a notification comes through on his phone.

"I doubt they'd name her if she was a minor," Eleri says. There's nothing more about the assault, but lower down the page is another article about the school. A more recent one.

Drinkwater High nicknamed "Suicide School" after spate of tragedies.

"Look at this," she says.

But Beni isn't listening. "There's an email from Mr Roberts."

"What does it say?"

"They're having a memorial at school for Nina on Monday, where people can lay flowers and stuff." He looks up at her. "Maybe the Secret Santa will go."

Sonja makes lunch for them, a breathtakingly hot chicken casserole that leaves Eleri weeping and sniffing. After the meal Beni is clearly keen to be somewhere else, so after scraping the remains of her meal into the cat's bowl (it has a missing ear and an iron stomach) they leave the house and walk to the bus stop together.

As Eleri's bus pulls up, Beni tells her that he won't be around tomorrow as he has church in the morning, but will see her at the memorial. She asks if he wants to go with her, but he says, rather sheepishly, that he's already asked Hendrick.

Back in the flat the afternoon passes slowly. With every intention of keeping her promise to Everett, she turns her phone on to silent, so she won't even know when the message comes through.

Falling asleep in front of a documentary about the Chernobyl disaster, she wakes to darkness. She goes around lighting the lamps, then flicks through the channels for something upbeat and inane. All the while her phone lies face down on the coffee table, as if it has fallen unconscious.

It's her turn to make dinner but as they missed each other

this morning, she's not sure what time Mum will be back. She's probably messaged, unless she's still angry. If so, then maybe she's planned to go out with Adam again. But then she definitely would have texted.

Reaching forward, Eleri turns her phone over.

Her heart contracts at the number of messages and missed calls, but most of them are from Beni asking if she's OK. There is one from Mum saying she and Adam are going for a pizza, and would Eleri like her to bring back one for her lunch tomorrow. It's a peace gesture, so she says yes, though she can't imagine ever being hungry again.

Mum replies at once, as if she has been watching her phone.

```
What flavour?

Pepperoni please

Ok x
```

She exhales with relief at the x. Perhaps that means she is forgiven.

The final message was sent earlier than the others. It had slipped to the bottom of the notification screen and she didn't spot it until her phone locked again and the light was still flashing.

```
Door 18.
```

It is followed by a smiling cat emoji.

She frowns. Is it another cat-themed gift, like the collar? Did Nina have a cat? Is it a metaphor about cattiness? Or a pun on *pussy*? This makes her hands go cold.

Then she realizes she hasn't seen the kitten since she got back in.

"Lav?"

She feels self-conscious calling the thing by its ridiculous name as she walks through the flat, plus she's certain the kitten has no idea what it's actually called, as neither she nor Mum can bring themselves to use it very often. The kitten's cushion, in a corner of the kitchen, is occupied only by drifts of silver fur.

"Lav? You'd better not be crapping in the laundry basket again."

She checks the basket, and though there is a kitten-shaped depression in the pile of used bedding, the fabric is cold to the touch. Neither is Lavender in Mum's bed, or Eleri's, or the airing cupboard, or the warm crevice behind the fridge.

She checks increasingly unlikely spots: behind books on the bookshelf, in the kitchen cupboards, under the wardrobe, her heart beating faster.

Her phone trills with another message. She is so agitated by now, she almost doesn't check it, but when she does her blood turns to ice.

There isn't much light, so it takes her brain a moment to make sense of the image – little black buttons running up to a black trapezoid.

Then Lavender creeps tentatively into the frame. The angle shifts and now Eleri can see that the black trapezoid is not a shape on the wall, it is a hole in the floor: the lift shaft. And the little buttons leading up to it are kitten treats.

There is no time to call DI Everett or Beni, and if she did it wouldn't matter what they said. If she doesn't go over to Gibea right now, Lavender is going to fall eighteen floors down the lift shaft and die.

Bursting out of the flat, she sprints to the lift. It has to be quicker than the stairs, but in the agonizing minute it takes for the thing to chunter up to her, horrible images fill her head: the kitten's broken body at the bottom of the lift shaft, not quite dead, little chest fluttering, blood leaking from its pointy ears.

When the doors creak open, she throws herself inside and hammers the ground button. The lift judders down through the floors and when it stops at the second she has to ball her fists in her pockets to stop them lashing out at the fit looking young woman who has hailed it rather than walk down four flights of stairs.

Squeezing between the doors before they fully open on the ground floor, Eleri bursts out of the building and flies across the grass to Gibea.

When at last she emerges on to floor eighteen, she forces herself to slow down and get her breathing under control. If the kitten is startled it will bolt.

"Lav?" she calls in a wavering voice as she creeps through

the darkness. "Here, kitty kitty…" She makes smacking noises with her puckered lips, not that any cat in her experience has ever found such a noise appealing.

Panic makes her lose her bearings and she forgets where the lift is situated, wandering hopelessly in and out of the bars of half shadow thrown by distant street lights, her heart pounding in her ears. But finally, turning a corner, she hears a sharp scrabbling.

She blinks, staring into the gloom.

Yes. Down there on the floor. A pale shape outlined against the abyss of blackness. Perfectly still, huge eyes glinting warily.

Cursing herself for not having brought a single scrap of food, she crouches on her haunches and reaches out her fingers, rubbing the tips together as if there is a tasty morsel between them.

"Come on, Lav, there's a good girl…"

It wouldn't matter if some axe-murderer was creeping up behind her now, her attention is wholly focused on the kitten and the lift shaft yawning just centimetres behind its little rump, a brutal mouth stretching wide to gobble it up.

"Come on, beautiful girl, come home now…"

No wonder it's reluctant to approach. Eleri has never been anything but hostile to the cat, shoving it off her bed, snarling at it, prodding and teasing it. If she takes a single step forward, the kitten will leap back to its death. Tears spring to her eyes as she thinks how cruel she has been to the creature, bought to keep Mum company and then forgotten when Mum found better company. A little life with no value to anyone, except to keep Eleri jerking on the end of her string.

The big eyes gleam and then the kitten lets out a soft mew. A single question mark. Eleri thinks then of Lavender's distress in the basket, of Adam's crooning song...

"*Lavender's blue, dilly, dilly,*" she begins tremulously.

The kitten raises a paw.

She tries again, attempting to keep the desperation out of her voice. "*Lavender's green. When I am king, dilly, dilly, you shall be queen.*"

After a moment's hesitation, the kitten makes a decision. It pads across the concrete floor and butts Eleri's outstretched fingers. Agonizingly slowly, Eleri slides her hand under the kitten's belly, holding her breath, certain that it will twist away from her at the last second. But no, the kitten allows herself to be picked up.

For a moment Eleri can only press the warm fur to her face and breathe in the sweet, musty smell. The kitten's heartbeat is like the precious clockwork of a fine watch.

And then she turns and flees the tower.

As they are riding the lift back up to the flat, it occurs to Eleri that she has been wrong to think that the Secret Santa is leaving her gifts. They are not gifts, they are messages. Some more clearly communicated than others. This one is to reiterate that if she doesn't keep coming, something bad will happen to those she cares about.

Whatever DI Everett says, or Beni or Calista, she has no choice but to keep playing the Secret Santa's game. She may not know the rules, or have any clue how to win, but she at least has a fair idea how it ends. In six days' time.

Sunday December 19

The kitten sleeps the night on her pillow. At just past midnight she hears Mum come in, clumsy but trying to be careful, therefore obviously drunk. She closes her eyes when Mum tiptoes into the bedroom. Leaning down to kiss her goodnight, she puts her hand on the mattress to steady herself, and Eleri's heart lurches. The hand lands right next to the carving knife she has tucked beside her body.

Before she went to bed she had a large and very strong coffee to ensure that she could stay awake until at least dawn, because while there was a slim possibility that the Secret Santa somehow managed to get Mum's heart pills from the pharmacy, there's no question that the only way he could have got hold of Lavender is if he let himself into the flat.

Hours later, as the ceiling lightens to a golden pink, she finally allows herself to fall asleep, only to be woken by her mum barging in and whipping open the curtains.

"Morning! I thought we could have breakfast together?"

"Sure," Eleri says groggily. Levering herself out of bed, she trudges to the kitchen and slumps down at the table.

The dark tower is wreathed in early morning mist. Lavender bumps her ankles and she lifts her on to her lap.

"What did you do last night, then?" Mum says, horribly cheerful.

"Nothing much. Watched TV."

"You know Lav slept on your pillow?"

"Yeah."

"And you didn't mind?" Mum laughs.

"No, it's fine." The kitten claws at the cord of her hoodie and she dangles it for Lavender to attack.

Mum brings over two plates of scrambled egg on toast.

Eleri can't meet her gaze as she chats happily about the restaurant and recounts another Adam anecdote about when he got hit by falling masonry while travelling through Rome. Part of an ancient brothel, he was told. Ha ha.

After a while she peters out and silence falls. Eleri wonders, with mixed feelings — half relief, half dread — if her mum is finally going to register that something's wrong and demand to know what it is. But when Mum opens her mouth to speak she is looking down at her plate.

"I was thinking of asking Adam to spend Christmas Day with us."

The fork stops on the way to Eleri's mouth.

"Not all day. Just for lunch."

Last year they had Gran over, and it was hard because she was ill and confused and kept needing to be taken to the toilet, and Eleri had to do most of the cooking. After Gran went back to the home, Mum had promised that next year they'd have an easy one, just the two of them.

"What do you think?"

What she thinks is, *No! Screw Adam*, and she opens her mouth to say as much. But her mum's face is so poignantly hopeful that she can't bring herself to watch it fall.

"Sure," she intones. Mum beams.

"Right. I'm working another late one tonight. You'll be OK, won't you?"

"Eleri? What's wrong?"

Eleven o'clock is one of the supermarket's busiest times and Mum's supervisor had to summon her from the shop floor. She sounds anxious.

"I lost my keys. I went out for some bread and I thought I left them on the counter but when I went back they were gone."

Mum groans. "OK, you'll just have to come to the store and get mine. I'll get a new one cut for you tomorrow."

"We need to change the locks."

"Why? Our address wasn't on them, was it?"

"No, but what if someone pickpocketed me and knows who I am? They could follow me back and let themselves into the flat."

Her mum laughs uneasily. "Unlikely."

"I don't know, Mum. I wouldn't feel safe. What about that homeless man that was almost murdered?"

There's a moment's silence, then her mum says, "Fine. I'll get a locksmith out. It'll cost a bloody bomb. You really must be more careful."

"Sorry."

The locksmith arrives an hour later. An hour in which she's been sitting on the cold lino of the corridor, pretending to be locked out. The man is ridiculously old, with a few sparse wisps of white hair and a dewdrop that quivers at the end of his nose as he works. He says very little, and at the end of the proceedings hands Eleri three shiny brass keys. Eleri thanks him and holds them tightly while the man writes out his invoice, before shuffling off down the corridor, bent over to one side by the weight of his tool bag.

She goes back inside, shuts the door and puts the chain on, then curls up on the sofa and finally falls asleep with Lavender nestled against her chin.

She's woken by her phone. Groggily she feels for it on the coffee table and squints at the screen.

Ras.

She lets it ring out.

Can we talk?

Ignoring it, she turns on the TV. She could be doing some work – they have mocks in the first week of term – but she can't seem to motivate herself to do anything at all.

An hour later, Beni calls. When she admits that she went to the tower, and why, Beni is silent for a moment, then he asks, "Did you call Everett?"

"There wasn't time."

"What about afterwards?"

"No. You heard what she said. She thinks it's a prank and they have *limited resources*."

"This psycho tried to kill your cat!"

"He didn't. He was using her to get me to toe the line. To make sure I keep coming all the way to the end."

"Which is … Christmas Eve?"

"I don't know but I think so – oh, wait a minute, I'm getting a call. Let me drop it."

"Is it Calista?"

"No. Still haven't heard from her. It was Ras."

"I'll get off so you can call him back."

"I'm not going to."

"Why?"

"Because he's a dick."

"What did he do?"

"Him and his mates were laughing when they found out what happened to Nina. He's just as bad as the rest of them."

"It probably wasn't him laughing. He liked Nina."

"But they're his mates. The people he chooses to spend time with. That says a lot."

"But you really liked him."

"Yeah, well, not any more."

The line goes quiet.

288

"What?" she says.

"El, you can't expect people to be perfect. They make mistakes. Like with Cal. You have to cut them some slack. Half the football team used to call me the F-slur, and then I started scoring goals for them and now I'm "Bend it". I could've held a grudge, but I didn't. And we're all happier because of it."

"You think I should *forgive* her for breaking in to my locker and destroying my invitation?"

"Maybe she was trying to protect you."

"I don't need protecting! I can look after myself!"

"Only cos you never take a risk though, right?"

She does a sharp intake of breath. "What's that supposed to mean?"

"You've been sitting on the same lunch table with the same people ever since you were at primary school. You never go when someone invites you somewhere—"

"Because Cal won't let me!"

"You don't need her permission! You can't keep using her as an excuse because you're too scared to engage with the world. I know it can be a cruel place but we have to—"

"Scared? Every single bloody night I've been going to that deathtrap of a tower, to get these stupid gifts, in case they help lead us to what happened to Nina. And you think I'm a coward?"

"I didn't mean—"

"Forget it, Beni. Let's just leave it. I'm having a stressful time and I don't need any more shit, from you or Cal or Ras, OK?"

"I'm not giving you any—"

She hangs up, hurls her phone on to the table, then rises from the sofa and strides to the window. Staring blindly out over the estate, she takes deep gulps of air until her heartbeat has settled back to its normal rhythm.

Cal, her mum, Ras, and now Beni. All her relationships seem to be falling apart.

There's a soft butt against her shin. She bends down and picks Lavender up, holding her warm furry body to her face. "At least I've still got you," she murmurs.

The text comes in right on time. No emoji today. The Secret Santa must be satisfied that his message has come through loud and clear. For a moment she considers just not going – after all, the locks are changed so he can't get in any more – but then she thinks about her mum shuffling home in the dark.

If she goes now there might be some vestiges of daylight left by the time she gets to the nineteenth floor, so she pulls on her jacket and lets herself out of the flat. But halfway to the lift, she stops and goes back for the pepper spray Ras gave her. She may have to do what the Secret Santa wants, but she doesn't have to be completely vulnerable.

By the time she gets to the tower the sun is setting. The light falling through the windows of the stairwell lies in red pools on the cement floor. By the time she emerges on to the nineteenth floor it has darkened to a lurid indigo. Old blood, congealing under the skin.

She walks through the door to the flats, then freezes.

Up ahead she can hear soft footsteps. They're coming her way.

She has never arrived this early before. Perhaps the Secret Santa wasn't expecting her and is still in the building. On this very floor.

Heart pounding, she turns to run back the way she came, but then she stops.

Beni was wrong. She's not a coward. And if this is her chance to know who's been tormenting her these past three weeks, she's going to take it. Sliding the pepper spray out of her pocket, she holds it out in front of her like a cocked pistol and sets off silently down the corridor. There's just enough of the bruised light to make out the layout of the floor, the depressed oblongs of the doorways, the meeting of ceiling and wall, the corner that leads to the next stretch of doors.

A figure walks round it.

Before it has the chance to even register her presence, she whips the canister up, depresses her thumb and sprays. The figure drops to its knees, like it's been shot, but she keeps on spraying, until it collapses on to its back, gasping and choking and clawing at its eyes. Finally the can is empty. She could run now, but she has to know. Getting out her phone, she lights up the screen and shines it on the face of the prone figure.

Sinking against the wall, she lets the empty can fall to the floor. So Calista was right. This has all been some elaborate prank to make her look a fool. She's probably being filmed right now by the odious Teddy P.

"I can't believe I fell for your bullshit."

Ras moves his hands away from his eyes, to reveal a face screwed up in agony "Not..." His cheeks are scarlet and shining with tears. "Not. Me."

"What?"

"Came to check ... on you..." he manages. "You weren't answering ... your phone..." He stops to gasp a breath. "Saw the light. Came up."

"What light?"

He stretches a trembling arm behind him and now she can see a pale glow coming from one of the doorways. It's not as bright as usual, but it's not wavering like the candlelight did.

"Don't!" he gasps.

Sidestepping him, she approaches the doorway, but when she gets there she stops dead on the threshold.

On the wall are words. Ugly, violent words that make her stomach twist.

SLUT. SKET. DIE BITCH. LYING SLAG.

HOPE U GET RAPED. NO ONE BELIEVES

U. PRICK TEASE. U DESERVED IT.

A hand closes on her arm and she spins round.

Ras has managed to peel open his streaming eyes a little, revealing slashes of scarlet where the whites should be. "Come away."

"No!" She turns back to the vile wall.

How can someone think she is any of these things when the only person she's ever even kissed is him?

Her fractured brain finally reassembles itself enough to form coherent thoughts. She recognizes the format of the messages. They are Snaps. But she has never received anything like this. Fumbling in her pocket, she checks her phone. No messages. If she never received them, perhaps they weren't ever intended for her.

Now she notices the projector at ground level on the other side of the room. She snatches it up and dismantles the box to reveal a smartphone. As she does so, her fingers brush the screen and the light goes out. The words wink out of existence as if they have spontaneously combusted or dissolved in their own acid, and the room falls into darkness.

There is no lock code, and she searches the phone for any sign of the owner, but the apps have all been deleted except for the photo gallery, and it holds only that single image. She taps in her own number, but a message comes up that the number is unavailable. Presumably this is the phone she blocked after the pills went missing.

"Must be a burner phone," Ras croaks. "Looks like they screenshotted the messages and put them all together."

He's breathing like the old men in Gran's home who were attached to oxygen tanks.

"Come on," she says. "Let's go back to mine and we can try and wash the stuff out of your eyes."

"Any better?"

Ras is bent over the bathroom sink, sloshing warm water on to his face.

She's trying not to feel guilty – her reaction was entirely understandable given the circumstances – but when he raises his bloodshot eyes to hers she can't help but feel a pang. She could have stopped when he collapsed, not emptied the whole can on him.

"As good as it's going to get for a while, I think. Can I have a towel?"

After he's dried off, she leads him to the living room and leaves him sniffing and coughing on the sofa as she goes to fetch him a glass of water. He claims it helps the stinging in his throat, but she's pretty sure he's just saying that to make her feel better.

"So what do you reckon they were about?" he croaks, putting the glass down on the coffee table. "Those messages?"

She hesitates before replying. She might be wrong. "I think they were sent to Nina."

"From who?"

"I don't know. The bullies from her last school, maybe."

"Did she ever mention anyone?"

294

"It's just a guess, but it might be one of the reasons she left. Me and Beni saw this article online."

She explains about the assault claim, and Mr Gamal beating up the teacher.

"It seems like Newham was really popular, and one of the messages said *No one believes u*."

"Could it be them doing this whole thing?"

It doesn't seem to make any sense for them to turn on Eleri, but maybe people like that just enjoy causing suffering, and with Nina gone they had to find a new victim.

"Did you go to the police?"

Eleri tells him how DI Everett downplayed what was happening, saying it was more likely to be a prank than stalking. "Sometimes it feels like he's watching me, though. Like, he knew we were going to get Lavender before I did. And then yesterday he actually came into the flat and took her."

Ras stares at her. "What?"

"It's OK," Eleri adds. "I had the locks changed this morning."

"He came in? When you were here?"

"I was at Beni's."

"But you *could* have been in."

"I guess. But I think he just used Lavender to force me to keep coming. He must have planned it for when I was out. Maybe he was watching the flat."

"But that wouldn't have told him you were getting the kitten."

"Maybe he got access to the computer somehow. He could be a hacker?"

Ras gets up, rubbing the last of the pepper tears from his eyes. "I want to see the gifts. All of them."

Sitting cross-legged on the floor of Eleri's room, Ras picks up each item, turning it over in his hands, scrutinizing every part of it intently, even sniffing it, like some kind of scrappy Sherlock Holmes.

"Any ideas?" she says when he lays the last gift down and leans back against her bed.

"Is that everything?"

"Oh wait, hang on." Eleri gets up, and her heart skips a beat. The elf is leering down from the top of her wardrobe.

"It's moved again," she mutters.

Following her gaze, Ras jumps to his feet and snatches the elf down, making its head waggle violently.

"This was from him too?"

"Yeah."

"And it's been here all the time?"

"No. It sort of moves around the house."

Before she can stop him, Ras is twisting the grinning face round and round, until with a ripping sound like machine-gun fire, the doll's head detaches from the body.

His expression thunderous, Ras thrusts his fingers into the white padding spilling from the elf's neck, then pulls out a black rectangle about the size of a sim card and holds it aloft.

"What is that?"

By way of answer, Ras brings the rectangle closer to his mouth. "Listen, arsehole," he hisses. "Lay one finger on Eleri and I'm gonna tear *your* head off too, OK? This shit stops here and now."

He drops the device on to the floor, raises his foot and brings it down hard, again and again, until the plastic finally shatters. Then he picks up the shards, goes to the window and throws them out into the night.

Eleri sinks down on to the bed. "He's been listening to us, all this time?"

Ras sits beside her. "You changed the locks so he can't get in, and now he can't listen to you either."

She nods miserably.

"El, you don't have to deal with this alone any more, OK?" He takes her hand. "We're going to find out who's doing this and I'm going to communicate to him in a way he will definitely understand that he will stop screwing with someone I care about. It'll be OK, I promise." And then his arms are around her and for an exquisite few minutes, before the knock at the door, she has never felt so safe.

It's only Mum, harassed looking, with a bag of groceries she's having to carry like a baby because one of the handles broke on the way home.

"He's done a good job, then," she says, coming in. "How many spare sets did he give you? Oh, hello."

Ras is sitting on the sofa.

"Mum, this is Ras. Ras, Mum."

297

"Hi, Mum." He grins.

"Hi! I'm Kerry." Putting down the bag, she hurries forward and reaches out her left hand. There's no brief hesitation as Ras's brain processes that her right is too twisted to shake, he just squeezes it warmly and says that it's nice to meet her.

"You too!" Mum says, far too enthusiastically, and Eleri shrinks with mortification. "I'm making moussaka. I can make it stretch if you'd like to stay for dinner?"

"Oh no, I should get back. Thanks anyway."

"Another time, then?"

Eleri inhales. *Shut up shut up shut up.*

"Yes, definitely. If I'm invited." He smiles at Eleri.

"OK, well, I'll just go and get started then." Picking up the bag, she bustles in the direction of the kitchen. "I'll close the door, so the smells don't get out. See you later."

The kitchen door closes firmly, and a moment later the radio is turned up full volume.

Ras smiles. "Do you think she did that so we can make out?"

Eleri shrugs.

"Shame to disappoint her then, eh?"

Eleri wrinkles her nose. "Yeah."

For the rest of the evening her tongue tingles with the heat from the pepper spray.

Monday December 20

Eleri stares out of the bus window at the falling rain. The expressions of the pedestrians are grim from being jabbed by clumsily wielded umbrellas or drenched with grimy water thrown up by the passing cars. Bedraggled toddlers in bright wellies refuse to take another step; dogs shiver, their tails between their legs. It's a perfect day to remember the dead.

Eleri hasn't bothered asking if Calista is going to the memorial. It would be totally fake of Cal to pretend she cared anyway. When Eleri thinks of how Cal treated Nina last year, it fills her with rage that's also directed at herself. She's made excuses for Calista for so long, willfully ignoring what was obvious to everyone else: that Calista is just a bitter, unhappy bitch who has to drag everyone else down to her level. The anger is a useful distraction from what is to come. It's not just that the memorial is going to be unutterably sad, but she can't shake the feeling that maybe Beni's right: the Secret Santa might be there.

In crime dramas, killers can never keep away from the funerals of their victims, and TV cops always stake them out, in the hope of seeing a mysterious figure flitting between the graves. It will be hard for a stranger to pass unnoticed among the students, so she might come face to face with him.

The thought makes her skin crawl.

Ras has promised to wait for her at the gates, and as the bus trundles into the stop she can see him playing keepy-uppy with a stone, as groups of black-clad students trickle into the school grounds, huddled against the rain.

There's nothing more bleak than a school out of term time – the buildings grey and abandoned, litter blowing across the cracked asphalt of deserted playgrounds – but on a day like this it's desolate as a nuclear winter. The sunken area of concrete on the main path to the headmaster's office has become a lake you can only avoid by stepping over the sodden grass.

"Hey," Ras says.

His face is pinched as if he's been crying, though it's probably just the cold. He's shivering under a threadbare black suit, the shoulders dark with rain, and he holds a drooping bouquet of white roses. Eleri is wearing the black dress she wore to Gran's funeral, under a smart coat Mum used to wear to the office.

"There aren't many here," he says. "But it's still a bit early."

Eleri's heart aches. Dead teenagers are supposed to have churches filled to bursting with sobbing friends eulogizing about the amazing wonderfulness of the dead-too-soon, but as they approach the head's lawn she sees that Ras is right. Aside from the teaching staff, in a tight group, talking quietly, the only people that have turned up are the geeks and the unpopular kids, and the prefects who were probably told to come. Ray is there too, standing at the back in his grubby gardening clothes, heavy head bent against the rain.

A trestle table has been positioned outside Mr Roberts' window. On it is a large photograph of Nina, printed on polyboard. Taken from her school pass, it's about the worst picture they could have found. Her face is lumpen and grey, and her attempt at a smile looks pained. The clear glasses press into the flesh of her cheeks, and the amber eyes behind the lenses are weighed down with sadness.

A tear rolls down Eleri's cheek.

Ras walks forward and lays his bouquet next to the four or five others lying on the table. A few candles in jars are scattered about, their flames sputtering.

Behind the table, Mr Roberts' blinds are down, and shadows move between the slices of light.

More people arrive, including most of the art club members and Miss Hanson, with a handsome white-haired man that could be her husband or her dad.

Ras raises his hand at Kika walking up the path with Rebekah. Eleri experiences a rush of gratitude as Rebekah approaches the table and fastens a silver balloon to the leg.

The script printed on the foil reads *Always in our hearts*. Coming beside her, Kika lays down an intricate origami bird made of white paper. A dove. It won't last long in the rain.

The time ticks over to eleven, and then past it.

Beni arrives with the new boy. He blows her a discreet kiss and then the pair of them go to stand at the margin of the art club group.

In her sodden court shoes and thin black tights Eleri can't feel her feet.

At last Mr Roberts' door opens and a woman emerges. Presumably his wife, she is in her forties or fifties and looks Malaysian or Philippino. The embroidered flowers on her high-collared black dress shimmer in the light from the tea lights in glasses on the tray she is carrying. She walks round and everyone takes a candle. Eleri cups her hands around the warm glass, shielding the flame with her bent head.

There's a sharp whistle behind her.

Teddy P and a couple of other boys are slouching through the gates, wearing tracksuits and trainers. They scan the crowd, spot Ras and amble over, kicking through the puddle and laughing like a pack of hyenas. They take it in turns to clasp Ras's hand in greeting but don't even acknowledge Eleri's presence.

"We're gonna head to Nandos after. Coming?"

Ras glances at Eleri. "No, I should probably…"

"It's fine," she says quickly. "I've got stuff to do anyway."

"I'll come over later, then?"

"Sure," she says. This morning her mum announced she was going to a film with Adam tonight. And after the discovery of the listening device, Eleri doesn't want to be alone in the house, even with the locks changed.

"OK." Ras looks unhappy, but before they can say anything else, the door opens again and Mr Roberts comes out. Without his usual sparkly eyed smile he looks twenty years older, his bald pate wrinkled with distress. Following behind him is Pierre Alexandre, the soloist in the school choir. Though he's in the year below Eleri, Pierre's voice still hasn't broken. His eyes droop at the corners and his lower lip connects directly to his neck, with no recourse to a chin. A person might not give him a second glance, if they hadn't heard him sing.

At a nod from Mr Roberts, Pierre goes to stand by the table. The speaker on the upper corner of the building crackles into life and a tinny piano starts up. Mr Roberts joins his wife, who snakes a slim arm around his waist, and he lets his bald head drop on to hers. Raindrops quiver there, then trickle down his temple.

The introductory bars finish and Pierre opens his mouth.

"*Abide with me, fast falls the eventide,*" he sings in a voice like light. "*The darkness deepens, Lord, with me abide.*"

Some of the female teachers start to dab their eyes.

"*When other helpers fail and comforts flee, help of the helpless, oh, abide with me.*"

Eleri glances over at Beni, knowing he will have dissolved into tears. She's right. His whole body is shaking.

She glances at the new boy to see if he has noticed, but Hendrick's face is expressionless. As handsome as he is, he is not attractive. His bland good looks are like those of a statue or a game character. He seems bored.

The headmaster's door opens once more and the crowd shifts and murmurs, because now Nina's parents emerge, pausing to take in the scene. Mr Gamal's arm is around his wife's shoulder as Pierre's voice soars up into the overcast London air. It pierces a hole in the cloud cover and a single ray of sunshine breaks through to fall on the table, catching the raindrops and turning the glossy polyboard to an oblong of pure light.

An upswell of emotion fills Eleri's chest.

How could she have forgotten Nina so quickly? Perhaps that's what the Secret Santa is so angry about: that after her disappearance, in the bustle and stress of the academic year, Nina's only real friend at EHS barely spared her a thought. Why didn't she try to *find* Nina? Why wasn't it her putting up the posters, handing out the flyers? What kind of friend *was* she anyway?

No kind. But perhaps it's not her fault. She hardly knew Nina: there just wasn't time in the single term they had together. Maybe if Nina had stayed they would have got closer. Perhaps she might even have supplanted Calista as Eleri's best friend. She was much easier company after all, not always slagging people off, belittling their achievements, seeking to control her, to dominate her time. If Eleri knew then what she knows now about Calista, perhaps she would have ended their friendship completely. And if that had happened, and she and Nina had become close, then maybe Nina wouldn't have done what she did.

Is it her fault?

Pierre stops singing, and there are audible sniffs and throat clearings, then Mr Roberts steps forward to speak.

As he eulogizes about *the lovely young woman whose company the school was blessed with for such a short time*, Eleri can't help but wonder how she ever suspected Jimmy Gamal of being involved in Nina's death. He is a broken man, grey-faced, slack-mouthed, bent at the waist as if something is gnawing at his insides. His wife stands straight-backed beside him, like a bamboo cane supporting a frail plant. While her eyes are fixed on Mr Roberts, her gaze is unfocused, as if her attention is actually on something far beyond him.

After he's finished speaking, Miss Hanson steps forward and reads a poem about a ship sailing over a horizon. Ray looks up for this and his eyes meet Eleri's. He nods in sombre greeting and Eleri raises the hand at her side.

In the silence following the poem there is a sly shutter sound. Eleri turns. A man with an expensive looking camera around his neck stands under a large umbrella beside a thin blonde woman in a fuscia suit and heavy make-up. Her head is cocked to one side, her eyebrows tilted in exaggerated sympathy

The poem was clearly too much for one of the younger students and she starts sobbing loudly. After a hushed discussion with Miss Hanson, Mr and Mrs Roberts lead her, half collapsing, back into his office.

Beni is now standing alone, panting and fanning his face. Even Teddy P and his odious friends had the decency to stay till the end, but Hendrick has vanished, leaving Beni in obvious distress. She's about to go over to him when a strident new voice cuts through silence.

"You must miss Nalina very much." The woman in the suit is talking to one of the prefects.

The girl glances at her friends and then nods. She is in a different year, so would probably never have spoken to Nina.

"Did she ever talk about her time at Drinkwater School?"

At the mumbled *nos* the reporter nods earnestly. Under the glare of the blinking lens, the normally boisterous girls are cowed.

"They call it *Suicide School*, though I guess thanks to her, you could say the same for Elsinore House now."

The girls share bewildered glances.

"Were you aware of the incident that caused Nalina to leave her last school?"

They shake their heads.

Ras comes over to speak to her, but Eleri hushes him with a raised hand.

"She falsely accused a teacher there of sexual assault."

"Oh my days…" murmur the girls.

"Mr Newham had this hanging over him for months while they investigated. He almost lost his job. His wife,

Lauren, and his baby were put through so much, it's a wonder there wasn't another suicide to add to the tally. Hasn't the whole *Me Too* thing gone too far, when the slightest gesture can be labelled assault? Don't you think the shift towards always believing the accuser has just given more power to malicious liars?"

There is a cry of inarticulate rage, and Mr Gamal comes barrelling through the crowd.

"Not false! Nina is no liar!" His hands chop the air with a violence that makes the reporter wince.

"I must ask you to step away from me, Mr Gamal," she says, with such exaggerated shock she might be a shrinking heroine in a silent film. "The other students disagreed. They testified that Nina had pursued the teacher in question, and then made up lies when he rejected her. Lies that nearly ended his career."

"*They* are the liars! Because she is pretty and they are jealous!"

The girls watch the scene with wide-eyed amazement.

"She come here to get away from them! All the bullying!"

"Bullying she brought on herself."

"No!" Jimmy cries. "No!"

Eleri steps forward and addresses the reporter. "*Brought on herself?*"

The woman turns her wide blue eyes on her. "And you are?"

"I was Nina's friend."

Jimmy Gamal is standing directly opposite her, pale and

panting so hard she can smell his sour breath. "Did you actually just say that Nina *deserved* to be bullied so badly she had to leave the school and change her name?"

"Mr Newham's career was almost ended by the accusation. It could have spelled the end of his marriage. The students of Drinkwater were upset for his sake. That a girl like *that*—"

"You shut your mouth!" Jimmy Gamal bellows.

The reporter smiles. "Shut my mouth? Or what? You'll put me in a coma like you did Mr Newham?"

She lands heavily on her neat, gym-honed backside with a grunt of surprise, and for a moment can only flap her glued-on eyelashes.

Then she gives a shrill laugh. "You just assaulted me!"

Eleri is unable to answer. She just stares at the outstretched hands that just slammed into the reporter's tailored jacket shoulders. For someone who prefers to go under the radar it was a pretty bold move.

"Too right she did." Kika comes to stand beside her. "And I will too if you don't piss off right now."

"Don't worry, Sienna," says the photographer. "I got it all on c—"

Approaching him from behind, Rebekah deftly slips the camera strap over his head and drops it on to the concrete.

"Oops," she says.

"You'll be paying for that!" the photographer splutters. "And anyway" – he smiles nastily – "the memory card will be fine."

"Double whoops," says Ras and kicks the camera down the path into the puddle that's so deep it comes halfway up the lens.

The photographer rushes to retrieve it, swearing as the thing bleeds water, and makes sad little clicking noises as he hammers the buttons. The reporter gets to her feet. There is a dark stain on the back of her pink skirt.

"You shat yourself!" Teddy P jeers.

Ignoring him, the woman picks up the umbrella, and heads for the school gates as fast as her stilettos will carry her. A single well-aimed tea light strikes her on the back of her head, spattering hot wax down her perfect Kate Middleton curls. There is a bark of laughter, and then others join in.

By the time they are out of sight, the sun has broken through the clouds, and the students start to disperse. They have done their duty and now they can slough it off. It's nearly Christmas. There's shopping and eating to do, fun to be had. Ray begins to gather up the tea lights abandoned on the walls and benches.

Ras takes his leave of Eleri, quickly and shamefacedly, promising to be over by three, then a red-eyed Beni comes over and hugs her. "I've got to go to the theatre tonight, but I'll come over tomorrow, OK?" He limps away with some drama club girls.

Rebekah raises an eyebrow at Eleri: *Are you OK?* Eleri nods. They can go.

Soon Eleri is alone except for the teachers talking earnestly under black umbrellas.

But not quite alone. Jimmy Gamal's black eyes are fixed on hers. For a moment they hold one another's gaze, and then he inclines his head. In acknowledgement perhaps, or thanks. A moment later, with infinite gentleness, Mrs Gamal touches her husband's arm and they shuffle towards the road, like two octogenarians.

Eleri walks up to the drowned shine. Somehow a single candle flame survived the onslaught of rain. She picks up the picture of Nina and wipes the rain off it with her sleeve.

Four days, Nina. Four days and then I'll know what really happened to you.

Ras is late. As the sun starts to sink and the shadows creep across the carpet, Eleri feels the first stirrings of fear. Instead of turning up obediently to collect her gift, she allowed Ras to threaten the Secret Santa. And now she's alone in the house and four o'clock is rapidly approaching. What will he do to punish her this time?

The sharp rap makes her jump. If visitors buzz in at the main entrance, their faces swim up on the little screen on the wall, but the screen is dark as she walks over to the door. She's glad she hasn't yet turned on the lights – she was watching YouTube with her earphones, so there will be no sign that's she's actually in.

Standing in the gloom, she listens intently.

"El? You there?"

She opens the door.

"Hey," Ras says, looking anxious. "Sorry. Ted needed

me to help him fix his bike. It took longer than I expected, sorry."

"It's fine. How did you get up here?"

"Someone was going out as I was coming in. There was no light on when I came down the path. Have you got the message yet?"

"No." She steps back to allow him into the flat.

But the message comes through on the dot of four.

```
Door 20.
```

They go to the kitchen window. A light is burning on the twentieth floor.

"It's fine," Ras murmurs. "We'll just stick something on the TV and ignore it, OK?"

He goes back to the living room while she makes tea. But when she returns, the TV is off and Ras is perched on the edge of the sofa cushion.

She puts the tray down on the coffee table. "I thought we were watching TV?"

"I've been wanting to talk to you about something."

She sits down on the armchair and folds her arms defensively. *Tamara's asked me out, so, sorry, but can we just be friends...?*

"I know you think Teddy's a twat and everything, and I had a real go at him for what he said the other day."

She shrugs. *Not my business.*

"But he's been a good friend to me over the years, a

311

really good friend. Especially this year, which has been … incredibly shit."

He takes a deep breath and runs a hand through his hair. "So, um, last year, we talked about our parents. Do you remember?"

She nods.

"I told you how my mum was sick?"

"Yeah."

"Well, something happened, at New Year. A few people know about it, Kika and Ted and some teachers, but I didn't want it getting around, because … well…"

"You don't have to tell me."

"I want to. It's important. And I hope it explains why I wasn't myself for a few months."

She nods, waiting.

"So, last Christmas Mum met this guy," Ras begins, looking down at his hands. "Online. Some bloke she used to know who was working out in a bar in Thailand. He invited her out there for New Year, but she thought she'd changed so much since they last saw each other that he wouldn't fancy her any more. The anti-psychosis tablets made her put on weight, you know?"

Eleri nods.

"So she came off them. My brother thought it was a bad idea, but she seemed fine to me. She started looking like her old self again, and she could fit into her old clothes so her mood was great. I told him we should give her a chance. That maybe she was better."

He stops, inhaling deeply, gazing at the dark TV screen.

"The day before she was due to fly out she'd gone to get her nails done and she was waiting at the bus stop when she saw someone pointing a gun at her from a window over the road."

Eleri's mouth opens. Then she understands.

"She called me and I told her to stay where she was and Hish would come and pick her up. But when I was on the phone to him, she called back and left a message to say that the sniper was coming after her and she had to run."

He pauses again, breathing heavily, as if the air in the room has lost some of its oxygen.

"I called her again and she'd gone into a multi-storey car park. She was going to hide there until Hish arrived. I told her…" He inhales. "I told her that it was fine, and he wouldn't be long. I figured she'd just hide under a car or something until he got there. He was out with some mates from work and said he'd just finish his drink and then he'd be down there. We didn't think there was any reason to hurry. She'd been like this before, you know?" He looks at Eleri, his eyes pleading, and she nods weakly, thinking of her own mum walking haltingly through a car park, unable to run or defend herself.

"I shouldn't have told her to wait. I should have called an ambulance." He closes his eyes. "The CCTV footage showed her jumping out from behind a Range Rover. She went to run down the exit ramp but they must have been coming up after her, so she went the other way, up to the next level, and the next and the next, until there was nowhere else to go. She was up against the barriers, cornered. She screamed at them to go away and then, as they were coming towards her, she got out her phone and texted me."

He takes his phone out and unlocks it, then he opens his messages and scrolls down, past Hish and Kika and Ted and Eleri, to *Mum*. He opens the last message.

```
I love you. Im so sorry.
```

Eleri stares, appalled.

"She was so scared. She didn't know what to do. So she … she…"

Almost inaudibly, Eleri completes the sentence. "She jumped."

Ras nods.

Eleri can't help herself. She needs to be sure that she hasn't got the wrong end of the stick. "They … they weren't really there, right? The snipers?" She winces, waiting for his anger, but when he replies his tone is one of aching weariness.

"They were for her. And for me they might as well have been, because they killed my mum."

In his hand his phone darkens and then winks out, then it slides out of his grasp on to the sofa cushion.

Eleri kneels down beside him and takes his limp hand. "I'm so sorry."

They sit like that for a long time, and then he kisses her, and then they kiss for a long time.

When they finally part, the flat is in pitch-darkness. It's gone six and there have been no other messages. She texts her mum to make sure she's OK, and she sends back a picture of her and Adam grinning behind a huge bowl of mussels.

Perhaps it's really over this time. Like with all bullies, maybe all she ever had to do was stand up to the Secret Santa and he would give up and go away.

She gets up from the warm nest of the sofa and stretches, inhaling the cool evening air. Ras smiles at her. "You OK?"

"Yeah. You?"

"Yep. Really OK. Really, *really* OK."

"Good." She blushes. "Want some food? I've got pizzas in the freezer."

"Sure, yeah."

Leaning on the countertop waiting for them to cook, she feels oddly light, as if she might float up to the ceiling. In the living room, Ras has put the TV on: some jingling Christmas advert for a supermarket.

They desperately need a new cooker: this one is hotter at the back than at the front, and when she takes the pizzas out they are burnt on one side. Hoping he won't mind, she slides them on to plates and carries them back into the living room.

Ras is watching *Scream*. The opening scene where Drew Barrymore is on the phone to the killer. Flirty at first, thinking it's all a prank, she starts to become uneasy, and then scared. And the next thing the viewer knows, her bloodied corpse is hanging from a tree.

Eleri averts her eyes from the screen. "Sorry about the pizzas." She lays them down on the coffee table. "The oven's crap."

Ras grins and pulls off a charred crust. "The black bits are my favourite."

Then his face falls as he registers the scene on the TV.

"Oh wait. Let me turn this off."

He switches channels and they settle down to watch *Gogglebox*. But as the evening goes on, she can't seem to relax. She's super aware of his presence beside her, and yet when he tries to put his arm around her she jumps. She laughs it off but the weight of his arm on the back of her neck makes her tense. Like she couldn't get away if she tried.

And then she realizes why she's feeling that way.

In *Scream* nobody suspects Billy, the loyal boyfriend. How could he be the killer when he has watertight alibis? He's even with Sidney when some of the murders occur.

But that's because he's not doing it alone. He has a friend helping him. A friend that finds the whole thing completely hilarious. A friend that laughs like a hyena.

Wasn't there something theatrical about the way Ras growled threats into the recording device? *I'm gonna tear your head off!* Almost like he was enjoying himself. Having a laugh with his mates. The mates Eleri has never liked or trusted.

She turns her head a fraction to look at him out of the corner of her eyes. He's laughing at something on-screen. Despite everything he claims happened to him, Ras is always laughing, as if the world is a very funny place indeed.

The programme ends and he asks what she wants to watch now, but she tells him she's really tired.

The goodbye kiss feels different, more insistent, the arms coiled around her waist like bindings. She pulls away and he blinks in surprise. *Are you OK?* Just tired. She smiles. Closes the door on him. Then she pulls the chain across and goes to the window. A minute or so later he emerges from beneath the building, wheeling his bike. When he gets to the path he climbs on and switches on the lights. Then he gets out his phone and starts to text.

Tuesday December 21

Next morning, over the steaming cardboard cups of hot chocolate Beni brings round, Eleri describes everything that has happened since she last saw him: the listening device, and her new suspicions about Ras.

Beni almost spits out his mouthful. "What are you talking about? Of course it's not Ras! How would he have access to any of Nina's stuff, and why would he want to anyway? You must be out of your mind! That boy likes you, and he's trying to protect you in that cute alpha way they have – all brawn, no brains – but he's trying. Come on, El, you don't seriously think it was him?"

She groans and throws herself back on the sofa. "I don't know what to think!"

"You're scared. I get it. But you're not thinking straight."

"I'm trying, Ben, I really am, but none of it makes sense.

318

I just don't understand what I'm supposed to have done. Why me?"

Beni exhales, shaking his head. He looks tired. Sometimes she forgets that other people are going through stuff too. She makes herself smile.

"So how's it going with Hendrick?"

Beni doesn't return the smile. "I just don't know. He blows hot and cold. One day he's texting me every two minutes, the next he totally ignores me."

"He didn't stay for the memorial."

"I know, right! I look round and he's not there. Without a word. I mean, I know it's boring if you don't know the girl, but still… I guess he's just not really into me."

There is silence.

"He's not even that good-looking," Eleri says.

Beni gives her a rueful look. "You and I both know that is BS."

"Yeah, but he's not attractive cos there's nothing behind his eyes, no spark."

Beni sighs again. "Well, he's the first guy to show me any interest since ever, so I'm gonna keep trying."

Lavender struts into the living room yowling. A scrap of paper is pinioned on one of her claws and she mews piteously as Eleri picks her up and carefully extricates it. It's a corner of wrapping paper from one of the Secret Santa gifts. She thought she'd thrown it all away, but a piece must have ended up under her bed.

"What is that?"

"I think it's supposed to be the angel Gabriel. Oh wait, you don't think he's some kind of religious extremist, do you?"

"Have you sinned recently, then?" He takes the scrap of paper and starts folding it flat on his knee.

"I don't think so." She blushes a little. Ras's hand did stray to her breast last night.

"That's not Gabriel," Beni says after a pause.

"How do you know?"

"Going to church every bloody Sunday for sixteen years. It's not just conversion therapy, you know. See the sword in his hand, and the family in the room through the door." He points.

"I thought that was Mary and Joseph."

Beni shakes his head. "They're Egyptians. And the angel is an avenging angel sent to punish them for their sins." He frowns. "Now we're on the subject of the Bible, those ten pence coins we picked up the other day. That's what Judas was paid for betraying Jesus. Thirty pieces of silver."

Eleri stares at him.

"But ... but I didn't betray Nina! How? How would I have done that? I was her friend, Ben. I never did anything—" She can't finish the sentence for hyperventilating.

"At least we know," Beni says later when Eleri's calmed down and washed her face and is sitting back on the sofa with a steaming cup of sweet tea. "At least we know why he's targeting you."

"But I never did anything to her, I swear." She can speak without her breath hitching now, but her throat feels tight, like she's having an allergic reaction.

"Babe, I know. The guy has got completely the wrong end of the stick."

"I need to tell him. I need to explain that I never did anything, but there's no way of replying to the messages!"

"You could leave him a note, in the tower, when you collect the gift. He'd see it when he went to pick up the light."

"I don't want to go back there again."

Beni takes her hand. "You don't deserve this, and this is the only way to let him know."

He helps her compose the letter.

I don't know who you are but you seem to
have a connection with Nina Mitri.

In the short time I knew her, Nina was my
friend. I never did anything to betray
her. I cared about her, and I miss her, and
I wish there was something I could have
done to stop her doing what she did.
Please leave me alone.

It seems inadequately vague, but she can't be more specific in her denial because she doesn't know what she's *supposed* to have done.

The afternoon crawls by and they watch Christmas movies with feel-good endings that just make her feel even more bleak. There is an ending coming, in just three days now, but she suspects it's not going to be a feel-good one. If she hadn't used up all the pepper spray on Ras she could take it with her tonight, but at least Beni will be there.

The message comes through right on time.

Door 21.

Lack of sleep and appetite has taken its toll. By the time they've trudged up to the twenty-first floor of Gibea Tower, Eleri's lungs ache and her legs are lead. She trudges after Beni as he follows the dull yellow glow that leads them, like the star of Bethlehem, to the open door of flat 214.

In the middle of the floor lies a little box wrapped in the angel paper.

Inside is a coloured bead.

"What's that supposed to mean?" Beni says, peering in.

"God knows." Replacing the lid of the box, she takes the letter from her pocket and leaves it on the floor by the light, then they go back.

It takes them a long time to find the exit.

It's the shortest day, Eleri realizes, as they step out of the splintered door into a blackness so dense she can barely see her hand in front of her face. The deepest, longest dark of winter. After today the nights will start getting shorter, as the earth turns its face to the light. But here, on the dark side of the tower, all is black, the cloud cover so dense that not a splinter of moonlight can escape to catch in the windows. They are empty eye sockets.

It's not as if she was expecting a message saying, *I'm terribly sorry, this has all been a dreadful mistake*, but as the evening passes, the silence from her phone removes any last vestige of hope that this might all end. When Beni leaves, she drags herself to bed, so bone weary that she leaves the chain off the door so Mum won't have to wake her to get in. Lying shivering on her pillow, too tired to get up and turn up the thermostat, she texts Ras, making up a lie about being too busy with a family visit to talk before. He doesn't bother to reply.

But around midnight her ringing phone shrieks her awake. Bleary-eyed she squints at the screen. It's not Ras, it's Beni. And a call in the middle of the night is never good news.

Wednesday December 22

St Frances Hospital was built in the eighties when bright colours and playground shapes were all the rage. With its entrance constructed from huge royal-blue pipes and capped with a bright green triangle, it looks like it's been built by some oversized toddler.

The bus drops Eleri at the other end of the car park and as she hurries across the tarmac, her raised hood does little to shield her face from the horizontal sleet, blurring her vision already clouded with exhaustion. After speaking to Beni, she didn't sleep a wink, just lay ramrod straight on the mattress, staring up at the ceiling, until she was sure that Mum had gone to work.

As she approaches the cold lights of the hospital, she can see Beni standing just inside the sliding outer doors. He dashes out to meet her, pulling her into a hug, but she pushes him away.

"This is my fault."

"How do you work that out?"

"The bead, in the box. It's like the ones Ras has on his bike spokes."

Beni murmurs, "Oh my days…"

"It was the Secret Santa."

"Jesus, El, this was attempted murder. We have to tell Everett."

Eleri snorts. "Firstly, do you think she's going to believe us? And if she does, do you really think she's gonna find whoever's doing this before Christmas Eve? Because if not, if he's still out there and he knows we've told the police, then what will he do next? Kill my mum?"

"So you just wait for him to kill *you*?"

"I don't know, Ben, OK? I just… I have to see Ras. He might know who's doing this."

The smell of the hospital reminds her immediately of Gran, of those final interminable days where they barely went home except to shower, living on the dried-up cheese sandwiches from the concession stand in the corner. It is still manned by the same slack-mouthed woman with nicotine-stained fingertips, who only ever filled your coffee cup halfway.

At the other end of the reception area corridors lead off, left and right, and there's a large sign directing you to the different departments: Radiology, Neurology, Cardiology, etc.

They hurry down featureless corridors, past beds and

wheelchairs and yellow-faced old men wheeling oxygen tanks. It must be breakfast time because the whole place reeks of burnt toast. Eleri thinks of the way Ras said he liked the black bits best.

It was a hit-and-run. He was airlifted here last night with a head injury.

What if he has brain damage, and instead of pizza he has to be spoon-fed puree for the rest of his life, his mum wiping the spills from his chin as his eyes roll back in his head? No, not his mum. His mum was killed by snipers. Oh, Ras.

They turn a corner and come to a set of royal-blue double doors. The sign above reads *Critical Care Unit*. Eleri presses the button on the wall. It takes several minutes for a crackly voice to come on the line.

"We're here to see Ras Mandip. He was in a bike accident."

"Are you family?" says the voice.

Girlfriend, Beni mouths furiously, but Eleri can't bring herself to utter the lie.

"Just friends."

"It's family only for the time being."

"Is he going to be OK?"

"The doctor will come by later, then we'll know more."

"Can we speak to them?"

"Only next of kin."

Eleri's shoulders droop. "OK. Thanks."

A row of bright yellow plastic chairs are bolted to the

opposite wall and Beni sits down, patting the seat beside him. "We'll wait for the doctor," he says firmly. "And this time you say you're his bloody girlfriend, OK?"

She nods. But she can't sit down, can only pace from the doors to the chairs and back again, her stomach knotting. As the hours crawl by, Beni scrolls through his phone, looking up at her anxiously every now and again.

At just past eleven a porter comes around the corner, wheeling an empty bed. Considering he must spend his time with the dead and dying, he seems remarkably cheerful, with glossy ebony skin and bright black eyes. He looks fifty or sixty, and an earring sparkles in his left ear and his shirtsleeves are rolled up to reveal tattoos of what look like babies' birth dates.

"Scuse me, madam," he says, with a little bow. Eleri sidesteps and he goes past her and holds his card up to the pad on the wall. There is a soft clump and the door opens. He wheels the bed inside.

As the door closes Eleri tries to glimpse inside the ward, but all she can see is a nurse's desk and beyond it, pale blue curtains pulled around a bed.

She paces back to the chairs.

A while later the doors open again and the porter reemerges. This time there's an old lady occupying the bed. Her skin is the colour of old parchment, her hair so fine that the current of air as the porter sets off down the corridor makes it swirl around her head like seaweed.

"Excuse me." Eleri steps into his path. "There's a boy in

there. Ras Mandip. He was knocked off his bike. Can you tells us how he is?"

The porter kicks the bed's brake on. "You his friends, are you?" The badge on his uniform says *Porter Jack*.

She nods.

"She's his girlfriend," Beni says, getting up and coming over. "Has he woken up yet?"

"Oh, he won't."

Seeing Eleri's expression, he adds hastily, "He's in an induced coma to protect his brain. Once the swelling has gone down they'll bring him out of it."

"What, so he was conscious when he came in?" Eleri says.

"He had a nasty knock, and was drifting in and out. Look, I really have to get this lady to the ward now."

"Did he say anything?"

"What?"

"When you were with him, did he say anything?"

"I couldn't really make it out."

"So he did?"

"Like I say, he wasn't making much sense."

"What was it?" The intensity of Eleri's gaze makes the man take a step back.

"Something about a *trick*," he says. "That's what it sounded like to me."

The blood drains from Eleri's face and she sits heavily on a plastic chair as the porter trundles the old lady back down the corridor, humming to himself.

"What do you think he meant?" Beni says softly, coming to sit beside her. "That he knew who was tricking you?"

"Or that he was part of it."

"How can he have been involved? He's lying in the bloody ICU."

"Maybe he wanted to stop. Maybe he only started it because he was upset about the invitation. His mum died, Ben. She had this hallucination where she thought people were trying to kill her and she jumped off a multi-storey car park."

"Jesus."

"Maybe he just flipped at being called a psycho."

"What, and then he waits a whole year to get his revenge?"

She shrugs. "Effective though, right? I'll never enjoy Christmas again. If I get to see another one, of course."

"Don't say that. Ras said it was just a trick. A prank gone too far, like Everett thinks. Come on. Let's get you home. You need some rest."

But at that moment there's the sound of footsteps approaching around the corner. Eleri jumps up, in case it's the doctor.

It's not.

Pure instinct, a lifetime of trust and closeness, makes her fall into Calista's arms, and for a long moment she just hangs there, while Calista rocks her and strokes her hair.

Then she remembers and pulls away.

In the week that has passed since Eleri last saw her,

Calista has lost a shocking amount of weight. Her skin is grey and flaky, her hair greasy and lank. In the tracksuit and an oversize puffer jacket she must have borrowed from her dad, she looks frail and shrunken.

"I'll just go and get some cans from the vending machine," Beni says and scampers away down the corridor, leaving the two girls standing perfectly still, staring at each other.

"El," she whispers. "El, I'm so sorry." A tear snakes down her sallow cheek. It should provoke some pity in Eleri, but it doesn't. What right has Calista to cry?

"Sorry for what happened to Ras, or sorry for what you did to us last year?"

"For both."

"Why did you do it? You knew I liked him."

Calista's face twists in pain. "I was scared. That you and him would get together and I would lose you. I needed you, El, with Mum going. You were all I had left."

Eleri shakes her head. "Well, congratulations on picking the one sure-fire way to make sure I'd never want to see you again. We are through, Calista. Everything anyone's ever said to me about you is true. You're toxic. You just want to suck all the happiness out of my life to make me as miserable as you."

When Calista breaks down into sobs, Eleri has to fight every instinct telling her to comfort her friend. Instead she picks up her coat from the back of the chair and walks away.

She's halfway across the car park by the time Beni catches up with her.

"I've called her dad," he says breathlessly, falling into step beside her. "She was in a really bad way."

Eleri turns on him. "And you're blaming me for that?"

"No, of course not. It was just sad, that's all."

"She brought it on herself." Eleri clenches her teeth and stares straight ahead, forcing a car to brake suddenly as she marches out in front of it.

"El."

Walking out of the car park on to the pavement, she becomes aware that Beni is no longer beside her.

"Eleri, don't do this."

"Do what?" She doesn't turn.

"I get that you're scared and that you don't know who to trust, but don't push everyone away. We care about you."

"Who's we?"

"Me. And Calista. She screwed up, OK. People do. They're not superhuman. You have to forgive them sometimes."

"Some things are unforgivable, Beni."

"They're not. Honestly. They're not. You get to decide—"

But Eleri doesn't hear the rest of his sentence because a bus roars into the stop and the doors hiss open. She gets on and sits down, her body angled away from the window, and the bus pulls away.

Now the only person she has left is the Secret Santa.

The razor blade is clotted with flakes of dark brown.

She wasn't surprised by what the angel left for her

tonight. The time for tricks – diamond rings and teddy bears – has passed. This is the truth, laid out cold and bloody. The Secret Santa means her harm.

It's probably the blade Nina used to kill herself, Eleri thinks dully as she replaces the lid of the box and folds back the angel paper. How could she ever have thought the angel carried a happy message? It holds a sword.

Eleri gets to her feet. She will take the ghastly thing home and put it with the other gifts. It will all be useful evidence for the police investigating her death.

She isn't afraid as she trudges back down the stairwell. In fact, despite the unrelieved darkness, she feels oddly safe. The Secret Santa removed the threat of the homeless man, and Ras, when it looked as if he would prevent her picking up the gifts. He wants her here, in two days' time, to witness the final act of the avenging angel.

But avenging what? A friend who was not friend enough to stop Nina from killing herself? It seems so trivial compared to what happened to Nina at the hands of Mr Newham. And yet he is walking around blissfully unaware, taking his baby to the park, kissing his pretty wife, while Eleri suffers.

Except that she doesn't suffer any more. She is resigned. What's done is done. There will be no forgiveness. Only her and the Secret Santa, face to face, at the end.

Easing out of the splintered door, she stands in the wind, tilting her head up to the heavy clouds, their swollen bellies threatening snow.

Thursday December 23

She has become a ghost.

Drifting around the flat, it is only Lavender that notices her, following her passage with large, liquid eyes from her place on Mum's lap.

Sometimes Mum speaks, but it is more to herself or Lavender than to her daughter.

"Does it still mean next day delivery if the next day is Christmas Eve…? Oh god, I forgot the bread sauce. Does anyone even like bread sauce…? Looks like snow. Wonder if it'll be a white Christmas…?"

Eleri drifts back to her bedroom.

The sun does not seem to have risen today. The clouds are apocalyptic, their bruised and swollen abdomens almost touching the roof of Gibea Tower.

Opening the window as far as it will go, she thinks about falling.

Far away on the high road, Christmas lights twinkle and figures move up and down, in and out of lighted shops. Between them and Eleri, the black obelisk of the tower is a door to a different world, one that she occupies alone, with the angel.

When she wanders back to the living room, Mum has gone. She must have said goodbye but Eleri didn't hear.

Later on Mr Vaseli slides their post under the door. Most are coloured envelopes that look like Christmas cards – she can't be bothered to open them – but one is marked *Kingdom and Chute Legal Services*. It must be from Adam's solicitors. Their first bill perhaps: thousands of pounds that they can't afford. In two days' time Mum will have enough to worry about to deal with this too. Eleri's tempted to just drop it into the bin, but in the end she just hides it among the pile of papers on top of the microwave.

Time drips like a tap with a faulty washer. Sometimes the hands of the clock seem stuck, and sometimes an hour will jump past in the space of a minute.

As four o'clock approaches she feels a kind of serenity. It's so close now.

But when her phone springs to life it's with a call not a message.

"Hey, Eleri? It's Adam."

It takes her a moment to make the connection.

"Oh. Right. Hi."

"I just wanted to call and make sure you're OK with me coming for Christmas dinner."

There is a pause. Eleri's thoughts seem to be taking longer to coalesce than usual.

"Yeah, it's fine."

Another pause, this time from Adam. "Doesn't sound fine. Look, I understand."

I doubt it.

"It must feel weird after it's been just the two of you for all this time, and maybe you're worried about your mum. That's natural, and right. But I know how lucky I am to have met her and…"

Zoning out, Eleri gets up off her bed and goes across to the window, gazing down at the darkening landscape. A figure is moving across the grass from the direction of the railway line. It is dressed in black, with a hood pulled up. She lays a palm on the window to steady herself and at the same moment the figure stops, as if it's walked into some invisible wall.

Its head tilts back.

From here the face is just a dark mask, but she can feel its gaze, ionizing the air between them.

"You," she murmurs.

"… you only have to say the word… Sorry, what?"

The figure moves behind the building and is gone.

"Nothing."

"Oh right, cos—"

"I'd love you to come for Christmas dinner, Adam."

Mum will need you.

"Really? Well, if you're sure, that's great. I'm really

looking forward to meeting you properly. And seeing Lavender again. Worst-behaved kitten of the whole litter. I guess I should have told you, huh!"

He has a nice laugh.

"Right, well, if that's OK, I'll see you in two days."

On the twenty-third floor a yellow eye flashes open, and now it has a vertical pupil. The angel is standing by the window looking across the abyss at her.

Hurling the phone on to her bed, she runs. Out of the flat and down the corridor, taking the stairs two at a time and bolting out of the main doors into the sleet. She doesn't feel its bite on her bare arms as she flies across the gap between the buildings, doesn't feel the burn in her chest or the racing of her heart as the floors tumble like dominoes before her, a single thought beating like wings in her mind: he is there, he is waiting.

The mug is brand new. It still has the sticker on the base with the name of the shop, one of the ones by school that sells absolutely everything at rock-bottom prices. She turns it over in her hands, running her fingertips across the cold porcelain. Beneath a picture of a shiny red apple are the words *I Love Teacher.*

This is surely the last gift, and yet it feels like simply a bad joke, a poor-taste reference to the assault on Nina by her teacher. She frowns, disappointed, then strides to the door.

"Is that it?"

Her voice echoes down the darkened hallway.

"Is that really all you can manage after all this time? A *pathetic mug*?"

Is it the angel whose presence she can feel, lost in the shadows? If she listens hard she can almost hear the rustle of his wings.

"You're here, aren't you?"

The dark listens.

"I'm not scared any more." Eleri walks out into the corridor. "But you are. You're a coward, aren't you? If you're not, come out and face me now."

She hears something then, the scrape of a shoe against concrete, not far away. She sets off in pursuit of the sound.

"FACE ME!" she howls, her bare feet slapping against the concrete.

She knows the anatomy of the building like an old friend now.

"WHY ARE YOU RUNNING?" she bellows, pounding around a corner in time to hear a quiet whump, as of a huge bird taking flight. Stumbling on, she rebounds off the walls, ricocheting like a stray bullet.

"WHAT ARE YOU AFRAID OF?" Her voice has an unusual echo and then a cold breath stirs her hair. Skidding to a halt, she throws out her left hand and clutches the edge of a wall. She can feel the yawning chasm opening up beside her.

The lift shaft. One more step and it would have all been over.

Backing away until she comes up against solid brickwork,

she begins to feel her way, painfully slowly, back out of the building.

She lied to the angel. She *is* scared. Very scared indeed.

The light goes out. Standing at her bedroom window, she peers into the darkness to catch a glimpse of a figure leaving the tower, but all she can see is her own spectral face staring back at her from the glass.

By the time she goes to bed an hour later, the mug is on her bedside table.

The octopus is on her pillow.

The headless elf lolls on her shelf, propped against the photograph of Nina. The travelcard and the postcard from Wales are tucked into the frame.

Lavender is chasing the wind-up mouse around the floor, wearing a beautiful jewelled collar.

The friendship bracelet is fastened with a safety pin around Eleri's wrist. Threaded on to it is the coloured bead from Ras's bike wheel.

The key hangs on a chain around her neck.

The soil is scattered across her carpet like confetti.

The thirty pieces of silver weigh down the pocket of her pyjamas, dragging at her hip.

The ring is on her finger.

Now, finally, she picks up the witch mask and pulls it down over her face, breathing in the chemical smell of the plastic, gazing out at the limited view allowed by the eyeholes. The pattern is complete, all but one of the doors of the calendar are open. They should allow some illumination, some understanding of why she was chosen for this. And yet she is still in darkness.

The razor blade sits in her open right palm and now she closes it, squeezing tight. The pain is sharp and clean and lucid. It slows her racing heart, calms her breathing. There is nothing more she can do.

She is in the hands of the angel.

Blood seeps from her closed fist to fall like tears on the carpet.

Friday December 24

CHRISTMAS EVE

Mum never came home. Eleri woke to a message saying she had decided to stay at Adam's as she had an early start in the morning and he lived closer to the store. She'll be working the whole of Christmas Eve, as it's double time, and will bring dinner back.

The long day passes.

Somewhere out of sight, behind the snow clouds, the winter sun draws a bloodless arc across the sky.

Beni doesn't call. Calista doesn't call. Ras sleeps on, according to the WhatsApp group set up by Kika, which Eleri was added to. In another world, another time, this would have made her happy.

The wound in her hand throbs like a heart.

Darkness gathers.

Mr Vaseli has the radio on: a choir singing Christmas carols.

"*The angel Gabriel from heaven came. His wings as drifted snow, his eyes as flame.*"

She doesn't need to look at her watch to know. She can feel the angel's approach: a flutter of wings in her chest. She goes to the window.

Gibea has never looked more dead. Blackened like a very old bone.

Lavender wanders in and gives an attention-seeking mew. Eleri picks the kitten up and buries her face in her soft fur. They stay like that for a long while and then a harsh electronic trill cuts through the contented purring.

Door 24.

The yellow eye opens.

This is it. The final door. The last and best gift in the advent calendar. It's waiting for her just a few paces from where she stands (as the angel flies).

The eye stares, pupilless.

Mr Vaseli switches off his radio and the silence throbs like a fresh wound. Her mouth is dry as the dust that covers the floors of the abandoned flats.

And then her stomach drops. The Secret Santa has threatened her mum before, and surely a razor blade covered in dried blood has only one meaning.

*

The store phone rings so long it eventually cuts off. They must be busy, of course they must: it's Christmas Eve. Too busy to call home if Mum didn't turn up for work. She's already called her mum three times, but her finger hovers over the redial button for a moment, then she thrusts the phone into her pocket, and goes in search of Lavender.

The bus is mired in traffic from the moment it leaves the stop on the high road. She stands by the doors, hopping from foot to foot, hissing at the lights to *hurry up and change*, and the car in front to *put its foot down*, at gormless pedestrians to *get out of the bloody way*. But the world is against her tonight and in the end she hammers the emergency button above the doors and jumps out into the road. Narrowly avoiding a moped weaving its way through the stationary vehicles, she makes it to the pavement and sets off at a sprint. But the pavement is just as clogged as the road and she finds herself ricocheting off lamp posts and rubbish bins, hurdling takeaway boxes and the legs of rough sleepers. Sometimes she has to run into the road to avoid a pushchair or wandering toddler, but the angry hoots and squealing brakes make no impression on her imploding mind. The Christmas lights draw crazy lines against the lowering clouds.

Finally, the orange glow of the supermarket comes into view. She thrusts through the flood of shoppers swilling around the entrance.

The place is a fluorescent-lit cathedral, the worshippers bowing down to the shelves of crisps and booze.

A security guard leans against an advertising board featuring a family around a heavily laden Christmas table. She runs over to him.

"Have you seen Kerry Kirdar?"

He stares at her as if she has spoken in an alien language.

The woman behind the tobacco and lottery desk overhears and calls over that she's not sure if Kerry's in today, but Eleri could try asking the manager, who might be in the office, or might have gone on break, or maybe— Eleri doesn't wait to hear any more and sets off up the first aisle.

Every burgundy uniform makes her heart leap. She recognizes some of the staff from her mum's camera roll. But the cheerful old ladies and mischievous teenagers now look tired and drained under their bobbing Father Christmas hats. Exhausted Christmas elves, sick to the stomach of Mariah Carey and the stench of freshly baked mince pies.

None of them know where Kerry is.

She runs up and down the aisles, vaulting a yellow sign propped up beside a smashed bottle of mulled wine, sidestepping a tantrumming toddler, thrusting between a couple arguing about cheese. By the time she reaches the freezers at the far side of the shop, her vision is blurred with tears of despair.

Mum is the last gift.

Carved up by the razor blade and served to Eleri as a final punishment for a crime she has never understood.

If she calls the police now the angel will see them approach. He will have all the time in the world to finish what he started. They won't have the manpower to search each floor thoroughly so he will elude them and make his escape, leaving Mum to bleed out. Or perhaps he will push her out of the window and the police will find her broken body on the path. Then again, perhaps her mum isn't the gift but the lure. If Eleri gets back there now then maybe she can save her, and deliver the real prize. Herself. Yes, she must get back to Gibea, if she has to sprint all the way.

She skids around the corner of the last aisle and staggers to a halt.

Because there, behind a display booth like a Punch and Judy stall, pouring out plastic cupfuls of beige liquid, is her mum.

Eleri leans against a wall of gift cards, panting.

"Cream liqueur, sir?" Mum says to a grey-haired man in canary-coloured trousers. He ignores her.

"Cream liqueur, madam?" This woman rubs her hands and takes the little cup and they begin a conversation.

Eleri watches her, smiling and chatting, the fairy lights woven around the booth sparkling in her hair. She looks happy. Love for her mother swells in her heart, pushing out all the resentment and irritation, all the trivia of the normal world. Mum always used to say that having a child was like having your heart walk around outside your body, and here is Eleri's heart, surrounded by light and warmth.

When she steps out into the night, everything looks

different somehow. The lights are friendly, the faces of the pedestrians shining with expectation. She wants to go home, but before she does she must rest. All the adrenaline that had kept her going up until now is draining away. Leaning heavily against the plate-glass window of the supermarket, she closes her eyes and breathes in the cold night air. Mum is safe, Lavender is curled up on Mr Vaseli's sofa: there's nothing more the angel can do to her. She thought she had to play this game until the end, but the angel no longer has any power over her. Perhaps he was never as much of a threat as she feared: just a prankster, like Everett said. As the noises of the city wash over her: car engines and sound systems, crying babies, distant church bells – her legs give out and she slides down the window on to the cold pavement.

"Merry Christmas, darlin'."

She opens her eyes. A wizened rough sleeper is holding out a bottle to her.

"Reckon it'll be a white one." He nods his grizzled head up at the clouds.

A closer look reveals him to be nearer forty than seventy. His hair is snarled and the legs she can see under brown trousers that may once have been jeans are covered in sores. But his eyes are hopeful and at last, Eleri thinks, there is something worth toasting.

She takes the bottle and swigs, wincing as her throat catches fire and burns all the way down to her stomach.

"There you go," he says with satisfaction. "There you go."

It takes less than a minute for the spirit to hit her brain and soften her thoughts.

"I haven't got any change," she says, offering it back to him. "I'm really sorry, I came out in a hurry."

"Can't I buy a drink for a pretty girl on Christmas Eve?"

She smiles. "Yes," she says. "You can." Another sip and then she hands the bottle back. He takes it with a shaking hand and tucks it into his coat.

"I hope it doesn't snow," she says. "Or you'll be cold."

"Yeah, but it'll be beautiful." He gives a toothless grin.

Her phone trills with a message and her heart clutches. But the message is from Kika.

```
Ras is awake. Doc says no brain damage
(cos he doesn't have 1). They r moving
him out of ICU but keeping him in obs
4 a few days.
```

This is followed by three prayer hand emojis.

Her vision blurs with tears that she quickly scrubs away as another message pings underneath Kika's.

```
Thanks K. U just made my xmas.
```

This is from Teddy P. Perhaps he isn't such a piece of shit after all.

Another message comes through, but this one is not on the group chat. It's a private one from Kika.

    Ras can have visitors now hes in
    Saturn ward any time between 11 and 6.

She quickly taps out a thank you to Kika, then scrambles to her feet, all the tiredness gone. But then she sees the time. 5.40. It will take longer than twenty minutes to get to St Frances. Will the hospital allow visitors on Christmas Day?

It strikes her then that she hasn't even done any Christmas shopping. Presumably she should get something for Adam too this year. After a farewell to the rough sleeper, she wanders along the pavement, past brightly lit shops and cafes. In the window of Primark are two mannequins wearing elf onesies. She recoils immediately (the headless elf has become an unwelcome resident of her mind), then she pauses. A onesie would be a good present for Adam, as long as he isn't too up himself to wear it. Well, this will be the test. She goes into the store.

An hour later she staggers on to the bus, laden with bags. As well as the onesie for Adam, she has bought Mum a pair of cashmere socks, a bottle of organic muscle soak and a jar of salted caramel hot chocolate flakes. She doesn't normally get presents for friends, but this year she decided to get something for Beni. Though he is the boy who has everything, she thought he might like some Calvin Klein underpants – last season's design from TK Maxx, so not too pricey. She considered getting something for Ras, but the thought of giving it to him brought her out in a cold sweat.

She is dozing against the window when her phone

347

announces another message. Sliding it out of her pocket, she knows it'll be just another addition to the group chat, but she can't help hoping that just maybe it's Ras.

It's neither.

The Secret Santa has sent her video.

The two towers thrust upwards into the swollen bellies of the snow clouds: the shining sword of Shiloh, beside its dark doppelganger. Positive and negative. Matter and antimatter. Good and evil.

As she steps off the pavement an unnatural silence swallows her up. The estate is completely deserted. It must just be that people have gone home early to prepare for the stresses and strains that tomorrow will bring, and yet as she sets foot on the flickering path she feels like the only living person in the whole world.

The lights of the path go out.

She stands in the darkness, trying to control her breathing.

At the top of the black tower the yellow eye is open. Every cell in her body screams at her to turn around, to flee back to the warmth of humanity, to wait out this night in the glow of a cafe or pub, to call Adam to come and pick her up: they could both stay at his tonight, and wake to Christmas morning in that cheerful flat that smells of incense and cats.

But she never really had a choice. She starts walking towards Gibea Tower and the gift that's waiting for her on the twenty-fourth floor. Halfway along the path she thinks she sees a flash of movement at the corner of the black tower, as if someone peered around the building and then darted back. She stops and stares until her vision goes fuzzy, but she must have been imagining it. Why would the angel wait for her down here anyway? He knows she must come up and go through the final door.

The stairwell windows look out over nothing but darkness. This must be what hell is like, she thinks, as she sets foot on the first stair: being completely alone in the cold and dark. When this all began, the stars would sparkle as she climbed, lighting her way with their friendly curiosity: what new gift would be waiting for her? But she knows what this gift is.

It's Beni.

At first she thought he was asleep, but then she noticed how blue his lips were. He was still breathing, though. The angel had wanted her to see that, his chest rising and falling: *you can still save him.*

Her footsteps echo on the stairs and something in the architecture of the building makes it sound like someone is coming up behind her. Her skin prickles and a spike of adrenaline energizes her heavy legs with its binary choice: fight or flight. She can't fly, the angel has made sure of that, and she has nothing to fight with. Why didn't she bring a weapon? A kitchen knife? A hammer? Hell, her bloody hockey stick would have done.

The door to the twenty-fourth floor has been propped

open and a yellow glow seeps across the concrete floor, like sickly starlight.

She follows it.

Beni is lying in a foetal position on the floor of flat 240.

She runs over and crouches beside him, attempting to lift him from the cold concrete. "Beni? Ben? Wake up. Come on. We have to get you out of here."

He is a dead weight, flopping like a corpse as she turns him on to his back to check for injuries. There is nothing, but his breathing is shallower than it was in the video and his normally warm skin tone is now shades of green and grey.

"Merry Christmas."

She spins around. A hooded figure is framed against the black oblong of the lift shaft. It lowers the hood and she stares at the handsome face, cold as marble, beautiful and terrible as a fallen angel.

Not a *trick*, Ras, no. The porter misheard you.

"I've given him an opiate overdose," Hendrick says.

Eleri realizes this is the first time she has heard him speak. His voice is smooth and warm.

"This is the antidote." He holds out a syringe with a yellow cap. "But if you want me to give it to him, you have to do something for me."

"What?" she whispers.

He steps aside to allow her a complete view of the lift shaft.

"Oh my god…"

A noose dangles over the forty-eight-storey drop.

"You get what you give, Eleri."

"I… I don't understand." She gets to her feet shakily. "What am I supposed to have given?"

"Every moment you waste is a moment closer to his heart stopping."

"Please, Hendrick. I don't understand."

And then, suddenly, she does.

Hendrick Jameson. James Hendrick. JH. The initials carved on the tree, next to Nina's.

"You were Nina's boyfriend."

"I was her soulmate and she was mine. When you find the one – and you never will now, Eleri – you just know. And we knew from the moment we met."

She swallows hard to moisten her dry throat. "I'm sorry for what happened, I really am. She was my friend. But how was it my fault?"

"Think, Eleri. But don't take too long about it."

She has thought. For the past month she has racked her brains about why she was selected for this horror; Beni has too, and Ras and Calista. And none of them could work it out. There was just that one thing – the lipstick – and that was only when she thought Nina's dad was involved. But it's all she has.

"The Secret Santa gift?"

Hendrick slow claps. "It must have seemed so funny. A clever way to be cruel, to make her realize that she hadn't escaped, that she could never escape."

"It was a misjudgement, that's all!"

"And the timings worked out perfectly in the end because I had others to deal with first. The cyberbullies, the sexual harassers. I made their lives as much of a misery as they made hers. Insults and threats morning, noon and night, filling their feed so they could never escape. And for the boys, a stream of dickpicks and propositions after I released their details to hardcore gay dating sites. They didn't like it much. Some of them chose the same route out Nina did."

Eleri gasps. *Suicide School.* "You hounded them until they killed themselves."

"I gave them what they gave Nina. Just as I'm doing now. You were her Secret Santa." He gives a little bow. "I'm yours."

"But this isn't suicide, Hendrick. This is murder."

"You murdered Nina." A twist of his perfect mouth is the first sign he has given of any emotion. "*You* were the worst of all of them, because she thought she'd finally got away. She begged me not to do anything about the ones at Drinkwater. After what happened to her dad, she said she didn't want to lose me too."

"What did happen to her dad?" Eleri breathes.

"After the rape, Jimmy went after the bastard."

Rape? The popular, handsome Mr Newham, with his pretty wife and beautiful baby, *raped* Nina?

"Beat the shit out of him. What choice did he have? The authorities weren't going to do anything. I planned to do the same with the rest of them, all those kids who had waited for the chance to bring her down, who made up the lies about her, sent those messages, made her life unbearable. But she said that she'd change schools, keep her head down, and get through it, and then at the end of it we could finally be together. We'd waited so long, always keeping our relationship a secret because her mum and dad wouldn't have accepted it. There'd be time, she said. Time to bring her parents round. She loved them. But in the end I hated them as much as the others, because there *wasn't* time. And now your time is up too, Eleri." He holds his hand out.

She's so afraid that her whole body trembles – but she's also angry.

"All this for a lipstick? You're out of your mind."

He blinks at her.

"She *wore* lipstick; I saw it in the pictures."

"Lipstick?" His marble brow furrows, and then his expression darkens. "Enough!" His roar reverberates down the lift shaft and now he moves towards her. If she won't go of her own accord, then he will drag her to the noose.

She has no choice. It's the only way to save Beni.

She steps forward to meet him.

At the same time a black shape hurtles from the darkness. Hendrick falls to the ground and a violent struggle begins, throwing wild shadows against the walls. Eleri cannot make out who has come to her aid until, at last, Hendrick gains the upper hand, his adversary jerking under the rain of blows.

Now Eleri can see clearly.

She gasps.

Calista's body is limp, her eyes rolling, her nose streaming with blood.

Kneeling over her, Hendrick draws his fist back to deliver the killer blow. Eleri only has a moment, this single moment while his balance is off, teetering on the edge of that terrible drop.

At the flash of movement, he turns his head, but there is no time to react. His eyes widen, and then he gives a grunt of surprise as Eleri pushes him down the lift shaft.

Only then does she remember the syringe. Throwing herself on to her belly she reaches out across the abyss, but it's too late. Time slows to a crawl as Hendrick falls, his pale face oddly serene, the hand holding the syringe stretching up from the lake of darkness. The drop is too far: the glass reservoir will shatter and Beni will die before the ambulance gets here. But then Hendrick loses his grip on it. His hand opens and the syringe arcs into the air. Caught in the light from the tripod, Eleri follows its shining passage, then stretches out her hand.

Saturday December 25

CHRISTMAS DAY

Her room is filled with light. Not the yellow stain from the tripod lamp but a pure white brilliance.

The flat is quiet, though she can hear Mr Vaseli's radio through the wall. Checking her phone, she sees that it's only just past seven. Given the events of last night, Mum and Adam will probably sleep in.

Mr Vaseli is pleased to see her and makes her stay for a glass of thick yellow liquid with the colour and consistency of egg yolk and the flavour of chemical custard. Dipping her finger in, she lets Lavender lick it and the kitten gives a delicate sneeze before coming back for more.

Mr Vaseli tells her about his children who have emigrated to Australia and are building a house that will be big enough for him to move in to. He shows her pictures of cement mixers and breeze blocks and then finally a picture of a little girl blowing a kiss.

"My granddaughter." He beams. "This time next year we will all be together."

She thanks him for looking after Lavender and goes back home, pouring the kitten a saucerful of the cream Mum bought to make the trifle. After she's finished lapping up the Christmas treat, Lavender curls around Eleri's legs and she picks her up, settling her on to her lap in the spot she cradled Beni's head last night, as they waited for the police to arrive.

Calista had to administer the opiate antidote because Eleri's hands were shaking too much, and afterwards she looked so ill Eleri had been seriously worried. Every few seconds Cal's body was racked with violent shivering and she gnawed compulsively at her torn fingernails. Eleri took off her coat and offered it to her, but she shook her head.

"Come on, you're going to make yourself ill."

"I deserve it."

"Why? You saved me."

"It was me. I caused all this." Her head was bent, the lank blonde hair falling in a shroud across her face.

"I could see how well you and Nina got on and I was jealous and scared that I might lose you. I thought that if Nina realized people at EHS knew what had happened then she'd leave our school too. Then she couldn't take you away from me."

And then Cal finally admitted the truth.

Last year, she had swapped the Secret Santa gifts, removing the lipstick Eleri had been so worried about from Miss Merrion's gift bin, and replacing it with the *I Love Teacher* mug.

It had been Cal who took Nina's travelcard. Tracing the journeys, she had discovered where Nina went to school before EHS. She found out that someone had accused a teacher there of rape, and looked through the socials until she found the name of the accuser.

Nalina Gamal. Nina Mitri.

Beni was sick then. Eleri had wiped his mouth with her sleeve but the hand that did this seemed to belong to someone else. Her whole body felt numb as Calista's voice went on and on.

"I never meant for her to kill herself, El, I swear. After she went missing, I told myself that it couldn't have been because of what I did: that she was screwed-up because of the rape and the bullying. But then when all this started happening I realized that it *had* to be my fault. I was too scared to tell you because I thought that would be the end for us. And then I was scared because I thought Nina would come back to get her revenge, and then I just didn't know what to do, so I hid at home and waited for it all to be over."

Eleri's mind scrambled to catch up but it kept hitting obstacles. Her best friend was capable of this?

"But after what happened to Ras, I realized that you were in real danger, and I couldn't let anything happen to you, so tonight I waited for you here and then—"

357

"You did that to Nina?" Eleri said finally. "Knowing what happened at Drinkwater. And then you kept it a secret, let the Secret Santa think it was me, knowing I was scared and in danger? That my family was in danger because of what you did?" She blinked in wonder. "How could you, Cal? How could you do that?"

But Calista did not get the chance to answer, because then there were sirens, and blue light rinsing the walls, and the thunder of boots on the stairs.

The police interview took place by Beni's bedside as Christmas Eve turned into Christmas Day.

The parents waited outside, Mum and Adam, Beni's parents and Calista's dad (her mum was on holiday and didn't answer any of the calls), while the two girls sat beside one another on plastic chairs next to Beni's bed. He was pale but alert and the doctors said there would be no lasting effects from the opiate overdose.

It was Eleri who recounted the events of the evening, with Calista nodding miserably when asked to confirm certain facts. Beni remembered nothing after Hendrick texted to meet him for a Christmas drink.

"At the time, we didn't know she had a boyfriend," Everett admitted.

"Well, *we* found out pretty easily," Beni snapped bitterly. "And anyway, would you have bothered investigating if you did? I mean, you didn't look for her very hard, did you?"

"Nalina was a troubled girl. We did the best we could with the resources we had and it would seem that if we had

358

the full information from James Hendrick, then perhaps we could have found her in time."

"It wasn't Hendrick's fault," Eleri said, and she felt her friends' gazes snap to her face. "He tried to find her and it was too late."

"He should have reported her death. Given the family some peace."

"I don't think Hendrick was all about peace," Beni muttered.

"OK, let's focus on what's important going forward. What matters is that you are safe until we manage to pick him up."

As they were led from Gibea Tower by Everett's officers, Eleri had expected to see a bloodied broken body under a blanket, but there was no sign of Hendrick. Later police discovered a net strung across the lift shaft. Hendrick must simply have climbed out of it on to a lower floor and fled when the police were on their way up the stairs. The noose had been fastened with bulldog clips: it would have fallen with the slightest weight.

"I don't think we're in any danger," Eleri said. "Not any more. He's done what he intended."

"Which was?"

"To make us suffer, like we made Nina suffer." Beside her, she felt Calista shrink.

The questions went on until Beni's mum came in and declared that the interview was over. Kissing Beni on the cheek, Eleri walked out into the corridor, into her mum's arms. The shock and dismay was gotten over with earlier, when Mum first arrived at the hospital and Eleri told her exactly what had been going on over the past twenty-four days. There would be more time to talk it through so Adam had said it was time they all went home to bed.

There had been moments, over the past few weeks, when Eleri thought she would never sleep again, but she was out cold from the moment her head hit the pillow.

And now she is wide awake. And there is something she needs to do. Leaving a note for her mum, she pulls on her trainers. Adam's huge, fur-collared parka hangs on the hooks by the door. She slips it on and leaves the flat.

She scents the snow before she sees it, a clean, blue hugeness spangled with ice crystals. Cosy in the parka, her face is the only part of her that feels the sting of the cold, and now that her eyes have adjusted she sees that the world has been covered in an enormous white eiderdown that stretches, unblemished, as far as she can see.

Every window of Gibea Tower is lit up, glinting in the sun shining down from a cloudless, powder-blue sky.

She sets off towards where she thinks the path is, leaving the very first indendations in the virgin snow.

If it weren't for the bandages wrapping his head and the stylish pale blue robe, Ras could simply be slumbering peacefully, like any other teenager this early in the morning. There are no tubes or wires connecting him to any equipment, and on the table beside the bed are a crushed Coke can and a half-eaten packet of Jaffa Cakes.

The young Chinese nurse didn't mind that she wasn't family, or that she arrived a bit before visiting hours were due to start. She just beamed, wished her a Happy Christmas, and led her to the window bed, smiling and nodding all the way, her red and green bauble earrings bobbing.

A pale blue plastic chair sits beside the bed, with a black jacket slung across it, and she is about to sit down when there is a voice behind her.

"Morning."

She turns to see a tall, slender and very handsome young man in a black T-shirt and jeans. In one hand is a plastic cup of black coffee, the other he stretches towards her.

"Hish," he says. "Ras's brother."

"I'm Eleri Kirdar," Eleri says. "I go to school with Ras."

"Eleri?" Hish smiles. "Right."

"Is it OK for me to be here?" she says quickly. "I mean, is he well enough to have visitors?"

"He's absolutely fine, as you can probably tell." Hish gestures to the Coke and biscuits. "Just being a lazy bastard, as usual."

"Shut up."

Their heads turn to the bed. Ras is struggling to sit up.

"About time," Hish grumbles, helping him into a sitting position, but Ras's pale eyes are focused on Eleri.

"Hi," he says.

She smiles. "Happy Christmas."

"You made it through," he says softly.

She nods.

Now Ras turns to his brother. "So, if it's Christmas, where are my effing presents?"

"At home. Still bagged and boxed, so I could get refunds if you pegged it."

"Yeah, well, bad luck. Go and get them, then."

"Piss off."

"I'm in *hospital*," Ras complains. "I nearly *died*. What kind of monster are you?"

"Chrissakes." Hish sighs heavily, gives Eleri a little salute, then grabs his jacket from the chair and heads for the doors. On the way out, the pretty Chinese nurse shares a joke with him that leaves her beaming.

When Eleri looks back at Ras his face is serious. "I'm so sorry I wasn't there for you, to the end."

"It wasn't your fault."

"Hish says I must have been doing something dumb, like riding no hands or something. He's probably right. I can't really remember anything after leaving the house to visit Ted. But you're OK, so I guess the whole thing *was* a prank after all."

Eleri shakes her head slowly.

"In that case, you'd better fill me in on what I missed."

"It's a long story."

"Make yourself comfortable, then." He shuffles up to leave a space for her on the bed.

She hesitates for the briefest of moments, then climbs up beside him.

Outside the window the snow has started to fall once more: huge, fat flakes like the drifting down from a pillow fight. At some point in the story Ras falls asleep, because the next time she glances at his face his eyelashes have sunk down on to his cheeks. She should go. It's past nine now and her mum will be up, but for the moment she is so comfortable curled against his warm body, his breath on her cheek. She will just stay a few more minutes.

She's woken by Hish's return, with two bulging Lidl bags.

"I know, right?" he says, grimacing. "There's nothing like your brother almost pegging it to make you part with your cash on a massive scale. I'm going to be paying this off until next Christmas."

Eleri slides off the bed. "I should go home. My mum will be waiting."

"Of course. Thanks for visiting. I know it meant a lot to him. Have a great Christmas, yeah? And I'm sure I'll see you again. Come round the house sometime. But give me some warning, cos the place is a shit hole. No thanks to His Lordship."

Eleri laughs, "Thanks", and turns to leave. But then she hesitates.

"I'm so sorry, about what happened to your mum."

Hish smiles sadly. "She was a special person. Like all mums, eh?"

"Yeah." And then on impulse, Eleri rises on her tiptoes to kiss his cheek. He smells of hair products and deodorant and the bitter coffee from the hospital machine.

"Happy Christmas."

"Happy Christmas, Eleri Kirdar," Hish says.

On the next ward along, Beni's parents and grandparents are gathered around his bed with a couple of pink-cheeked nurses. They are drinking champagne from real glasses and eating Celebrations from a box resting on Beni's legs. Beni is due to go home as soon as the doctor does his rounds, but none of the Brown family seems in any hurry. Sonja is deep in conversation with the nurses about hospital hauntings, while Beni's dad and granddad discuss the bed's engineering, pressing the remote control to make it rise and fall and pitch and yaw while Beni sits there stony-faced.

When he sees Eleri, Mr Brown hails her like an old friend. He has spoken to a colleague at Shelter, he tells her, and they've found a studio flat locally for Ray, the rent and heating to be covered by the council. Today he will be going for Christmas dinner at a local hotel with fifty other old people. Apparently it gets quite raucous.

Beni's family can be overwhelming on a normal day, but today Sonja keeps grabbing Eleri, hugging her to her ample bosom, and trying to force champagne down her, and after a full ten minutes of this she's ready to go.

While Sonja is busy dancing around the other beds, offering champagne to all the patients while the nurses try and fail to stop her, Eleri takes the opportunity to leave.

She leans in to kiss Beni goodbye, but as she pulls away his fingers close around her wrist. "Be careful," he says in a low voice. "I know you think you're safe now, but I thought I knew Hendrick too."

"If he heard us talking, then it's Calista who should worry," Eleri says.

"Have you spoken to her?" he asks.

She shakes her head.

"Are you going to?"

"She killed Nina, Ben."

"No, she didn't. Nina was screwed-up by what that teacher did to her, and then what happened to her afterwards. What Cal did, yeah, it was bad, but it was just one link in the chain. She couldn't have known what Nina would do."

"Well, she should have thought. I have to go."

Slipping past Sonja, who has produced a bunch of mistletoe and is planting a smacker on a delighted octogenarian, she heads out of the ward.

Waiting for the same lift down to the ground floor is the porter they spoke to the night Ras was admitted. He is stewarding a bed where a frail, bald-headed child lies, connected to a drip.

As she goes to stand beside him, he doesn't recognize her. He is too busy helping the child squeeze the red nose of the Rudolph on his Christmas jumper. When finally, with a little help from him, the nose lights up and plays "Jingle Bells" the child's face crinkles into a smile.

The world is full of good people, Eleri thinks. For every toxic teenager who sends a message urging someone to commit suicide, there is a porter in a Rudolph jumper, a Mr Brown, a Hish Mandip, a Kika Aliadiere, a Will Roberts, a Miss Merrion. And, she thinks, as she comes out of the lift and passes the area where the parents waited last night, an Adam, at the side of a woman he has known for a matter of weeks, as she sobs over her child.

Time to go home.

But when the bus pulls into the stop, she doesn't get on. Instead she takes her phone from her pocket and taps out a message to her mum, then she crosses the road to the stop on the other side.

The blanket of snow has made her think of another sleeper.

The Muslim part of St Jerome's cemetery is at the far end, past the ranks of crosses and shields and praying cherubs. The graves are different here. There are stone teardrops and domes and elaborately carved scrolls, some inscribed in English, others in a flowing Arabic script. The snow-covered ground makes it impossible to identify any fresh soil, but over at the furthest line of graves the ground is raised in neat ridges.

She picks her way over, leaving deep prints in the snow.

Nina's is the second to last grave on the row. The black stone glitters with mica in the morning sun.

Nalina Gamal, reads the English script. *To Allah we belong, and to him we shall return.*

Beneath it are lines of sweeping gold Arabic.

"Hi, Nina," she says quietly. "I know you probably don't celebrate Christmas, but I didn't want you to be all alone today." She crouches down on her haunches, laying her hand down at the head of the raised ridge. The snow sighs away beneath the warmth of her palm. "I wanted you to know that you were loved. And you are missed. And I wanted to tell you that I'm sorry. For not seeing what you were going through. For not being able to help you."

Most of the trees lining the cemetery perimeter have dropped their leaves, but a single yew stands bent, as if in mourning. The breeze ripples its glossy needles, like a voice just at the edge of hearing.

For a long time it is the only sound. The snow starts to fall more heavily, covering her hand as if another white hand has laid itself over hers. Clouds keep blotting out the sun, casting fleeting shadows on the ground, like spectres moving in and out of the graves. Even in Adam's parka she is starting to shiver, but she can't bear to go, not yet. To leave Nina here, alone in the cold.

And then there is another shadow, but when this one falls across the grave, it remains perfectly still.

She turns.

A hooded figure stands at the end of the grave.

She glances around for anyone that might come to her aid, but it's Christmas morning, people are lying in or enjoying leisurely breakfasts, children are examining their presents for the telltale rattle of Lego or the disappointing squish of clothes.

Slowly she gets up. "Please," she says.

"I was never going to hurt you," Hendrick says, in a voice soft as snow. "The net was there to stop you falling."

Her lips part but words fail her.

"Death is a way out, Eleri. Nalina knew that. Some people don't deserve ways out. Some people deserve to live and suffer."

"What are you going to do to us?"

"Nothing. Perhaps you didn't deserve it after all, and your friend has made a hell for herself without my help. No, there are others who need my attention now."

"Hendrick, whatever you're planning, please don't. Just go and live your life. I won't say anything about seeing you."

"My *life*? That ended last year, and yet here I am." He opens his arms, then lets them drop by his side. "And that's the way it will be for him."

"The teacher?" Eleri breathes.

Hendrick gives a quiet chuckle. "I saved him for last."

"You won't kill him, or his wife, or his baby? You have to promise me, or I will go to the police, Hendrick."

He pulls down his hood. She was wrong about him being unattractive. He's as heart-stoppingly beautiful as Nina was. A fallen angel forever locked out of heaven. His smile takes her breath away. It lights up his brown eyes, dimples his angular cheeks, promising wit and fun and warmth and love, but it is completely soulless.

"I'm getting to know Lauren Newham quite well. Because, you see, it turns out that sex attackers don't make for such good husbands after all. She was lonely. She's not lonely any more. But *he* will be. And when Lauren has gone, and baby Ruby, and he's all alone, then he might just understand. And if he doesn't, then the lessons will just have to carry on."

"You have to let this go, Hendrick. For your own sake. You have to forgive—" She stops because it's not true. You don't *have* to forgive. Like Beni said, you choose to. Hendrick chooses not to.

"Come back with me. You won't go to prison. There's no proof that you were responsible for what happened to Ras, and I can convince Beni not to press charges."

"I've gone way beyond that, Eleri, and it's too far to go back. I'm nearly with Nina now."

Then, because he is so lost, because it's Christmas Day and he's all alone, and because the intimacy they have shared over the past few weeks has been the most intense experience of her life, she puts her arms around him. Time and space and the rest of the heartless world crumbles and blows away in the breeze, until it is just the pair of them, the snow falling silently around them.

After a few moments he pulls away, and without another word turns to leave.

"James," she calls after him. He looks back at her. "What shall I do with all the things? All the … gifts?"

"Whatever you like."

"But … but what about the ring? Don't you want it back?"

"Give it to someone you love." And then he pulls up his hood and walks away, vanishing into the mist of falling snow.

She arrives home to find her mum in tears. Adam is beside her on the sofa with his arm around her. Rushing across to the sofa, Eleri drops to her knees.

"Mum? What is it? Didn't you get my text?"

But now she notices the envelope on the coffee table. The one she tried to hide with all the others on the microwave. It has been torn open and the letter is crumpled and damp in Mum's hand.

"I'm sorry," Eleri says desperately. "I didn't want it to ruin Christmas. I was going to tell you about it afterwards."

Her mum touches her face. "It's fine." She's smiling. "They've settled."

"What?"

"AWP," Adam says. "My mate put the frighteners on them, and they changed their mind about going to tribunal, because they knew they'd lose."

"So what does that mean?"

"They've offered me a payout," Mum says.

Eleri's eyes widen. "How much?"

Mum unfurls the piece of paper in her hand and shows Eleri the figure halfway down the page of dense type.

"Oh my days," Eleri breathes.

"I know, right?" Now her mum is beaming, even as the tears continue to stream down her glowing face.

Eleri squeals and pulls her mum into an embrace.

They have champagne for breakfast, and then Adam insists on playing them his Spotify *liked songs* list and he and Mum dance to the 80s classics that were, apparently, the anthems of the Ilford Pally. Eleri is soon too tired – and hot, now that Mum's turned the heating up – to continue, and sinks down on to the sofa to enjoy the excruciating sight of her mum twerking to Duran Duran with her new boyfriend.

Fortunately this performance has to be cut short by the dinner preparations. Eleri heads to the kitchen to make a start on the veg, but Adam follows her, taking the peeler from her hand and shooing her back to the living room, telling the two of them to relax while he demonstrates the culinary skills he learned on the silk trail to Kashgar.

"Do you think he's actually done all this stuff?" Eleri whispers, as Mum gets out the Scrabble board (no TV is allowed on Christmas Day – Gran's rule).

"I don't know," Mum whispers back. "And I really don't care." She grins.

"I heard that," Adam says from the doorway, Mum's Daniel Craig apron tied around his waist. "And you two have just volunteered for a special Boxing Day slide show."

Half an hour later the turkey has been spiced with an eclectic blend from the much neglected selection in the larder, stuffed with a concoction of raisins, apples and breadcrumbs, and is sitting in a bath of the remains of the champagne. Adam slides the tray into the oven, slaps his hands in satisfaction and says, "Right. Present time!" Then he adds hurriedly, "Unless you have, like, a special time you always do it?"

"Not at all," Mum says, then she turns to Eleri. "Do we?"

Eleri smiles and shakes her head, then she gets up and goes to her room. But ignoring the socks, bath soak and hot chocolate sitting in a bag by her desk, she slides the pillowcase out from under the bed.

Mum has bought her a laptop. She stares at the white box with the glinting silver apple, then bursts into tears, which sets Mum off too.

"Twenty pounds, you said!" Eleri cries. "This isn't twenty pounds!"

"I know," Mum sniffs. "I was going to pay it off in installments, but now I don't have to."

Adam has bought Eleri some reindeer poo and a bath bomb, which she hugs him for, and when he takes the onesie out of its bag, he insists on getting straight into it.

Then Eleri presents her mum with the small velvet box. Mum's eyes widen as she slides off the hair ribbon, which was the only thing Eleri had to hand to make it look like a proper gift.

She opens the box, and for a long moment there is silence.

"Oh," she says finally. "Oh, Eleri. Oh wow."

"I found it in a charity shop," Eleri says quickly. "The lady said it's probably glass, but I thought it looked quite classy."

"It does." Her mum sighs, gazing at the stone as if entranced by the glittering lights. "The diamond looks just like the ones in Gran's ring."

"Yeah," Eleri says. "I thought so too." Then she leans over and kisses her mum on the cheek. "Happy Christmas."

"Well, I'm not sure how I can follow that." Adam grins.

It turns out he has got them all a trip to Paris, and this sets Mum off again, and she says she needs a drink to recover. Adam pours out some glasses of Baileys, but before he has the chance to sit down, Eleri says, "How much have you had to drink?"

"Not enough, why?"

"Can you give me a lift somewhere? Though you're not allowed to get out of the car in that." She flicks the elf's bell on the onesie.

A little boy answers the door, a yellow paper hat pulled down over one eye, the other filled with madness. His mouth is stained blue and scraps of wrapping paper and Sellotape are stuck to his Spider-Man pyjamas. From a room beyond, Eleri can hear screaming and a TV at full volume, and the shrill complaints of an old woman.

"Is Calista there?"

He turns and runs off down the hall. A long time passes and Eleri wonders whether he has even passed the message on, but then Calista appears, shuffling up to the door in leggings and an ancient T–shirt Eleri recognizes from their primary school days. Her eyes are dull and her face pallid.

As she steps into the doorway, she doesn't speak, only winces slightly, as if waiting for more pain.

"I was wondering," Eleri says, "if you fancied coming over to ours for Christmas dinner."

Calista blinks her bloodshot eyes, then frowns, as if waiting for the punchline to a joke.

"There's enough food. Adam's with us too, but he's OK actually. I checked with Mum and she'd love to see you."

A tear trickles from the corner of Calista's eye and snakes down her pale cheek.

"Will your nan mind?"

"I think…" Calista croaks, "I think she'd be delighted actually."

"Do you wanna go and ask her?"

Calista turns and stumbles up the hall. Behind Eleri a passing car blares out "Last Christmas". The snow on the road has been churned to grimy slush and on the pavement it has compacted to dangerous icy patches. On the way here from the car she almost slipped over. A man comes striding past the box hedge, his arms full of presents.

"Merry Christmas!" he calls, as if this isn't London at all but a friendly little country village where everyone knows each other. She raises a hand.

The Calista that reappears is different from the one that left. There is colour to her cheeks and a brightness to her eyes as she scurries back to the door, a net of brazil nuts swinging at her side.

"Nan said I could take these cos they get under her dentures, but that's it, I'm afraid. Can we stop on the way so I can get some stuff to bring? The Indian shop on the corner's open till midday."

"Mum said you don't have to bring anything," Eleri says. "Just yourself. That's enough."

Calista ducks her head, in shame or gratitude, or perhaps just to slip the scarf around her neck, and then she steps out on to the front step, closing the door behind her. The two friends set off down the path, passing out through the tiny garden gate that felt so big when they were small, and then out on to the pavement.

In the lit windows of the houses they pass, Eleri can see families enjoying their Christmas morning, wild-eyed children bounce on sofas, resplendent in their princess and superhero costumes, while the faces of the adults look strained or tired as they endure the irritations and tensions of family life, biting their tongues, looking at their watches. And yet each year they keep coming back. With hope and forgiveness for the frailties of the people they love, because perfection is only for the angels.

Hendrick has taught her a lesson, but it's not the one he intended.

She slides an arm into Calista's and they cling to one another to stop themselves from falling as they head back to the Saab idling on the kerb.

Acknowledgements

As ever, love, respect and eternal gratitude to my agent, Eve White, along with the incomparable Ludo Cinelli and Steven Evans. Thanks, gang. This one made my year.

I am immensely lucky to be working with the fantastic team at Scholastic: Yasmin Morrissey who commissioned the book and was a joy to edit with; the positively exhilarating Tierney Holm; Harriet Dunlea (Empress of Harlow) and the enormously patient and diplomatic Sarah Dutton. Thanks also to copy editor Susila Baybars and the cover designer Jamie Gregory.

Thanks to Shelley Routledge who was kind enough to read the outline of YBWO and give me her usual perceptive and incisive feedback.

To the teenagers that helped me sound less like a 47-year-old – Dainton John, Phoebe and Raffi Jay and whoever else happens to be in my house playing Fifa when something comes up – luv gs.

My husband, Vince, has been a rock, i.e. rough, grey and not much of a reader, but there's no one better to discuss the intricacies of plot with.

And, finally, love and gratitude to my Mum, Jill Smith, who will read this to the very last full stop.